Narrow is the Way

By the same author

A NARROW ESCAPE
ON THE STRAIGHT AND NARROW

Narrow is the Way

Faith Martin

ROBERT HALE · LONDON

© Faith Martin 2006
First published in Great Britain 2006

ISBN-10: 0-7090-7967-2
ISBN-13: 978-0-7090-7967-5

Robert Hale Limited
Clerkenwell House
Clerkenwell Green
London EC1R 0HT

The right of Faith Martin to be identified as author
of this work has been asserted by her in accordance with the
Copyright, Designs and Patents Act 1988

2 4 6 8 10 9 7 5 3 1

Typeset in 10½/13pt Sabon
Printed in Great Britain by St Edmundsbury Press
Bury St Edmunds, Suffolk.
Bound by Woolnough Bookbinding Ltd

chapter one

Detective Inspector Hillary Greene slammed on the brakes of her ancient Volkswagen Golf, and snarled an insult at the BMW driver who'd cut her up. Although flagging the prat down, showing her ID card and scaring the hell out of him might make her feel a lot better, it would also make her late for work. Besides, if she indulged in this bit of petty vengeance every time some idiot in a bigger car tried it on, she'd never get from point A to B.

Even though she had barely a mile to travel from her canal barge, moored permanently in the small village of Thrupp, to her desk at Kidlington's Police HQ, the traffic approaching Oxford was notoriously bad, and this little infringement of her personal space was nothing compared to some days. So she contented herself by giving the BMW driver (was the cheeky sod on his mobile phone as *well*?) a one-fingered salute, which he pretended not to notice, and sighed heavily.

Alongside the road, the hawthorn hedges were turning a vibrant orange. Dry yellow leaves swirled around the kerb, doing a dance in the wake of passing cars and brightly coloured berries and lowering grey skies were the order of the day. Keats would have loved it. Hillary Greene just hoped that the autumnal fogs would keep off for a while yet, because then driving in to work would become an absolute nightmare.

The number of times she'd nearly been rear-ended in a November pea-souper didn't bear thinking about.

She turned on the radio, relaxing to a sixties golden oldie –

somebody bewailing the fact that trains and boats and planes had taken their loved one away.

Hillary snorted. They should be so lucky.

Travelling down Kidlington's main road, past the set of traffic lights that led off to the local airport, she glanced across at the turning to her old house. Or to Ronnie's old house to be more accurate, her late and extremely unlamented husband, now nearly two years dead. Now if only some nice train, boat or plane had taken *him* away, say ten or even twelve years ago, she'd cheerfully have paid the fare.

Arriving safely at the HQ, she had her usual trouble finding a parking space, and wondered idly whose backside it was that you had to creep around nowadays in order to get your own slot.

She finally parked under a sumac tree that was going out in a blaze of glory, and glanced up at an uncertain sky. Well, not all that uncertain really. It was bound to rain in Britain in the autumn. Or summer for that matter. She only hoped the seals on Puff the Tragic Wagon held out. The last thing she needed was to finish work tonight and find herself the proud owner of a soggy car.

She scooped up that morning's unopened mail from the passenger seat and swung out a pair of surprisingly good legs, for a middle-aged gal like herself. She mentally crossed her fingers that her tights would stay unladdered. For some reason, she seemed to spend a fortune on replacing bloody nylons.

'Morning, guv,' she heard someone say, just as she pushed in through to the main lobby door. Turning, she found the hulking presence of DC Tommy Lynch looming up behind her and grinning widely.

'Tommy. We catching the same shift?'

'Looks like it.'

They walked up together into the main office, where Hillary shared a corner with DS Janine Tyler, Tommy, and DS Frank Ross.

Her team.

'You're due in court this afternoon, right, guv?' Tommy asked, noticing that his DI was wearing one of her more tailored outfits, a crafty concoction of navy and white which seemed to hide her curvaceous figure better than her usual, less mannish outfits.

Tommy hated suits like this one.

'Yeah, the Gordon case,' she admitted glumly, and Tommy grimaced in sympathy.

Randolph (Randy) Gordon was a two-time loser who specialized in forged passports, credit cards, sick notes, hell, even gun licences for all they knew. This time, Hillary had caught him bang to rights with a stack of falsified papers destined for illegal immigrants, but his barrister had come up with a glitch in the arresting officer's procedure, and now it looked as if Gordon was going to walk.

'Tough luck, guv,' Tommy commiserated quietly.

Hillary sighed an acknowledgement, but was already shrugging out of her coat and slinging it across the back of her chair. Across the way, the door to DCI 'Mel' Philip Mallow's office remained firmly closed, and she wondered if her immediate superior, and friend for the last twenty-odd years or so, was even in yet. If he wasn't, it served the silly sod right.

The whole station knew that the twice-divorced DCI Mellow Mallow and her sergeant, Janine Tyler, were all but shacked up together. And rumour also had it that it was this naughty relationship that had helped to scupper Mel's chances for a superintendency when their current boss, Marcus Donleavy, had been promoted.

Way back in January, Marcus was supposed to have been booted upstairs, but due to some snafu or other, it was only now happening. And Hillary wouldn't have been human if she hadn't wondered if her own chances of steeping into Mel's shoes, as a new detective chief inspector, might just have been in the offing.

But there'd been serious obstacles to that happening back then. Ronnie, the bastard, had died in a car crash, and with his death had come serious allegations of corruption. Corruption, moreover, that had been subsequently investigated and corroborated. Worse still, the internal investigation team had had her firmly in their sights too, for a while. But, long since separated from Ronnie, Hillary had had nothing to do with his animal parts smuggling operation, as the investigation had finally proved. It had hardly been auspicious for her promotion chances though, had she not also solved a particularly nasty murder case going on at the same time.

Now, of course, she'd long since put all thoughts of a promotion behind her. Mel wasn't getting booted up, so there was no opening for a DCI slot.

Hillary gave a mental shrug and put all thoughts of Mel to one side. No doubt he knew as well as everyone else what a mess he'd made of things, and she knew that her friend was nothing if not ambitious. So why was he still, after nearly a year, sticking to his relationship with the unsuitable Janine Tyler?

And speak of the devil, Hillary thought wryly, smiling inwardly as she watched DS Tyler swing through the door. In truth, there was no real mystery as regards Mel Mallow's ongoing relationship with his junior officer. Janine was almost the archetypal blonde bombshell. She was young, not yet twenty-seven, and had long, pale-blonde hair, the almost obligatory blue eyes, and a slim, athletic build that was the envy of many.

Hillary had not been best pleased when she'd first learned of their affair. Janine, as a humble sergeant, was supposed to answer directly to Hillary, who answered to Mel, who answered to Donleavy, and so on, up the food chain. The thing was, Janine tended to think that having the DCI's ear (as well as every other part of him) circumnavigated Hillary's part in the link. An error that had caused some friction between the two women in the past. Now, though, things seemed a bit more settled, although Hillary was well aware that Janine would have preferred to work with another DI.

But that was life for you. Give it half a chance, and it would bite you in the arse.

'Janine,' Hillary greeted pleasantly, as her pretty blonde sergeant settled herself down at her desk. 'Making any headway with the warehouse fire?'

'Arson, boss, clear as day,' Janine said, and for a while, they went over her previous day's interview with the fire marshal, the witnesses, and the warehouse owner.

Tommy, busy typing up his notes on his own cases, paused momentarily when Frank Ross, reeking of cigarettes and booze, shuffled by. The poisoned cherub, as he was universally known behind his back – and sometimes to his face – was looking even more hung over than usual. He slumped down at his desk and began to initial pages on a report, which even Tommy could see he was barely making a pretence of reading. The sooner Ross took early retirement the better. It was a sentiment unanimously held at Kidlington nick, from the desk sergeant up to the chief constable. Only Frank Ross never seemed in the mood to oblige.

Hillary, going through her own paperwork with rather more diligence, finally took a break after an hour or so to open and read her mail.

There were the usual suspects of bills, flyers and promises of a change of lifestyle courtesy of mail-order catalogue subscriptions, and these were quickly binned or set aside. But Hillary felt her heart jump as she recognized the familiar logo on the last envelope. It was from her solicitor, Graham Vaughan, an old crony from years back. She sighed and opened it, and read the short, neat letter with a sinking heart.

Over six months ago, just when she'd thought the house was going to be freed up after probate, and the internal investigation team had finally cleared her name, she'd had a letter from the Endangered Species Animal Army (or ESAA for short) informing her that they were suing her for possession of the house.

Their argument was simple. Ronnie Greene had made his money via the illegal trade in endangered species. Ergo, they considered that they had a moral and legal right to seize his assets to help fund their own fight on behalf of endangered animals. It had sounded all well and good, but Ronnie had very carefully hidden his ill-gotten gains, and not even the police team that had uncovered so many of his scams had been able to find it. That had left ESAA with only one real asset to go for: Ronnie's house.

Her house, dammit.

So far, Graham had been doing everything to stall them and keep the process from getting to court. His letter today informed her that ESAA, in the form of the Chairman of the Oxford branch, had finally agreed to a face-to-face meeting with Hillary and Graham the day after tomorrow to see if they couldn't come to terms.

That promised to be a real barrel of laughs.

Hillary shoved the letter, along with the bills, back into her bag, and looked up as Mel Mallow finally made it in. He looked, as ever, as if he'd just stepped out of the portals of a male modelling agency.

Janine, she noticed, watched him with a proprietorial air that made Hillary wonder uneasily if wedding bells might not be in the air. If so, Janine was almost certain to be moved to another division, which meant Hillary would have to break in another sergeant: a not totally unpleasant thought.

In his office, Mel unloosened his grey silk tie and undid his gold and onyx cufflinks. He settled down with a cup of his own-brew coffee, made from the coffee machine he kept permanently in his office, and went over his immediate plans, now that the new super was due to arrive today.

No two ways about it, when he'd first learned that Marcus was being booted upstairs and was being replaced by some high-flyer from the Met, he'd been as sick as a dog. Even more so when Donleavy, never one to pull his punches, had come straight out and told him that part of the reason he'd been overlooked for the promotion, had been down to the situation with Janine Tyler.

Of course, Mel knew that his previous two divorces had never sat well with the top brass. Even though practically everyone else over the age of thirty was divorced nowadays, the fact that he'd got two such divorces behind him was considered to be particularly careless on his part. But it was hardly his fault.

He'd made the classic mistake of marrying too young to begin with, a problem that had been quickly and more or less painlessly resolved by a mutual, and largely amicable divorce, less than two years later. And it wasn't as if he'd done anything stupid after that. He hadn't rushed into another marriage, nor made the same mistakes twice. In fact, his second marriage, to a very wealthy widow, had had the brass purring. Mel and his new wife had quickly produced a son, and for over ten, good, solid years, everything had been hunky-dory. It had been his wife who'd become restless, who'd said that she couldn't take to life in a back-water like Kidlington, and who'd yearned to get back to London and her gallery-owning, Sloane-ranger friends. What had he been supposed to do? Contest the divorce? Hardly. As it was, he'd come out of it very nicely indeed. For once, it had been the male partner who'd come up trumps in the financial quagmire that was a modern divorce court. He now had a detached, des res. in The Moors area of Kidlington, and no alimony payments to make, since his first wife had also since remarried.

It was not as if he was a Casanova, for Pete's sake. OK, so Janine was younger than him by twelve years or so – and was blonde and beautiful and a mere sergeant. His worst sin, he knew, had been in poaching in his own back yard. But he wasn't a monk. He was damned if he was going to give her up.

Yet he wanted to rise high, if only to show his second wife a thing or two, and for the boy's sake, too, of course. It did a lad good to have a father to be proud of. And yes, he could admit it to himself, he'd always rather fancied himself as top brass. He might look and dress the part of a sucessful middle-class executive-type now, but lurking in the back of his mind were memories of his extremely humble beginnings. To make matters worse, Janine was constantly hinting at wanting to move into his house, and the fact that he was always pushing back to avoid just such an event happening, was surely a clue that something was not right in the house of Mellow Mallow.

Time to get to work. He sighed and picked up the dossier detailing the possible murder of one Jean Radcliffe. A middle-aged, single woman, who might (or might not) have been bumped off by her married, harried and much poorer sister, who was the sole recipient of her sister's quarter-of-million life insurance policy. As a trained nurse, she would know several fairly clever ways of getting away with murder. An unusually unclear pathology report wasn't helping matters. The CPS was dithering.

But he simply couldn't concentrate.

He glanced at the clock and wondered when Superintendent Jerome Raleigh would get here. Jerome Raleigh. Mel gave a mental snort. Now what the hell kind of a name was *that* anyway? Detective Superintendent Jerome Raleigh. He sounded more like a character out of one of those ridiculous romantic novels. Rome Raleigh, the tall, dark and handsome dashing police superintendent.

Mel slammed shut the dossier on the Jean Radcliffe case and paced restlessly to the office window to look outside. It had started to drizzle.

If he was strictly honest with himself, he believed that Jerome Raleigh, the interloper from the Met, had snaffled his promotion, and that he, Mel, had let him do it. But there was sod all that he could do about it at this point. The real question now was – would he let it happen again? Did he really intend to let himself rot in his current DCI groove for the rest of his career? Because if he was to make sure that the next opening to superintendent had his name written all over it, he had to dump Janine. Nobody had said so to his face, but that was what it amounted to.

Hillary climbed the stairs to the Oxford County Court House and wondered why she hadn't become an architect. Or a barrister. Or a librarian. Or a dental hygienist, if it came to that. She'd had a good education, and had even made it into

Oxford's Radcliffe College, so in theory, she could have done anything with her life, And when faced with an afternoon like this one, watching her case go down the crapper because some gung-ho young copper had made an honest and infinitesimal administrative mistake, she wished that she could be saying 'rinse please' to some poor sod who'd just undergone root canal work instead. At least then the pain would be someone else's and not her own.

And it sure as hell had to beat being the senior officer in the dock facing a grinning defence attorney on the attack and a bored, hostile, or woebegone judge, watching the proceedings with a jaundiced eye.

'You look like you expect to be sent down for ten years.'

Hillary shot a surprised look upwards, and saw, coming down the court steps towards her, the blond, smiling, handsome features of DI Paul Danvers. The man who'd investigated her for corruption.

Truly, her cup runneth over.

'Paul,' she greeted wearily. Although she hadn't been best pleased to learn that he'd been transferred to the Kidlington nick, they'd at least agreed to bury the hatchet, which, as far as she was concerned, was the end of the matter. So she'd have been genuinely surprised had she been able to read Paul Danvers' mind in that moment.

Paul hadn't wanted to be seconded to the investigation team into Ronnie Greene's illegal activities in the first place, and from the first moment he'd met Hillary Greene, he'd liked it even less. Although he and Curtis Smith, a long-serving investigator of other cops, had quickly found proof of Ronnie's corruption, there had been not a scrap of evidence that his estranged wife had been involved. A good thing, since Paul had found Hillary Greene fascinating, right from the start. Tough, competent, and sexy.

So it was perhaps not so surprising that when the investigation had wound down and he'd gone back to his native Yorkshire, he'd found himself becoming restless. When he'd finally applied for the transfer to Oxford, he had more or less convinced himself that the move had been a strictly strategic one. Moving around looked good on a CV, and it had been time for a change. Besides, everyone believed promotions were easier to be had down south.

He hadn't been at Kidlington long, however, before he'd invited Hillary out to dinner. He'd been surprised but delighted when she'd said yes, and he thought that the evening had gone well. But since then, things had somehow stalled between them. She'd turned down a second date, and although she was always friendly enough whenever they met, he could tell she was hardly panting for his company. But Paul wasn't the sort to give up without a fight. He had a confidence-boosting track record when it came to women, and his good looks didn't hurt either.

Now he saw Hillary glance across at the tall, good looking brunette by his side and quickly introduced them, pleased to note the speculative look in Hillary's eye.

'Sorry, Detective Inspector Hillary Greene, this is Louise Bennett, a junior barrister. Louise, Hillary.'

Hillary and the lawyer shook hands, Louise giving the older woman a far more speculative look than was perhaps strictly necessary. True, Paul wanted to remind Hillary that other women found him attractive, if only to nudge her out of her neutrality a little and make her take a fresh look at him, but he didn't want trouble!

Hillary shifted on the steps uncomfortably. Being sized up as a potential rival by Danvers' latest love-interest wasn't something she'd been expecting. Did the barrister seriously think that her boyfriend might fancy her? Hillary wasn't sure how she felt about that.

Danvers was both younger, not to mention prettier, than herself. She could hardly take him seriously, right?

'So, why the glum face?' Paul asked curiously.

Distracted, Hillary sighed and quickly related her tale of woe. Louise perked up a bit at this, and listened with interest, then told her that, in her professional opinion, her chances of a conviction were low, the technicality being serious enough to let Gordon walk.

Hillary didn't really need to be told. Still, as she smiled goodbye to the happy couple and walked inside the quiet, cold, legal halls of the Oxford Court House, she would do her damnedest to nail the old-time forger. She failed, of course. It was only in westerns that the underdog got to win. Or, depending on your point of view, where the forces of law and order always got their man.

Defeated and spitting mad, she returned to The Mollern, her fifty foot narrowboat, just after dark.

After her frustrating appearance in court, the constant grating of Frank Ross's poisonous harping, and the will-they-won't they see-saw that was the Mel-and-Janine cat and dog show, she was in the mood for a long hot bath and a long cold vodka. But she had fat chance of indulging in either.

The Mollern boasted a feeble shower only, and although she had a bottle of vodka in the fridge, she had the rather distressing feeling that she wouldn't be able to stop at just the one drink.

When she'd first moved onto her favourite uncle's boat, she'd thought of it as a strictly temporary measure, but then Ronnie had died, with all the subsequent problems of probate; then had come the internal investigation team; finally this threat from the barmy army animal people, and so, after nearly two years, here she still was, thinking of the Mollern as home, when she wasn't cursing it.

She poured herself a cup of coffee, glad that the boating season was almost over. During the summer, the Mollern was constantly bobbing about in the wake of passing tourist craft. Now, as she sat down in the single armchair in the tiny lounge, she closed her eyes and wondered if she could be bothered to put on the television. She couldn't remember if she'd run the generator enough to chance it.

In the end, her drooping lids made the decision for her. She turned off the lights and hit the sack. She felt bone weary and in need of a good solid ten hours' kip. Things could only look better in the morning.

Yeah. Right.

*

About ten minutes into the morning, just after midnight to be precise, she was woken up by the ringing of her mobile. She groped for the light switch, fumbled the phone to her ear and yawned a response.

'Yeah?'

'Hillary? It's Mel. We've got a suspicious death. Get yourself over to Three Oaks Farm, Steeple Barton. I've sent Janine and Tommy ahead of you.' He paused. 'Ross, too,' he added apologetically.

He, like everyone else, wished the aliens would come and take Frank Ross away. Rumour had it that the flatfoots up at the big house were all pooling in to buy a special radio that would transmit just that message, deep into outer space. He wondered where he could sign up to give a donation.

Hillary muttered an assent and again yawned massively.

'Oh, and Hill?'

'Sir?'

'From the few reports I've had in, it looks like being a bad one.'

Hillary closed her eyes briefly. Great. Just what she needed.

chapter two

Hillary was on the move barely five minutes later. She turned right at the main road, heading for north Oxfordshire and the cluster of villages named Steeple something-or-other. She knew where Steeple Aston was, and North Aston, but had the map open beside her to make sure she didn't bypass the turning for Steeple Barton. It was the smallest of the villages, culminating in a dead end deep in the middle of the lush Cherwell Valley that spread from Deddington to Rousham.

Once on the back roads, the headlights began to pick out yellowing trees, rain-wet shaggy grass verges and the occasional glowing eyes of either deer or foxes. But not, she hoped, anybody's cat. The last thing she wanted to do now was to run over someone's pet Tiddles. She was going a little faster than the wet conditions called for, and she was conscious of the narrowness of the road, and the high hedges on either side. Occasionally she caught the odd glimpse of a house light, but traffic out here was virtually non-existent.

But, as she passed a large collection of barns and sheds, and took a narrow, single-track lane to Steeple Barton, she quickly found the dark, deserted night giving way to a veritable light show. A big, square farmhouse was lit up like the proverbial Christmas tree, with lights blazing from nearly every window. Even with the car windows firmly rolled up against the autumnal chill, Hillary could hear the susurration of sound that only came from a large crowd, emanating from within the rooms.

She frowned, wondering why a small village farmhouse

should be host to so many gawkers on a weekday night in the middle of nowhere. Surely word of the death hadn't travelled that far, that quickly?

Since there were no signs of patrol cars or police personnel at the farmhouse, she carried on down the heavily mud-streaked lane, cursing tractors and farming machinery as she went. Abruptly the village ended with a five-barred gate, which was being guarded by a solitary, miserable-looking constable. She rolled down the window as he approached, but he obviously recognized her because he nodded his head respectfully and began speaking at once.

'Ma'am, it's about four hundred yards further up. The doc's already here, and SOCO are on the way.'

Hillary watched as he opened the gate, then drove through, wincing as she heard the mud from the farm track slam into the underside of her car. Puff the Tragic Wagon was going to need a visit to the car wash like never before.

She felt the uneven, stone-and-mud track lurch beneath the wheels and sighed heavily. Just where the hell was she going? If someone actually lived at the end of this pitted track, they'd have cause to make a hermit jealous. Come to think of it, there were no power or telephone lines this far out either. Then her headlights picked out a cluster of vehicles, some patrol cars, others civilian, and saw the floodlights.

The preliminary team had obviously been busy. The big lamps were all centred on what looked to her to be a large, corrugated-iron barn. It looked silver and ghostly in the artificial glare, like some unhappily constructed spaceship that had abruptly found itself the unwanted focus of attention.

She got out, glad that she'd thought to wear her oldest pair of flatties, as mud sucked around her insteps with each step she took. Outside, the wet air promised more rain to come and, as she approached the barn, she felt her nose begin to itch. There was a pungent aroma all around that she couldn't quite place, until she stepped onto the filthy concrete floor of the barn, and spotted the large black-and-white shapes moving around uneasily in their stalls.

Cows. Lots of cows. Some chewed at the hay in wire baskets unconcernedly, others, more skittish, shied away as she walked past. All, however, were curious and watched her with those heart-breakingly lovely, brown, bovine eyes. No doubt, the herd of Fresians weren't used to midnight visitors.

A gaggle of white-suited people were clustered in a group about mid-way down the huge cowshed, and Hillary paused, not sure if the area had already been designated a protected crime scene. She'd seen no duckboards outside to protect footprints, presumably because the ground which a herd of cows used on a daily basis, wasn't ideal for the preservation of footprints and other evidence.

She coughed loudly, and Janine Tyler's fair head appeared from the scrum and came forward. She was holding a sheaf of papers clipped to a board, the usual PDFs (personal description forms) and others, that were the bane of a sergeant's life.

'Boss,' Janine said, nodding towards the group, signifying it was safe to come forward.

'Hello everyone, I'm DI Greene, the SIO here,' she introduced herself without preamble. Most of those present she knew, but not all of them. 'What have we got then…. bloody hell!'

She blinked, not at all sure that she was seeing what she thought she was seeing. The small crowd had parted, giving her her first view of their victim. She stared at the sight in front of her, trying, and failing, to take it in.

For there, lying on a cow-shit splattered, foul and redolent concrete floor, was a young bride, dressed in a fabulous white gown.

She opened her mouth, then closed it again. For a split second, she wondered if now wouldn't be a good time to wake up. She'd had particularly vivid dreams before, that had abruptly wondered off in outlandish Monty Python-like directions, but this one took the biscuit.

Then the surreal moment passed, and she shook her head. 'What the hell?' she said simply.

The dead girl didn't look a day over twenty, and had a mass of glorious, red-gold hair, swept up onto her head in what had once been a magnificent chignon. Now it was spread out in an untidy mass, and lay against the foul concrete like an ignominious halo. The wide-open eyes were a velvet pansy-brown, and beneath the voluminous, snow-white dress, Hillary guessed was a five-foot eight or so, lithe and willowy figure.

The dress itself was sumptuous – all satin, lace, and hand-stitched pearl beadwork. The bodice had a wasp-like waist, with the skirt flaring out into ballooning shimmering satin. The only thing missing was a wedding veil and a bouquet.

'Boss, there's been a fancy-dress party up at the farmhouse,' Janine said, reluctant to explain, but supposing she'd better. She so rarely got the chance to see her super-efficient DI lost for words that she wanted to revel in it for a few seconds more.

'Oh,' Hillary said flatly, then nodded. That explained the presence of the crowd back at the big house then. 'Obviously this is one of the guests?'

'Yes, boss,' Janine agreed.

Hillary stared down at the girl, noting the congested and contorted face, the protruding bluish-tinged tongue and tightly clenched fists. Even so, Hillary could tell that this young woman had once been very beautiful indeed. Kneeling down beside her, dressed in white coveralls, was a dapper man, currently inspecting the bride's neck.

'Has all the appearance of a manual strangulation,' Hillary said out loud, not a question so much as an opening gambit.

Doctor Steven Partridge looked up, and smiled briefly. 'Looks like it. And before you ask, I'd say she'd been dead less than an hour. Poor cow.'

Everybody groaned. Even Hillary.

She wasn't shocked by the bad-taste joke, because morgue-humour was something every cop quickly became used to. And she wasn't fooled into thinking, as some did, that Steven Partridge lacked respect for the dead. In fact, she knew the pathologist was one of the most compassionate men around. It was just … dealing with stuff like this on a regular basis, most people preferred to use humour, especially macabre and politically incorrect humour, as a handy armour.

Behind her, she heard the approach of another pair of feet, and automatically glanced down. But she could see why duckboards hadn't been set up here either. The chance of finding recognizable footprints on filthy wet concrete, trampled daily by cows, was pointless.

Tommy Lynch and Frank Ross approached curiously.

Frank took one look and whistled. Tommy Lynch seemed to pale visibly, although the big constable gave no other outward sign of distress. 'Guv,' he said instead and waited patiently for orders.

Hillary turned back to the corpse. 'She's wearing a gold and what looks to me like a real, diamond ring. Also a gold locket, and a fairly expensive looking wrist-watch. Any sign of a handbag?'

'Yes, guv,' a uniformed officer, obviously the designated Evidence Officer, came forward with a pile of neatly tagged plastic evidence bags and a list of contents.

'Was there a purse?' Hillary asked, ignoring the lipstick and other items of make-up, perfume and assorted detritus associated with females.

'Yes, guv,' the evidence officer, a middle-aged WPC, said at once. 'Contents: forty pounds in notes, two pound coins, and forty-two pence in change. Also two credit cards bearing the name Julia Reynolds, an organ donor card and driving licence ditto, a pack of condoms and a national lottery ticket.'

Hillary nodded. 'So the motive wasn't robbery,' she stated simply. She glanced around, shivering slightly as she did so. A damp autumn breeze could be felt penetrating the gaps in the corrugated iron walls and high, arched ceiling. Despite the steam rising from the many cattle, it felt unnaturally cold. The thud of hoofs and the shuffling of large, four-legged bodies, for some reason made the hairs rise on the back of her neck.

There was something primitive about this particular scene of death that set off superstitious nerves she never even suspected that she had. Perhaps it was because of the bridal outfit the victim was wearing. Or the fact that she'd been strangled. Whatever it was, Hillary felt as if she'd wandered into some sort of bizarre Grimm's fairy-tale: *The Beautiful Bride, Sacrificed in the Cow Byre.*

'All right, let's get cracking,' she said sharply, more to reprimand herself than anyone else. 'Tommy, Janine, start with the interviews up at the farm. Call out some local help,' she put in, before Janine could start complaining. 'It sounds like they've got quite a crowd up there. Find me a local bobby, someone who knows the people and the area – I want a word. Doc, you'd better do what's necessary. I think I can hear SOCO arriving. We'll want to clear the place for them. Frank, find the farmer, or cowman, or whoever's responsible for this barn and find out the routine.'

Frank snorted. 'What's to know? There won't be any security around here – who's going to want steal cows? This ain't "Bonanza".'

She shot him a look, and he muttered something about a similarity between cows and senior women police officers, and shuffled off. As he did so, he kicked at the metal railings of one of the stalls, sending the harmless animal behind it jumping hysterically to the back. The whole barn boomed like the inside of a gong as it hit the side of the wall, the reverberation making everyone jump.

'Somebody ought to report you to the RSPCA, you wanker,' someone called out, but Frank Ross could be selectively deaf when he chose.

Hillary glanced across at Janine, who was busy sorting out witness statement forms. 'Anything else before I lose you?' Hillary asked, without much hope. She doubted Janine could have got here more than ten minutes before herself.

'Boss,' Janine muttered, the corner of one form gripped between her teeth as she rearranged others on top of her clipboard. She spat it out.

'The vic's name is Julia Reynolds, twenty years old, lived with her parents in Kirtlington. She was a guest of a guest at the party. She was found by the farmer's son, one Michael Wallis, and his girlfriend … er …' – she squinted at her notebook shorthand – 'Jenny Porter, and they ran back to the house to call it in. They're outside, in one of the cars. I think that's about it.'

Hillary nodded. She didn't envy Janine and Tommy their night of interviews. The guests would soon been clamouring to be let home to their beds.

'Oh and Tommy,' Hillary called, making the young DC hurry back expectantly. 'Gather up any cameras and film taken at the party and get the police lab to print them off. You never know your luck.'

Tommy nodded, jotting down the reminder in his notebook.

Hillary, seeing the first of the SOCO team arrive, crouched down beside Steven Partridge. 'Skin under the fingernails?' she prompted.

He held up one of the bride's hands in his gloved own, examining the pearl-pink painted nails judiciously. 'I wouldn't be surprised. You don't have someone's hands around your throat, strangling the life out of you, without putting up a struggle.'

Hillary grunted. That wasn't always the case, but she wasn't about to argue semantics now. She glanced around, and shivered again. 'Why would a beautiful young party guest want to come out here to this filthy, smelly hole?'

The doc grinned. 'You're asking me?'

Hillary laughed. Doc Partridge was well known for his fussy and sartorial elegance.

'Yeah, but let's face it: it's not the sort of place a pretty girl would agree to meet a lover, is it? And if she just wanted a breath of fresh air, this isn't the place for it.' And she coughed, the pungent bovine perfume making her point for her. 'And if she just wanted somewhere to have a quiet chat with someone, I'm sure the farmhouse had the odd quiet room — or even the garden, at a pinch. Could she have been kidnapped at the house and forced here?'

Steven Partridge shrugged, and nodded at the long, tight-fitting satin sleeves. 'Could be, but I'll have to get her on the table before I can do even a preliminary search for any bruising on the arms.'

'Ma'am?' a diffident voice interrupted her musing, and she glanced up, expecting the police photographer or another SOCO to hoick her out of it, but it was a fresh-faced uniformed officer who nodded down at her.

'Sorry, ma'am, I was told you wanted to speak to me.'

Hillary thought, I did? Then nodded. Right. 'You must be the local man I asked for.'

'Yes, ma'am. Dennis Warner. I live at Duns Tew, just across the way.'

Hillary nodded and stood up, trying to pretend her back didn't ache as she did so, and slowly walked away from the body. Once outside in the dark, wet air, she took a deep breath, promptly wished she hadn't, and nodded towards the lane. 'Come on, let's get out of here.' The sweetly corrupt scent of cattle was beginning to make her feel sick.

Dennis Warner grinned. 'You get used to it. Living out here.'

Hillary supposed you did.

'So, what can you tell me about the farm?' she asked.

'Ma'am. It's owned by a man called Owen Wallis. Local, born and bred. The Wallises have owned Three Oaks farm for yonks. Don't quite go back to the Doomsday Book, but you get the picture. Back in the 1500s, the Wallises were "Sirs" and the like, but they lost the title somewhere down the line. They still own several small properties in Steeple Barton though. Used to be for the workers, now they rent them out to city folk for weekend places and such. Makes a tidy sum from rent alone, I reckon.'

Hillary nodded. Most senior investigating officers would be chivvying him along by now, but she'd never found that having good background gen, even stuff that couldn't possibly be relevant, had ever hurt an investigation.

'Resented for it much in the village?' she wondered aloud.

Dennis shrugged. 'Not so's you'd notice. Nowadays, half the village is made up of strangers. It's not as if the farm employs that many. And those they do don't seem to complain. I reckon they're as happy to buy a council house on a mortgage as the rest of us.'

Hillary nodded. 'Big family?'

'Not any more. Just old man Wallis – well, not so old, he's in his fifties, I suppose. Owen Wallis, his wife, Wendy, and the one lad, Michael. It's their silver wedding anniversary – that's what the shindig's for.'

Hillary nodded. It was unusual to have a big party on a week night; most people tended to opt for a Saturday. Any particular reason for the Wallises to do it this way round? 'So, what do you know about the son Michael? He's got a girlfriend?'

'Yerse, local girl. Michael's been away at agricultural college, only coming home during the holidays. Seems happy enough to do his bit and eventually take over the farm.'

'It's in good financial shape?'

'Not as good as it was before the foot-and-mouth,' Dennis said quickly.

Obviously, Hillary thought, that particular disaster still cut deep. 'Oh? Did the Wallises loose their herd?'

'No. They were lucky. But still, the Wallises aren't quite the force they used to be. Rumour has it Owen Wallis is coming up with some sort of scheme to refill the family coffers. Nobody quite knows what it is, but it is said that Theo Greenwood is involved.'

'Greenwood?'

'He owns the Hayrick Inn, up on the main road. Probably heard of it?'

Hillary had. A big old coaching inn, catering to the Oxford to Banbury trade. A deeply attractive, creeper-covered inn, which had just had a big new annexe controversially built at the back of it. Doing a roaring trade with high-end conferences and the local elite.

'They recently hired one of those nearly-famous TV chefs, right?' she prompted.

'Right. The owner was at the party tonight – him and his son, Roger.'

They'd been walking steadily down the side of the muddy track, and were now approaching the gate. Wordlessly, Hillary turned and slowly began to walk back again.

'What do you know about the victim, Julia Reynolds?'

'Lived in Kirtlingon, ma'am, in one of them council house cul-de-sacs just off the road that leads to Bletchington,' Dennis said promptly. 'She runs her own travelling hair-styling business.'

Hillary raised an eyebrow. 'She seemed pretty young to be doing that.' Usually girls interested in that sort of thing went straight from school at sixteen to do some course or apprenticeship, and then into a hair-dressing salon where they swept the floors and answered the phone, learning the job from the ground up, and only progressing from hair-washing to the more interesting stuff much later.

Dennis snorted. 'Julia was never one to hold back,' he said flatly. 'Not that I knew her that well, mind,' he added hastily, in case Hillary Greene began to wonder. Dennis, who usually worked out of the Bicester nick, didn't know much about Thames Valley Headquarters personnel, but he, along with every other copper in Oxfordshire, knew about Ronnie Greene all right. And that his widow, so scuttlebutt had it, was as decent a copper as he had been bent. Rumour also said that she was highly rated as a detective (not always synonymous with SIOs) and that it was always a treat to work on one of her cases. So the last thing he wanted to do was get thrown off the case because he was deemed to be too close to the victim.

'It's just that we all went to the local comp, and one of my mates went out with her for a few months.'

Hillary nodded. 'So, what's her rep?'

Dennis paused and looked up, noticing for the first time that the misty drizzle was rapidly turning into fog. 'Well, she was always one of those girls who was gonna go places, you know?' he began, after a thoughtful silence. 'Always had big ideas, big plans. And she was a looker, so nobody laughed when she said it. It was typical of her to go independent, for instance, and nobody would be surprised to find out she was making a go of it. She got on well with people, and she knew how to use her looks, like. I mean, not just with the men –

although there were always plenty of them – but with women, too. You know, all these old dears she permed and primped, probably took one look at her and thought that she could turn them into an Evangelista overnight, and Julia would play up to that.'

Hillary nodded. 'So, what was she doing at the party tonight? She a friend of the Wallises?' On the face of it, that didn't seem likely. What did a working-class hairdresser (albeit one with charm and ambition) have in common with landed (if impoverished) gentry?

'No, ma'am, I don't think so. If I had to guess, I'd say she was almost certainly brought here by a man. It'd be just the sort of thing Julia would like. You know, so she could go to work tomorrow and tell all her old biddies that she'd been up at Three Oaks farm at the shindig of the season. That'd be the kind of thing that would give her a real thrill. To be in with the country set, so to speak.'

Hillary nodded. 'But she won't be going to work tomorrow, will she, Constable Warner? And all her old biddies will be gossiping about her, instead.'

Although she could understand why the young constable was excited to be working on his first murder case, and wouldn't have been human if he didn't feel alert and eager to help, it never hurt to be reminded that, for the victim, life, in all its variations, was now over.

Dennis gulped audibly and uncomfortably. 'Yes, ma'am,' he said woodenly.

'So, did she have any brothers and sisters?'

'No, ma'am, I don't think so.'

'All right. I want you to prepare a list of any friends you know she has, and give it to DC Lynch. Anything else you know about her that you think might be useful?'

Dennis Warner wondered how he should respond to that. He was well aware that he'd just been mildly reprimanded, and was reluctant now to speak ill of the dead. OK, if he was honest, he'd deserved it. He *had* sort of forgotten that the poor girl was really dead, and all that that meant.

'I won't bite,' Hillary Greene said in the darkness, her voice definitely sounding as if it was smiling.

And Warner suddenly remembered, with relief, that Hillary Greene wasn't said to be one of those moody sods who could snap your head off or pat you on the back for no particular reason, just as the fancy took them.

'She was said to be a party girl,' he began cautiously.

'Drugs?'

'More likely booze. She liked a drink, liked to get really rat-arsed. And she'd been known to keep two or more men on a string, when it suited her.'

'Right. So, by eleven, eleven thirty, she was likely to have been at least well on the way to being merry,' Hillary mused. 'Was she the sort who became more malleable, or more strident, when she got drunk?'

'Dunno, ma'am,' Dennis said frankly.

Hillary nodded. 'Right, see if you can find out. Well, that's all for now. You might like to join my team at the farmhouse, help out with witness statements if you like. I'm sure you know the drill.'

'Ma'am,' Dennis said, and left her, retracing his steps back down the rutted path. So that was the famous DI Greene. All things considered, he thought he'd come off very well.

Back at the cowshed, Hillary approached a platinum-coloured Mondeo which had its interior light on, revealing two dark-haired people sitting in the back seat. Unless she missed her guess, Michael Wallis and his girlfriend. A uniformed PC was sitting in the front passenger seat and he jumped when she tapped on the glass. He was one she didn't know, so she showed her card and, as much for his passengers' benefit as himself, said, 'Detective Inspector Hillary Greene, from Thames Valley, Kidlington. I'm the senior investigating officer here.'

She indicated with a jerk of her head to the uniformed officer that she wanted him to get out, and murmured quietly, 'Michael Wallis and Jenny Porter?'

'Yes, ma'am.'

'They been talking much?'

'No, ma'am. The girl's a bit upset, and been crying like. Then small chit chat. Nothing about the vic. Or the circs.'

Hillary nodded, then slipped into the passenger seat, turning around to face the young couple behind her.

Jenny was a rather plain-looking girl, with long dark hair and small, light-coloured eyes. She was dressed as Little Bo Peep, with cute, puffed sleeves of white, with a navy-blue and white pinafore dress. Her shepherd's crook, made of balsa wood, lay across both her lap and that of her companion. She also held a daisy-covered bonnet in her lap, twisting it compulsively this way and that. Hillary hoped it wasn't a rented costume, because she'd have to pay for the ruined hat if it was. In contrast, Michael Wallis was something of a looker, and was dressed as a pirate. He even looked a bit like Johnny Depp from that pirate movie. Even sitting down in the back seat, Hillary could tell he'd be tall, at least six feet, and he had heavy, slightly wavy dark-brown hair, high cheekbones, and big dark eyes that would give even his father's cows a run for their money. A black eye patch, pushed up to the top of his forehead now, gave him a rakish air. She wouldn't normally have put these two together. It just goes to show, she thought. Never judge a book by its cover.

'Jenny, isn't it?' she said, giving a small smile and thrusting her hand between the two front seats. The girl took it quickly and smiled, visibly relaxing. 'And Michael?'

'Right.'

Again, hands were shaken.

'So, what can you tell me?' She kept the question deliberately vague, and her eyes on Michael. She'd often found an open-ended question could produce more information than ones that could simply be answered either yes or no. Especially if asked of a man, in front of a girlfriend in obvious need of protection and succour. Some of Hillary's best interviews had been conducted in situations just like these. If either Michael or Jenny had something to hide, she'd have willingly bet her next month's salary that it would be right here and right now that she'd find out about it.

'Well, not much really.' Michael Wallis spoke with neither an upper class nor country yokel accent, which would no doubt serve him well in his chosen career in land management. 'Mum and Dad are having this big party for their twenty-fifth. Most of their friends are around their age, and to be honest, I expected it to be a bit of a bore, and it was.'

Jenny Porter giggled unexpectedly. Then she looked shocked and put a hand over her mouth. Hillary was fairly sure it was down to nerves, rather than to her being a natural giggler.

She smiled back. 'Don't worry. I know – it's just the shock. Don't worry about it.' Nobody looked less like a giggler than the plain and unpretentious Porter girl.

'Thanks,' she whispered back.

'So, Michael. Go on,' Hillary prompted.

'Well, it's because it *was* so boring that me and Jen decided to cut loose for a little while, and came up here.'

Hillary glanced out of the window pointedly. The cowshed didn't look any more salubrious for being festooned with the bright yellow and black police tapes being set up around it.

'I wanted to see the cows,' Jenny Porter said defensively, and in direct response to the police woman's obvious disbelief. 'I know that sounds silly, but I did.' Her chin rose in half-hearted belligerence, but Hillary merely nodded. In truth, she'd heard less unlikely things.

The trouble was, when you were paid to have a suspicious mind, it was sometimes hard to believe even the most believable of explanations. Over the years however, experience helped you sort the wheat from the chaff, and she was perfectly willing to believe that a plain young girl with a surprisingly good-looking and well-to-do (by most people's standards, at any rate) boyfriend, would be perfectly willing to go and look at cows, if it meant spending some time alone with the object of her desire. It would be better with a full moon and haystack, perhaps, but a cowshed in the rain would do if you were desperate enough.

'So you came up here and … what? Just found her?' she asked, letting a touch of scepticism creep into her voice now.

'But that's just what we did,' Jenny jumped right in, sounding just a little aggrieved. 'We walked up the path, talking about next year's summer holidays - we want to go somewhere nice, Corfu maybe, or somewhere in the Caribbean.' Jenny paused for a breath. 'And we came in here, and Michael pointed out what made a good milker,' she paused for another breath whilst Hillary hid a smile, 'and ...well, we kissed for a little bit, and then Michael said he could see something further down the barn and hoped one of the cows hadn't got out. We walked down ... and Michael used his lighter and ... there she was. This big white blob.'

Jenny Porter began to cry. Hillary handed over a tissue from the box of Kleenex she'd spotted on the car's dashboard.

As his girlfriend sniffled, Michael took up the story. 'I could see at once that things were bad, so I got Jenny out of there, and told her to wait, whilst I ran back to the house and phoned you lot.'

'You didn't have a mobile?'

'Not on me.'

'And did you go back inside whilst you were waiting, Jenny?'

The other girl shuddered. 'Oh no. I didn't want to go back in there.'

'Did either of you see anybody when you were walking up the track?'

They looked at one another then shook their heads. 'Did you hear a car start up, or did one pass you by as you walked out the house?'

'No, it was too early for the guests to start leaving,' Michael said.

'Did you recognize her?' Hillary asked, and saw Michael Wallis tense. He'd obviously been expecting the question, and Hillary was interested to see how he'd tackle it.

'Yes. Her name was Julia. She came with somebody. The son of one of Dad's cronies, I think. I've seen her around sometimes. I think she's a local girl.'

Hillary didn't miss the quick, worried look Jenny gave her

31

lover. But was that just a plain girl's insecurity, or did she have some other reason to think that Michael's off-hand admission was just a shade too casual? Hillary made a mental note to find out if Michael Wallis had ever been one of the men Julia Reynolds had liked to lead around on her string, then nodded.

'OK. You can take Jenny home now. But someone will be in touch to take a proper written statement.'

Michael nodded. He didn't look exactly thrilled at the prospect.

Hillary climbed out of the car and went back to the cowshed. SOCO were still going about their quiet business, whilst two men waited to remove the body to the mortuary. She had no doubt that she was looking for a man, probably a jealous lover or would-be boyfriend. When a beautiful young girl, not known for her monogamous ways, ended up strangled at a party, you didn't have to be Hercule Poirot to figure it out: one of Julia Reynolds' men had turned from a lover to a killer.

Now all she had to do was put a name to him.

chapter three

Hillary awoke to the sound of arguing starlings. She fumbled from the narrow bed, grabbed a twenty-second shower and dressed. Living on a boat made drinking and washing water especially precious, but she'd long since become expert at using the least possible amount of everything, including the batteries and the calor-gas cylinders.

She boiled the kettle (enough water for one cup exactly) and glanced at her watch, debating whether to head for the HQ or go straight back to Three Oaks Farm. She slung her bag over her shoulder and duck-walked up the iron stairs to avoid banging her head, and absently padlocked the doors behind her.

Over on Willowsands, her neighbour, Nancy Walker, was listening to something weird. Probably some 'new age' tape her latest conquest had given her. As a forty-something widow, Nancy trawled the male student body around the environs of Oxford like a killer whale on the lookout for seals.

Once in the car, she decided she'd better check in at the office, and was glad that she did. The moment she stepped inside, the desk sergeant nobbled her.

'Here, looks like your new super has just arrived,' the sergeant, an all-knowing, all-wise veteran of twenty years, tipped her the wink before the door had even shut behind her.

'And?' Hillary asked, veering off to the desk immediately. As any green flat foot soon found out, if you ever wanted to know what was what, you asked the desk sergeant. His knowledge was all knowing and indiscriminate – from who was boffing the tea ladies, to the latest gaffe to issue forth from the lips of the chief constable's good lady wife.

'Not married, but no odds yet on whether he's in the closet,' the sergeant said now with a quick smirk. 'Got plenty up here, though' – he tapped his temple – 'and didn't do the usual stints in press liaisons or records. Met rated him all right, but nobody's yet sussed out why he moved.'

Hillary shook her head woefully. 'And is that all you know?' she asked, rolling her eyes. 'You're falling down on the job, Harry.' Everyone called the sergeant Harry, although Hillary had heard that wasn't his actual name.

'Give us a chance, guv,' the desk sergeant grinned back. 'Give me another hour, and you can place your bets along with the rest of 'em.'

Hillary wondered what, other than the sexual orientation of the new super, would be available for the big house's gambling aficionados by lunchtime. No doubt there'd be some sort of pool on whether he'd been pushed or had jumped from the Met. Odds on there'd be much jockeying and shoving around about any potential scandals in his background. She might put a fiver down on him being a secret drinker, but she'd have to check the state of his eyes first.

She used her key-card and code to gain access to the main office, and made her way to her desk. None of her team was yet in, and she wasn't surprised. After pulling an all-nighter, who could blame them? She shifted through the paperwork, noting the preliminary interview reports handed in by the uniforms. She speed-read her way through them, feeling her spirits sink as she did so.

Apparently, the Wallises 25th wedding anniversary party hadn't confined itself to the main living-room, but had spilled over in to the kitchen, the new conservatory, the library, and various rooms in between. Some hardy souls had even been dancing in the garden, to the music of the live band.

So nobody would have an air tight alibi, unless they had stuck with one person the whole night. And who did that at a party? Any one of the – she did a quick mental assessment of the numbers – fifty-five to sixty or so male partygoers could have sneaked out for ten, fifteen minutes, and killed Julia Reynolds.

She began sorting through them, working up a pile of more-or-less non-starters. Into these she tossed the too old and the three physically incapacitated (one in a wheelchair, one with debilitating arthritis in both hands, and one who'd broken an arm at golf – a pity the report didn't say how the prat had managed to do that!) and, after a moment's thought, the two openly gay couples who had been at the party. She was not dismissing any of them as such, only putting them at the bottom of the pile.

That still left a depressingly large list of suspects. And since there was no such thing as a happily married couple – at least, not to a copper investigating a murder – she couldn't see how she could cull the list any further. The very young – how old did a lad have to be to be able to strangle a woman? – she also downgraded. Up to the age of fourteen, anyway. Still, teenagers were notorious for being prey to their hormones, and she couldn't see the beautiful, confident and ambitious Julia Reynolds being particularly kind to love-struck teenagers. There were five between the ages of fourteen and nineteen at the party, most of them sons of invited guests.

Naturally, the married men would have a lot to lose if Julia was threatening to tell the wife about their little fling and had to be prime suspects, until eliminated.

Then there was her boyfriend. She'd noted that several of the witness reports confirmed that Julia had arrived with Roger Greenwood, and that they were considered to be an item. He would have to be top of the list for now. Nor was she forgetting the farmer's son. Suspicion often fell on the finder of the body, sometimes with cause, sometimes without. The only thing in Michael Wallis's favour was that he hadn't been alone. Hillary supposed Jenny Porter could have been an accomplice, but she didn't think so. But there was nothing to say Wallis hadn't killed Julia earlier, then suggested the walk to Jenny in order for him to have a witness to the 'discovery'. It wouldn't be the first time that had happened. Killers knew a lot about the pitfalls of forensic evidence nowadays, thanks to pathology dramas on the television, and forensic-based thrillers. Wallis might have been afraid he'd have left traces at the scene, and returning there to find the body was as good a means as any of explaining away any traces of him found there.

She'd have to get one of the uniforms to press Jenny Porter on who it was who'd suggested the little sojourn in the barn, and who'd been leading the way.

Over the course of the morning, first Janine and then Tommy trickled in, looking heavy-eyed and slouch-footed. Of Frank, mercifully, there was still no sign. Perhaps the aliens had finally come for him and done everybody a favour.

'Guv,' Tommy said, glancing at the preliminary forensics reports Hillary was now reading. 'Anything good?'

'Not so far. As we thought, the cowshed floor was too contaminated for any really good evidence. There are still one or two things pending, but I think most of our bread and butter is going to come from the corpse itself.'

Tommy, who was drinking coffee, gulped a bit too much and began to cough. Janine half-heartedly slapped him on the back. 'Got to toughen up, Tommy,' she muttered, teasingly.

'Glad you think that way,' Hillary said sardonically. 'You can attend the post-mortem.'

Janine sighed heavily. 'Yes, boss,' she said. Then added immediately, 'Why can't Ross go?'

Hillary rolled her eyes. 'What have you got against Doc Partridge? You know we have to keep him sweet. If we sic Frank on him, the next four bodies we send over will be put to the back of the queue. That's what he did last time.'

Janine sighed again, but didn't argue with Hillary's logic.

'Tommy, I want you to get a list of all Julia's clients,' she carried on. 'And no, I don't think some silver-haired matron strangled her because she hated the colour of her latest rinse, but people talk to their hairdressers. And vice versa. You never know what titbits they might have learned about our vic and be willing to pass on. And since we're dealing with a strangling, and statistics show that we're almost certainly looking for a man and that sex is going to come somewhere in the equation, concentrate on her men friends. Stalkers. Some over-enthusiastic admirer. You know the drill.'

'Guv,' Tommy said. He wasn't sure, being big and black and male, that he was the ideal candidate to go talking to middle-aged or timid old ladies, but he'd give it his best shot. For Hillary Greene, he was always willing to give things his best shot.

He watched her now as she reached for the phone, and saw that she was allowing her hair to grow longer than her usual shoulder-length bob. Was that deliberate, or had she simply not realized? He thought she'd look good with long hair - it was a lovely, dark-brown colour, like a hazelnut. He imagined her walking across the car-park, a breeze blowing it back off her face, like one of those advertisements for shampoo. Then he saw Frank Ross pushing through the door and quickly got on the phone himself. The last thing he wanted was for that bastard Ross to know how he felt about the boss. His life wouldn't be worth living.

'Guv,' Ross said sourly, scratching under his armpit, leaving no one downwind of him in any doubt that he'd skipped his morning shower. 'The cowshed is never locked. The steel doors shut with a simple latch and there's some dim overhead lighting, for the winter months. There's no valuable milking equipment or anything, it's just a shelter for the cows, so there's no security alarm or system. It's just a bloody iron barn in the middle of nowhere.'

His tone said that he could have told her that without traipsing all over Steeple Barton to find the cowman and asking him about it.

Hillary nodded. 'Do they have a problem with dossers? Tramps sheltering overnight, new age travellers, that kind of thing?'

Frank hadn't thought to ask. 'No, guv, nothing like that,' he said firmly. He was buggered if he was going to go back to ask either. It was as plain as the spot on his nose that the vic had been done in by a jealous boyfriend. Everyone knew Hillary Greene went over the top when it came to checking out long shots. And she was always giving him, one of her oldest-serving and best sergeants, the scut work. He was getting sick and tired of it. No point in complaining to Mel though; he and the bitch from Thrupp were in each other's pockets.

Hillary nodded. So the passing-tramp theory didn't look likely. Still, it had been a wet and nasty night and couldn't be totally discounted. But even if some gentleman of the road had been kipping down there in the straw and body warmth of a dozing cow, why would he up and strangle Julia Reynolds? And come to that, why had Julia Reynolds been there in the first place?

She'd almost certainly rented the wedding dress, so the last thing she'd want to do is get it dirty and have to pay for cleaning. And a cow-shit infested shed was surely the last place she'd choose to go in a voluminous white gown. Voluntarily, that was.

No, she just couldn't see how an anonymous tramp would fit in the frame. Something of a relief, that, considering how hard it would be to track down an itinerant.

'Frank, I want.... Hey up, heads up. Looks like we've got company,' she hissed, straightening up in her chair and closing the folder in front of her, out of habit.

Janine and Tommy, whose desks faced hers, swivelled around in their chairs as Mel Mallow stepped out of his office and cleared his throat loudly. Beside him stood a tall, lean man, with neatly cut dark-gold hair. He was dressed in a dark-blue suit and anonymous tie. His eyes, which were scanning the room, didn't look as if they were missing much.

So this was the new super. The may be gay, may be scandalous man from the Met.

'If I could just have your attention for a minute,' Mel yelled, although the room had very quickly fallen silent. 'I'd like to introduce you to Superintendent Jerome Raleigh. Superintendent Raleigh, as you know, is taking over Marcus Donleavy's old patch. Sir?'

Mel stepped back and Janine winced, knowing how much he must be hating every moment of this. It was no secret between the two of them just how hungry Mel had been for the promotion.

'I won't keep you,' Jerome Raleigh said crisply, 'I know you've all got more cases on than you need, and the last thing you want is to listen to a speech. I just want to tell you that I'm a hands-on copper, and I look after my people. That means I want to be kept informed, and I want anyone with a problem to come to me immediately so that it can be straightened out before it becomes a problem for everyone. It'll take me a while to learn the patch, so I'd appreciate some patience. I've spoken for some time with Chief Superintendent Donleavy, and his methods and mine pretty much gel, so I'm not anticipating too many teething pains. Right, that's it.'

He nodded once, then glanced back at Mel, who walked him to the door. When he returned, DCI Mallow went straight back to his office and the room held its collective breath, wondering if he'd slam the door. But Hillary could have told them that he wouldn't. Mellow Mallow hadn't got his nickname through irony. But she and Janine weren't the only ones to guess just how much he must be smarting, right about now.

'Wow, what a hunk,' Janine said thoughtfully. 'Did you see the colour of his eyes?'

Hillary, who hadn't (and had been wondering, on and off for some time, whether she should bite the bullet and get an eye test) shrugged. 'Can't say as I noticed.'

'Sherry,' Janine said definitely.

Frank Ross snorted. 'You mean red? I bet he's a boozer. That's why the Met jettisoned him.' But he sounded cheerful at the thought of another kindred spirit, and one in a high-ranking position at that, occupying his nick.

Janine didn't deign to reply. Instead she transferred the brochures she had in her desk drawer into a plain beige folder and made her way nonchalantly to Mel's door. A few grins broke out as she knocked and entered, but nobody begrudged the DCI some loving comfort just then.

'Hey, he didn't look anything special to me,' Janine lied, shutting the door carefully behind her. 'I bet he'll be gone by the end of next year.'

Mel, who was staring out of the window, looked back at her and shook his head. 'I don't know. He's a close sod, I'll give him that. I spent nearly all day yesterday with him, and didn't get even a hint of what made him tick.'

'Never mind, darlin', you'll soon be picking over his bones,' Janine said cheerfully and, standing beside him, bent over to open the folder. 'I've been thinking about getting away for a weekend somewhere, just you and me. You know, one of those country hotels, where they serve four-star food and we can learn archery or something totally useless. What do you think of this one – it's in the Cotswolds, so it's not much travelling? Or maybe the New Forest, or the Norfolk Broads? The rates are cheaper out of season, plus places won't be so crowded.'

Mel glanced unenthusiastically at the brochures. He couldn't afford to be seen to take time off now, even if it was a legitimate weekend he was entitled to. Introducing Raleigh had been a salutary lesson that was going to rankle for some time yet.

'Come on, it'll be fun,' Janine pushed, sensing his distinct lack of enthusiasm. She was looking forward to a little pampering, and nearly all the hotels had spas and massages, aromatherapy treatments and beautician services as part of the package.

'Not now, Janine,' Mel said irritably. 'And you've got a big case on, haven't you?'

Janine's eyes flashed, and Mel knew what that meant. 'Look, leave these with me, and I'll see which ones I like the look of, and when things are quieter, we'll see,' he said quickly. He knew he was placating her, and the continual need to do so was becoming more and more annoying. 'Now, I have to get on. Anything new on Julia Reynolds?'

Janine gritted her teeth and smiled. She hated it when Mel pulled rank on her. But she should have known better than to pick a fight with him whilst she was at work. It gave him a heaven-sent opportunity to put one over on her. No, she'd wait until tonight to bring this up again. If Mel thought he was going to get away with this shit, he had another think coming. What was the point of having a better-off, older and good-looking boyfriend, if he couldn't splurge on her now and then?

'Sir,' Janine said negatively, and left. And all the office heard her slamming the door on the way out.

Jerome Raleigh finished reading the last of the personnel reports Marcus Donleavy had left for him, and pushed them away, putting the cap back on his pen and tossing it down restlessly on the folder. He had an office on the top floor, overlooking the leafy, rather pleasant streets of Kidlington. He wasn't sure he particularly liked it – either the office or the town.

Kidlington was, technically, a large village he supposed, although he expected the inhabitants looked on it as more of a town. It was certainly a far cry from the Capital, but then, that too, suited his purposes for the moment. Here he'd have far more leeway. And since all his friends had been left behind, and had no idea what he was up to, he'd be able to get on with things with a free hand.

But he'd have to be careful. And patient. Very patient.

All in all, he thought the morning had gone reasonably well. None of the faces he'd seen had been openly hostile, which was a relief. Philip Mallow wasn't a particularly happy bunny, but Jerome had a good idea why that was. His own speech to the troops had gone down well, striking the right balance between leadership and approachability. It would take some time for them to get to trust him though. He'd moved about enough in his earlier career to know that these things took time.

Still, he was reasonably confident that the team here was a good bunch. With the exception of one or two slackers, the usual time-servers and rank-and-file incompetents, the only really bad apple was Frank Ross.

Donleavy had warned him that the best friend of the notorious Ronnie Greene was universally loathed, and with good reason, though on occasion he could prove useful. The lowlives were scared of him, and he had an extensive list of narks that was second to none. He could generally be relied on when it came to the hard stuff, and was a good man to have guarding your back during a riot or public disorder. He was less of an asset otherwise, and Jerome had wondered (and very carefully asked) why he'd been assigned to Hillary Greene's team.

He'd had to tread carefully there, suspecting that Ronnie and Hillary Green might have had reasons of their own for keeping a man like Frank Ross close, but he'd been quickly disabused of that idea.

Every superintendent – if he was good, and Marcus Donleavy, Jerome had quickly realised, was *very* good indeed – knew his patch and his people like the back of his hand, and Donleavy had been very clear that not only was Hillary totally clean of any of her husband's dirty dealings, but was one of the best, if not *the* top cop, on his team.

Frank Ross had simply been foisted on her because nobody else could stand or deal with the bloke. Not that Hillary had appreciated the vote of confidence in her patience at the time, Donleavy had chuckled. Now, everyone supposed that she'd simply got used to having the poisonous little cretin around.

After reading DI Greene's file, Jerome had found himself similarly impressed by her capabilities. He knew, as did Marcus, that not every cop was a natural detective. Some worked strictly by the book because they lacked the imagination, skill, or experience, to do otherwise. Most played politics, with some seeing the catching of villains as barely a means to an end. Only a golden few had a flair for solving cases, and he could see from Hillary Greene's conviction rate, why the public prosecutions office regarded her, too.

He hoped they'd get on. If he had to baby-sit Philip Mallow's hurt feelings for any length of time, he'd need all the allies he could get.

Raleigh closed her file thoughtfully and leaned back in his chair, stretching. Whether or not she'd be useful to him, was another matter. She might be *too* good. *Too* clever. She might even find out what had brought him to Thames Valley, and that simply wouldn't do. No, it might just be that Frank Ross would be a far better bet after all. Men like him could be useful, if given the right incentive. He'd have to sound him out carefully and see, and if he seemed to be up for it, Jerome would then set about cultivating him – as distasteful as that might be.

Hillary watched the fox slink across the road a few yards ahead of her and lightly touched the brakes. In daylight, the single-track road to Steeple Barton seemed even more treacherous than in the dark. Clumps of patterned mud, fresh from a tractor's gigantic wheels, gave the surface a greasy look, and the high hedges on either side gave her a vague feeling of claustrophobia. The fox, spotting her at last, broke into a panicked run and promptly disappeared. Unlike many of her colleagues, Hillary had never felt the yen to leave Oxfordshire for the bigger, badder cities. At heart, she supposed, she preferred to see trees and fields than factories and housing estates.

As the hedges opened up to reveal the tiny village green, Hillary noticed a man climbing awkwardly over a field gate. There was nothing particularly odd about that, except that he didn't seem very comfortable doing it. People who lived in the countryside quickly developed an easy climbing manner for negotiating stiles, fences and gates, but this man looked clumsy. He wasn't helped by having gangling legs and arms, and being dressed in a green anorak that was too new. His wellingtons were also fresh-from-the-shop clean. He struck her as someone trying to look like a local, and not quite making it.

Press, Hillary thought grimly. Had to be. But she'd have thought they would be all gone by now. Those who had gathered like ghouls in the early hours, had taken their mandatory shot of the mortuary van being driven away, and had no doubt long since pestered the Wallises for an interview and filed their stories. Now it was the police press liaison officer who'd be taking the brunt back at HQ. There could always be scavengers left hanging about, she supposed.

She watched the sandy-haired man thoughtfully as he set off over the field. From her mental map of last night, she was pretty sure the pasture would lead towards Three Oaks Farm.

She went past the small cluster of pretty cottages, a tiny old schoolhouse (long since converted to a private residence) and single post box, and followed the road to the end. The gate to the cowsheds now stood unguarded, the police sentinel having been gratefully dismissed. If there'd been even a small gathering of press, the uniformed officer would have been obliged to remain and secure the premises, but nowadays, murders didn't get the sensational attention they once did. Although, Hillary suspected, once word got out that the victim had been dressed as a bride, they'd soon come traipsing back. The macabre always attracted them. She could almost see the gory and highly inaccurate headlines now.

She turned and parked the car facing back the way she'd come, then walked the short distance back up the road to the farmhouse itself. The sun had come out, and rosehips gleamed scarlet in the hedgerows, and a lonely jackdaw called for company as it flew low across the fields towards a colourful spinney.

The Three Oaks farmhouse was one of those solid, square, grey houses, that had once been unfashionable, but which would now probably fetch a breathtaking sum if it ever came up for sale. Built not so far back that it was uncomfortable, it was old enough for the workmanship to be immaculate and long-lasting. Hillary found herself comparing the edifice to the Mollern and almost seeing the funny side.

The door was answered by a young woman in jeans, who introduced herself, surprisingly as, 'Madge, I'm the daily.' Hillary stepped inside an old-fashioned hall that smelt of damp umbrellas and wet wool. 'The missus is in through there.' Madge pointed to a closed door. 'Want tea?'

'Coffee, if you have it,' she pleaded, never one to overlook a caffeine hit. Madge grinned and nodded.

Hillary knocked on the door and heard a startled summons to enter. Inside, a green-eyed, heavy-set man, with attractive waves of iron-grey hair, got up from the sofa, a question on his face. From the armchair opposite, a forty-something woman with carefully dyed blonde hair, wearing a tan-coloured silk blouse and clotted-cream coloured linen trousers also watched her curiously. The woman looked as if she should be beautiful, but when Hillary looked at her closely, she could see that, in fact, she was not.

'Mr Wallis? Mrs Wallis?' She reached into her bag for her wallet. 'Detective Inspector Hillary Greene. I'm in charge of the Julia Reynolds' murder investigation.'

'Ah, Inspector, glad you're here,' Owen Wallis said, even as his wife was opening her delicately pearl-pink lips to greet her. 'I've been trying to get someone to see reason about my cows, but everyone says I have to talk to the man in charge. But I've been ringing the station all morning and getting the run around.'

Hillary blinked. 'Sorry to hear that, sir.'

'Yes, yes, but can I see to my cows?'

Hillary, who now knew what Alice had felt like when she disappeared down the rabbit hole for the first time, blinked again. 'Er, your cows, sir?'

'Yes. They're being kept in the shed. But they're milkers, and pretty soon the poor sods will be feeling the pain from their udders. I need to move 'em out to the milking sheds, but those Johnnies in white overalls don't seem capable of seeing reason. Even after the last of 'em left, I was told I couldn't move 'em.'

Hillary nodded, holding up a placatory hand. 'Let me just see if I can do something about that, Mr Wallis,' she said, flipping open her mobile. A quick call the police lab confirmed SOCO had everything they needed.

'Please, feel free to see to your cows, sir,' Hillary said, on finishing the call. 'I'm sorry you've been worried.' The last thing she wanted was a hostile witness. As it was, Owen Wallis was already heading for the door, and she quickly added, 'Perhaps I can have a word or two with your wife, whilst you're busy, and then I would like a word or two with you later, sir?'

'Yes, yes, of course. I'll be right back when I've seen my cowman,' the farmer said, disappearing out of the room.

Hillary took a seat on the sofa, and Wendy Wallis smiled knowingly. 'My husband has a one-track mind, I'm afraid. I'm used to it. So, what can I tell you? I have to say this is the first time I've had any contact with the police. And I still can't believe that poor girl was killed in our cowshed. I mean it's so … so … bizarre!'

Hillary could well understand how Wendy Wallis felt. According to what she remembered from the paperwork, Wendy Wallis had been the daughter of the local schoolteacher. She'd married well, and no doubt had led a fairly comfortable and insulated life ever since. It remained to be seen whether or not she was the kind of woman who also liked to live with her head buried in the sand. Or if, paradoxically, her isolated life on the farm had given her a rabid interest in the outside world.

'What can you tell me about the victim, Mrs Wallis. Julia Reynolds. Did you know her?'

'Not really. I mean, I'd seen her about the village. A friend of mine, Davina McGuinness, has her in to do her mother's hair. So I've seen her once or twice at Davina's place – she had a granny flat added on for her, when she fell down the stairs at her own place. Her mother, I mean.'

Hillary nodded, having no trouble following the rambling explanation. 'So were you surprised to see her at your party?'

'Well, only at first. And then someone told me she was here with Roger Greenwood. So that made sense. My husband was closeted with Theo Greenwood, his father, for a good half-hour in the study, and I was not best pleased, I can tell you. At our silver wedding anniversary party! The things I have to put up with with that man,' Wendy said, but she didn't sound particularly angry.

Hillary had the feeling that her conversation was just a bit off, as if her mind was on something else. But then, she was probably just nervous.

'So, did you see Julia Reynolds leave the party with anyone? To go outside at any time?'

'Oh no. But then I wasn't paying much attention to her.'

'You didn't notice anything odd about her behaviour? Didn't see anything strange happening?'

'No, as I said ... well ... what do you mean by odd, exactly?'

Hillary felt a little jump in her pulse rate. It was often like this. You'd be interviewing a witness with no high hopes of anything good, and then, out of the blue, a little nibble. 'Oh, anything at all. No matter how insignificant.'

'Yes, but I mean, you don't want impressions, do you? I mean, you police like facts and things.'

'That's not altogether true, Mrs Wallis,' Hillary said carefully, not at all sure what she might be letting herself in for. 'At the moment I'm trying to build up a picture of the victim, and any information, no matter how unscientific it is, could come in useful. You said you got some kind of impression about Julia?' she prompted gently.

'Well, like I said, it's nothing definite. And I can't say it was important or anything. It was just that outfit of hers. It was quite stunning, and being a fancy dress party, she was so beautiful I can quite see why she'd chosen something spectacular. I rather got the impression she was a bit of an exhibitionist, but ... well, to tell you the truth, I felt that she was deliberately taunting somebody with that wedding dress of hers.'

Wendy Wallis stopped, then frowned. 'It's hard to put it into words. She was slightly tipsy, I know, and like all young things nowadays, not exactly discreet, but it seemed to me, once or twice, that she was sort of ... showing off ... no, not that exactly, but somehow making a point. Scoring off somebody. Oh, I don't know how to explain it,' she huffed in frustration. 'She was just up to some kind of mischief; yes, that's it: definitely up to mischief.'

'Could she have chosen the wedding dress as a kind of hint to Roger Greenwood, do you think?' Hillary asked, not sure what Wendy Wallis was getting at.

'No,' the farmer's wife said firmly. 'I didn't get the feeling that her boyfriend was the one she was tormenting. She seemed genuinely fond of him, and the boy was smitten right enough. No, it was someone else. But I may have been wrong.'

But Wendy Wallis didn't really believe she was wrong, and Hillary didn't know the woman well enough to gauge if her self-confidence was justified.

One thing was for sure, Hillary thought morosely; if Julia Reynolds *had* been up to mischief last night, using her costume to make some sort of point, then perhaps all her taunting and tormenting had proved far more successful than had been good for her.

chapter four

Hillary returned to Kidlington, and spent the next few hours dealing with her other cases, including a somewhat cold telephone conversation with the prosecutor of her now aborted fraud case. It wasn't often one of her cases fell down, and it put her in a nasty mood and just the right frame of mind to attack her tray of paperwork.

Mel seemed to be in as foul a mood as herself, and when they found themselves snapping at each other over a minor difference of opinion about the Radcliffe case, with Mel convinced in spite of only flimsy evidence that the middle-aged spinster had indeed been killed by her older sister for the insurance money, and Hillary urging caution, they both decided to retire to their corners and cool off. Apart from anything else, Frank Ross had been seriously entertained by their rare show of spite, and was wearing a sneer that would have cracked cutlery, and nobody liked to please the poisoned cherub.

So it was something of a relief when Tommy Lynch, answering a summons from the ground floor, told her that the 'best friend' of Julia Reynolds had come in, asking if she could help.

'I don't suppose she was at the party, too, was she?' Hillary asked, without much hope, as they jogged lightly down the stairs and headed towards the interview-rooms.

''fraid not, guv,' Tommy confirmed.

'Oh well. At least we'll be able to get a better picture of our vic.'

Tommy nodded. He was looking forward to this. Not only was he always grateful for any time spent alone with the woman he admired and – yes, fancied – above all others, but he was genuinely impressed with her various interview techniques. What the public failed to realize (since it didn't make good drama) was that more cases were solved in the interview-room than anywhere else. Sometimes the guilty just needed to get things off their chest and barely required a nudge in the right direction. Sometimes, they were too clever for their own good, and needed to be tripped up and tied into knots. Other times, it was down to the interviewing officer to tease nuggets of previously forgotten bits of information from witnesses, or help them bring to mind events that they hadn't thought relevant. Whatever, most cops needed to have the gift of the gab if they wanted to solve cases, but Tommy had seen Hillary tackle people with an almost paranormal ability to get the most out of them.

He knew he could learn a lot from Hillary Greene, and he was not about to waste any precious chance to watch and learn, not if he wanted to make sergeant by his next birthday.

As his superior officer pushed open the door, Tommy saw a small, nervous-looking girl sitting at the table. She had short dark hair and big brown eyes, covered by a pair of too-small, rectangular glasses. She wore a pair of jeans and a chunky, hand-knitted cream sweater. She was fiddling nervously with a cigarette packet, although she hadn't yet lit up. He knew that Hillary, a non-smoker all her life, would be relieved by that.

'Hello, Miss …?'

'Mandy Tucker,' the girl all but whispered, half-rising from her chair, obviously unaware of the protocol.

'Mind if I call you Mandy?' Hillary said, with a warm and easy smile. 'I'm Detective Inspector Hillary Greene, in charge of the Julia Reynolds' murder investigation. Please, sit down, Mandy. We're grateful to you for coming in like this.'

Mandy Tucker nodded, and sniffed, then sat down. 'I wanted to help. Although, really, I don't know what I can do.' She was still whispering, and almost maniacally fiddling with the packet. Tommy had the feeling she'd never been inside a police station in her life.

Hillary sat down and nodded to Tommy to use the notebook, not the recorder. She was sure that the machinery would send someone as timid as this into further paroxysms of shyness, and that was the last thing they needed.

'It's all right, Mandy, we know you weren't at the party, and so can't give us any practical help. We don't expect you to. All I need from you is to tell me about Julia. The kind of girl she was. You'd be surprised how much that will help us,' Hillary said brightly, with yet another reassuring smile.

Mandy Tucker gave a slightly tremulous smile in response, and Tommy could see her bony shoulders relax just a bit.

'OK,' she agreed willingly.

'So, how long have you and Julia been friends?'

Mandy Tucker laughed. 'Oh, for ages, ever since we were five. We went to the same primary school in Kirtlington, then to the Comp. I stayed on to do A-levels, but Julia left at sixteen. But she did my hair for me, and we went to the socials, and the pub for lunch, whenever.'

'Sounds like you were really close then. So, how would you describe Julia? And please, Mandy,' – at this point Hillary leaned over and gently placed a hand on Mandy's own, waiting until the shy girl looked her in the eye – 'we know that your friend is dead, and it still seems horribly unreal, and the last thing you want to do is talk about maybe some of the bad things about her. I know it would feel horribly disloyal. But the thing is, everybody has good and bad in them; I do, you do, PC Lynch here, everybody. It's what makes us human. And the chances are that it wasn't whatever was good in Julia that made somebody kill her, but whatever was bad in her. Do you see what I'm saying?'

She took her hand away slowly, and watched the other girl nod miserably. Although her hands had ceased destroying the cigarette packet, Hillary could see that she wasn't altogether convinced.

'You see, Mandy, as hard as this is to understand and

believe, your friend is dead. You can't do anything for her; you can't make it better; there's nothing you can say or do that will make things different. All you can do for your friend now is grieve for her, and help us to find whoever did this to her. She'd want that, wouldn't she? To know that whoever did this to her was caught and made to pay?'

'Oh yes,' Mandy Tucker said at once. 'She would.' She straightened a little more firmly in the chair and her eyes became harder. 'Julia wasn't a bleeding heart. She thought they should bring back the death penalty for killers. You know, like they have in America.'

Hillary nodded. 'A lot of people feel that way,' she said, with careful neutrality. 'So you know that she'd approve of you being honest with us. From what you say, I don't think Julia was the kind of girl who'd be afraid of the truth.'

'No, you're right. She was always honest, sometimes brutally so,' Mandy agreed, her own voice strengthening now as she remembered her dead friend's savvy. 'She always said what she thought,' Mandy added, managing another wry smile. 'Not everyone liked that, you know. But Julia always tackled things head on. Called a spade a spade. Like this immigration thing. She said everyone was afraid to say what they really thought, because they were terrified of being labelled a racist. But she thought immigration should be stopped. She said why should she have to give over a third of her earnings in tax, so that some foreigner who'd never paid a penny into the system could just waltz over here and get ahead of her on the National Health queue. She said nearly everybody thought the same, but just didn't dare say so.'

Hillary nodded. 'But she *did* say so?'

'Right. And like fox hunting. She said it was a big lie that everyone living in the country was all for fox hunting. She said that she'd lived in a country village all her life and she thought fox hunting was barbaric. She threw a boyfriend over, once, when she found out he'd ridden to hounds. She told him to his face he was a cruel bastard, and she hoped he fell off his horse next time and broke his neck.'

Hillary smiled and nodded calmly. 'And who was this, exactly? How long ago?'

'Oh, ages ago. We were still at school. She'd just had her sixteenth birthday party. His name was Jake Burdage. He's in London now, I think. A stockbroker or something.'

Hillary saw Tommy note down the name and nodded mentally. Although she thought this antagonized ex had been dumped too long ago to still harbour a murderous grudge, it would have to be checked.

Still, it sounded as if Julia Reynolds had no fears about rubbing people up the wrong way. She'd met her kind before – they were usually unimaginative people, secure in their own identities, who saw no need to cushion reality. They were almost always incapable of seeing a point of view from the other side, and this often led to an unseeing, unthinking and uncompromising outlook which invariably gained them enemies. Other, lesser mortals, thought this mentality was either brave or foolhardy, whilst others, more *au fait* with the world, considered it to be downright dangerous. Hillary was inclined to believe that it was a combination of all three.

Had Julia Reynolds' bold and unthinking personality blinded her to the dangers that night in the cowshed? Had she told somebody just what she'd thought in that dark, deserted place, and never even considered that perhaps discretion really was the better part of valour?

'So, she was obviously the kind of girl who could stick up for herself,' Hillary mused. 'And she was running her own business, even though she was still very young. Was it successful, her business?'

'Oh, yes. Well, she always had money to spend,' Mandy amended scrupulously. 'I mean, she was always dragging me to Debenhams to buy lipstick and stuff, and was always getting new outfits and CDs, but whether or not it all came from her business, I don't know. I think her boyfriends gave her money, too, sometimes. She was bored with her job, I know, because she often put down her old ladies when she talked about them, but at the same time, she always seemed to be out and about with a job on. I think she used to butter them up. She used to laugh about it, and say things like "You know that silly old dingbat what's-her-name. She showed me this picture of Jennifer Anniston the other day, and asked if I could give her a haircut like that. I mean really! The old girl's sixty if she's a day. Can you imagine it? I talked her into a page-boy instead." And the funny thing is,' Mandy went on, 'I would see the woman she was talking about afterwards in a shop or somewhere, and all her friends would be telling her how well the cut suited her, and you could tell she would be really chuffed. Because the cut *was* just right for her. That's why she was always in demand. Julia was like that. She got away with things, because she was good at everything she did. You know what I mean?'

Hillary did. 'Did she say anything else about her customers? About one of their husbands, perhaps? Or one of their sons, bothering her, pestering her, making a fool of themselves over her, that kind of thing?'

Mandy frowned. 'No, I don't think so. She didn't really ever meet the menfolk much. She'd go to people's houses in the day you see, when most of the men were at work. Oh, she did say something about … oh, what was her name? Mrs Finch. No, Finchley – that's it. According to Mandy, Mrs Finchley was always sozzled. She said she had to keep an eye on her when she sat her under the dryer, 'cause she was always dozing off. Anyway, she told Julia once, when she was drunker than usual, something really naff about her husband. Something about how he was doing something dodgy, only she didn't know what. You know, something criminal.'

Beside her, Hillary could feel Tommy perk up, and gave a mental smile, wishing she, too, could summon up a similar enthusiasm. But she doubted that this would come to much. Many drunk housewives had odd ideas about their spouses. It usually came from the bottom of a gin bottle. Still, this too would have to be checked out.

'Any idea would sort of crime she was talking about?' she prompted diligently.

'Nah,' Mandy said dismissively. 'I don't think Julia was really interested. She said she knew the hubby vaguely – he had a bit of WHT, but he was basically harmless. Probably fiddling his income tax or something, Julia thought.'

She saw Tommy's fingers move, and looked across to see him tapping the initials WHT and looking at her with an eyebrow raised in question.

'Wandering hand trouble,' Hillary murmured with a smile. And wondered if Julia might have been more intrigued than she'd let on to her friend. Had she checked up on Mrs Finchley's better half and found something juicy? Had she tried a spot of blackmail? It was always possible. She doubted Julia Reynolds would have felt much compunction about it, and travelling hairdressers didn't exactly earn a mint, did they? The temptation to earn some extra dosh could have been intriguing.

'I would imagine your friend was popular with men, wasn't she, Mandy?' she asked quietly, knowing she had to be careful, now, how she phrased things. She didn't want Mandy getting defensive, just when she was finally loosening up. 'We know she went to the party, for instance, with Roger Greenwood. Was she serious about him?'

'I'll say!' Mandy snorted. 'She thought Roger Greenwood was a really good proposition. Especially if his dad brought off this property deal that he's been wittering on about for the last few months. She said he could even end up being a multi-millionaire. Roger's dad, that is. And that Roger was almost certain to end up vice-chairman of his dad's company one day.'

'They'd been going out long?'

'Nearly a year. Longer than she'd ever been out with anyone before. She kept hinting about a diamond engagement ring, but I never saw it.'

Now it was Hillary's turn to shift restlessly on her chair. Now things were looking far more interesting. 'So she thought Roger was going to, or already had proposed?'

Mandy frowned, and began to back track. 'Oh, I don't think he'd actually proposed. Not right out and asked her to marry him or nothing. If he had, Julia would have been bragging about it no end.'

Hillary nodded. Yes, that sounded about par for the course. Julia Reynolds didn't sound the type to keep her light under a bushel.

'But I know she was hoping he would,' Mandy ploughed on. 'He was smitten right enough, I know that. Mind you, his dad was dead set against it. She said he'd once told Roger that he'd marry Julia over his dead body. *Tres* Victorian, as Julia put it. She used to tease Roger about his dad's old-fashioned ways a lot.'

'Do you think she chose to wear a wedding dress to the fancy dress party as a hint to Roger?' Hillary asked. 'Or do you suppose she wanted to cock a snook at his father?'

Mandy laughed. 'Probably both, knowing Julia. You know, now I come to think of it, I was with her when she tried on the outfit at the fancy dress shop, and she did say that wearing it would put old pig-features in a tizzy. I 'spect she meant Mr Greenwood.'

'Do you know what Mr Greenwood had against Julia as a prospective daughter-in-law?' Hillary asked, genuinely curious now.

'Oh, I 'spect he thought she wasn't good enough for his precious Roger, or something. He wanted him to marry some big land-owning farmer's daughter or some Sloane type. Not that Mr Greenwood is so upper crust himself, mind. Julia said he was no better than her or her family. His ancestors were some sort of feed-and-grain merchants. Nothing to be so snotty about, Julia said.'

'So Roger was the 'real thing' then? But she'd had plenty of boyfriends before him?' Hillary probed carefully.

'Why not?' Mandy shot back belligerently, instantly on the defensive. 'What's wrong with that nowadays? Julia was always careful about ... you know ... stuff. Getting AIDS and all that. Men have been sowing their wild oats for centuries. Now a woman can do the same.'

Although it was the slightly awkward and shy Mandy

Tucker who was speaking, Hillary could clearly hear the voice of Julia Reynolds. She wondered if Mandy had actually agreed with her friend's liberated, bold stance, or whether, at heart, the placid, shy Mandy had felt uncomfortable having such a voracious man-eater as a friend. If she had, she'd never admit to it now.

'So, she wasn't seeing anyone else? There'd be no reason for Roger Greenwood to feel jealous?'

Mandy ducked her head and began to fiddle with the cigarette packet again.

'Mandy? Remember what we talked about before we started?' Hillary chided gently. 'Your friend was strangled, which almost certainly means by some man who felt enraged by her, or betrayed. You can see why this is important.'

Mandy chewed her bottom lip unattractively, then sighed. 'Well, there was someone else. I don't know who he was. Julia just called him her bit of rough on the side. But she wasn't serious about him. It was Roger she was after.'

Hillary could see the other girl was getting ready to dig her heels in stubbornly, and decided to change tack. There'd always be others willing to talk about Julia's peccadilloes. And if she knew human nature (and she did), *plenty* of others. A girl like Julia was bound to have made enemies in the female community – girls who'd had boyfriends snaffled in the past, as well as girls, or even mature women, who envied Julia her beauty and independence.

'OK, so tell me what else you can about Julia. What did she like doing? Did she have any hobbies?'

Mandy, clearly relieved at the change in subject, shrugged. 'Well not really. I mean, the thing is, Julia would get really enthusiastic about things, but they never lasted.'

'For example?'

Mandy thought about it, then nodded. 'OK. There was this time at school, f'r'instance. We had this guest speaker in assembly once, one of these Greenies. He was all set to stand for the Green Party or Greenpeace or whatever. Anyway, he went on and on about how the countryside was being poisoned, and how each year there were less and less swallows making it back to the British Isles because the Spaniards kept eating them when they flew over the mountains. They catch them in these big nets apparently. Isn't that gross? And I mean, silly? How much meat could there be on a swallow? Anyway, Julia got really mad about it, and when this bloke said they were going to be doing a tree-planting out by Charlton-on-Otmoor, and called for volunteers, Julia signed up, and dragged me along. Of course, it was really hard work planting these little sapling things, and we only planted five or six, before Julia got fed up and we skivved off. That was sort of typical of her. But she really, genuinely, believed in the cause though, and later she bought some save the seal stickers and stuff, and demonstrated outside an animal lab once in Oxford, but only when she felt like it. You see what I mean?'

Hillary nodded.

'And it was the same with the shampoo,' Mandy went on. 'The stuff that wasn't tested on animals, and had no stuff in it that would harm the environment was too dear, Julia said. It would cut into her profits too much to use it. So she wrote a letter to the manufacturers, telling them it was no use producing stuff unless it could compete in the market-place. They wrote her a rather snotty letter back, and Julia used normal shampoo after that.'

Hillary was careful not to smile. But just how much of the spoilt child had been ingrained in the adult? 'She didn't like being challenged you mean?' she mused.

'Oh no. But don't get the wrong impression. Her heart was always in the right place,' Mandy insisted. 'Like when we went to give blood. That wasn't her fault either.'

'You've lost me,' Hillary said gently.

'Well, we'd just left school, and there was this mobile blood donor van parked up on the village green. You know, they travel about from town to town so people can volunteer to give blood? Well Julia thought it was a great idea, and we went in and signed up to be blood donors, and organ donors – you know, you fill in a card and put it in your purse?'

Hillary nodded, remembering that there'd been a donor card in Julia Reynolds's purse the night of her death.

'Well, I gave blood first, and I could see straight away that there was something wrong. Julia went sort of ... well, pale and greenish. And when the time came for her to be tested, just to have the little finger prick, to check for anaemia she just couldn't go through with it. Turned out, she had this phobia about needles. I remembered then how she'd cried and made a fuss when we were little and had to have our jabs. They were very nice about it on the blood van, even though you could tell they were a bit exasperated. Well, the nurse was. She was this old biddy who rolled her eyes a bit. It made Julia cross. But it really wasn't her fault, see, 'cause when she had to have her appendix out later, it was really awful for her. She hated the hospital, and couldn't stand it. She said it did her head in. She'd always hated anything to do with illness and stuff. She even discharged herself early, it was so bad. The doctors warned her, but she went straight to bed once she got home, and was careful not to do too much, and it turned out all right in the end. But I mean, it had to be real, didn't it? To discharge yourself like that? I couldn't have done it, I can tell you, I would have been scared stiff. And she was really in pain, just after surgery, but she said she just couldn't breathe in there. In the hospital. So it wasn't her fault. People were always blaming Julia, thinking she was pulling a fast one, when she really wasn't.'

Mandy paused to take a much needed gulp of air and Hillary once again placed a calming hand gently over Mandy's clenched fist. 'OK, Mandy, it's all right.' The other girl had worked herself up into a such a state of agitation in defending her dead friend, that she looked ready to burst into tears.

'Nobody knew her better than you did,' Hillary soothed. 'You must have been a good friend to her. Tell me, can you think of anyone who might have got mad enough at her to want to kill her?'

Mandy sniffed and finally pulled a cigarette from the carton and lit up. She puffed frantically and then shook her head, not noticing that Hillary had leant back in her chair, well out of the way of the billowing smoke. 'No. I mean, Julia had a lot of boyfriends, but only Roger recently. And he's too nice. You don't think he killed her, do you?' she added sharply.

But Hillary wasn't about to be drawn. 'We don't know yet, Mandy. What about Michael Wallis. The son of the farmer, where the party was held. Do you know him?'

Mandy wrinkled her nose. 'Vaguely. From around.'

'Did Julia know him?'

'I guess. But she'd never been out with him. She said he'd got a dog for a girlfriend now. Is that true?'

Hillary smiled and shrugged, thinking of poor Jenny Porter. 'Some people don't put looks high on their list of priorities,' she chided.

Mandy sighed somewhat wistfully, and Hillary suddenly realized that this shy, unassuming girl, couldn't have had it easy, always being in the shadow of her beautiful and ambitious best friend. She wondered what, if anything, Julia Reynolds had brought to their friendship.

They talked for another half hour but Hillary learned nothing more useful. Julia got on well with her parents, but expected to be moving out to live with Roger Greenwood soon. She'd had no family arguments or rows. Her father seemed the sort to be proud of his daughter's strong personality, rather than disapproving. She made a mental note to find out where Julia Reynolds' father had been at the time of the killing, just to make sure. It wouldn't be the first time a father had killed a daughter that he'd seen as bringing 'shame' on the family, although, luckily, that kind of thing was much rarer now than it had been. Still, in a murder investigation, you left no stone unturned.

When Mandy had finally gone, Hillary's stomach was rumbling, but lunchtime was long since past. She left Tommy to type up his notes, and made her way to the canteen intent on getting a drink and maybe a piece of fruit, but was waylaid on the stairs by a secretary.

The new super was 'having a chat' with his senior officers,

and it was her turn, apparently. Wearily, and a trifle apprehensively, she made her way to Superintendent Jerome Raleigh's office.

She'd worked under Marcus Donleavy for most of her senior years at Kidlington, and they'd always got on well; they understood each other, and Hillary had always regarded change, although inevitable, with a great deal of suspicion.

As she knocked on the door and waited for his call to enter, she wondered nervously what he'd been told about Ronnie, and the internal investigation into his corruption that had been conducted last year. Nothing good, that was for sure.

She had only recently discovered – or at least, strongly suspected that she might know – where her misbegotten spouse had stashed the majority of his dirty loot, but as yet hadn't done anything about it. But with a new super breathing down her neck, perhaps now would be a good time to get it sorted, once and for all?

'Come in,' Jerome Raleigh called, then looked up as the door opened and DI Hillary Greene walked in.

She was dressed in a deep burnt-amber two piece, with a plain white blouse, sensible brown shoes, and a pretty, tiger's-eye pendant. Her nut-brown hair gleamed in a slightly too-long bob. Her make up was discreet and casual. She had a surprisingly shapely figure, the kind film stars in the fifties had, and wary, clever, dark eyes. She was, he could see for himself, a very attractive widow.

So far, he'd picked up very little about her love life on the gossip train, except that she lived alone on a canal narrowboat in the tiny village of Thrupp. Scuttlebutt insisted that she was currently still very much unattached, although from what Jerome had been able to read between the lines, some at the nick thought that DI Paul Danvers, (weirdly enough, one of the men who'd investigated her for corruption) might have been sniffing around.

He could see why men would be interested. She looked to be in her thirties rather than her forties, and held herself well. She also walked well, which was something of a dying art. Jerome always noticed the way a woman walked.

Hillary Greene also had a degree from a non-affiliated Oxford college in English Lit., so she had brains as well as an understated, pleasant beauty. She'd done well to rise to the rank she had, especially considering she'd been hampered with the husband from hell.

Of all the officers working under him, Jerome Raleigh suspected this woman might turn out to be the most interesting of all – and potentially the most dangerous to himself. If she ever got wind of what had really brought him to Thames Valley, he could be deeply in the shit.

'Please, DI Greene, sit down. This is strictly an informal chat.' He watched her sit, noting the wary eyes and sharp observation, partly concealed behind a vague smile. He understood how she felt. He was the new boss – he could make things easy or hard for her.

'Marcus thinks very highly of you, DI Greene,' he began cordially. 'He said, of all his DIs, you had a flair for real detective work. Reading up on some of your previous cases, especially the Pitts case, and that of the French student just recently, I'm inclined to agree with him. You're currently working a murder investigation now, is that right?'

'Yes, sir. Julia Reynolds, strangled in a cowshed. She'd been attending a fancy dress party at a local farm.' Briefly she ran down the current status of the investigation although, strictly speaking, this was Mel's immediate province.

'Sounds straightforward enough,' Jerome said.

Hillary hesitated for a scant second, then nodded. 'Yes, sir.'

But Jerome didn't miss it. And after a moment's consideration, believed that Hillary Greene hadn't intended him to.

'You think not?'

Hillary shuffled on her chair. 'I'm not sure sir.' She opened her mouth to say more, then shut it again. The truth was, she wasn't really sure what was bothering her about the Reynolds case exactly, so how could she explain it to her new boss?

At first, it had all seemed straightforward enough. A beautiful girl gets strangled – so look for a jealous man. Nine times out of ten, the simple answer was always the right one. So when had she begun to have doubts? Talking to Mandy Porter, perhaps? Certainly, a whole different avenue of possibilities had opened up after that interview. Had Julia been blackmailing someone for instance? She'd certainly had the nerve and hard-headedness needed to carry it off. Or had she managed to piss somebody off in a way that had nothing to do with sex? Theo Greenwood, for instance, who didn't want his son marrying her?

She might not be sure of her ground, but she was glad she'd planted the seed of doubt with her new super. It meant that if things didn't pan out as quickly as she hoped, she would at least have a life-line, of sorts, left dangling.

Jerome Raleigh nodded, and Hillary wondered if he had read her far more accurately than she'd wished.

'Well, if your gut tells you something may be off, there's probably a reason. Keep me informed. I see you live on a boat?'

Hillary obligingly talked about the delights of houseboat living, and after a while, was dismissed.

She made her way back to her desk thoughtfully.

Jerome Raleigh was still definitely something of a mystery. He'd played his cards as close to his chest as she had, and she left the room feeling as if they'd been playing a game of chess that had ended in a respectable and mutually acceptable stalemate, with perhaps a few more points going to the super.

She definitely got the feeling that there was more to the man that met the eye. Now that she'd had a first-hand look for herself, she couldn't understand why he'd ever left the Met. A big city, with all its possibilities, seemed the ideal environment for someone like him.

'Been in with the big chief then,' Janine said, the moment she sat down at her desk. 'He's a dish, isn't he?'

She'd had her own interview with him an hour before, and was wondering if she might not be able to use the unattached Jerome Raleigh as a very handy stick to beat Mel with. She was sure it wouldn't take much to make Mel sit up and take notice, as jealous of the new super as he already was. If he thought

Janine's eye was wandering in Jerome's direction, her country weekend break was bound to be a sure thing.

'Yes, he is,' Hillary said absently. She'd have had to have been blind not to appreciate the man's attributes, and although she'd been celibate for far too long, after that confidence-busting shambles that was life with Ronnie Greene, she wasn't exactly immune from male charm, as she'd found out shortly after meeting a certain DI Mike Regis.

No. She wouldn't think of Regis now.

Tommy, staring at an interview form he was reviewing, felt his heart sink to his boots. Jerome Raleigh, so he'd been reliably informed by one of the janitors, was unmarried. And he'd be daft not to take notice of a widow as attractive as Hillary.

'So, is he a shirt-lifter or not?' Frank Ross demanded, with all his usual tact and diplomacy, and Hillary sensed those within earshot prick up their ears. It was gratifying to know that her opinion was so widely rated.

She glanced across at Frank thoughtfully. 'If I had to lay my bets now, I'd say not,' she said, calmly.

But she felt it was going to be a long time before anyone knew anything definite about their new super, and until she had him at least partially sussed out, she'd be treading on eggshells – and so would everyone else if they had any sense.

She had the distinct impression that Jerome Raleigh was not the kind of man to be messed with.

When Tommy got back to his desk he found a report waiting for him from one of the uniforms helping with the house to house inquiries in Julia Reynolds' neighbourhood. A woman bringing in her washing had noticed a purple Mini ('one of them new ones') parked in the lay-by outside Julia's house in the early evening. Needless to say, the witness could not remember any of the letters or numbers in the number plate. It was probably nothing, but it still had to be checked out.

Tommy sighed. It was going to be a long day.

chapter five

Gregory Innes cursed as the smell of cow shit wafted across on the damp autumn breeze and threatened to clog his sinuses. What's more, he was sure that the makers of the waxed so-called waterproof coat he was wearing could have been had up under the Trades Descriptions Act. His feet felt cold and damp in the unfamiliar wellingtons, and were threatening to develop blisters. To top it all, his nose wouldn't stop dripping. He was not very happy. It was not only physical discomfort that was making him miserable though. He wasn't looking forward to the next few minutes at all, either.

He crouched down even further behind the thick hawthorn hedge as the Wallises' cowman carefully shut the gates behind him, climbed into his disreputable-looking Land Rover and drove away. A black and white collie, sitting in the back of the open trailer attached to the van, went into a series of frenzied barking as it spotted him, making Gregory cringe and wince at every frenzied warning the sheepdog howled. Luckily for him, the cowman must have been used to the animal making a din, for he didn't bother to stop and investigate.

Eventually, the outraged barks were silenced as the cowman headed out on who-the-hell-knew, or cared, what task, and Gregory straightened up with a sigh. His back was aching.

He was a tall, rangy, fair-haired man, who looked older than his thirty-eight years. He rubbed his hands together, surprised at how cold they were. He should have worn gloves. This damp weather was far worse than frost or snow for getting into your bones. He should know – he'd become used to being out and about in all weathers during the course of his occupation. He rubbed his hands briskly to get the circulation back and cursed silently, acknowledging to himself, somewhat glumly, that he should have known better, and come better equipped.

Still, in his defence, it had to be said that he was far more used to Birmingham and the sprawling burbs than this. This was his first big job right out in the sticks, and if this was an example of country living, you could keep it. He simply couldn't figure out why plonkers wanted to retire out here, amongst all this filth and stinging nettles.

He glanced left then right, seeking a weaker spot in the hedge to push through, swearing as the thorns scraped bloody lines across the backs of his exposed hands. Once clear of the hedge, he trotted carefully over to the cowshed, and gave another quick look around. No matter how often he snooped – and snooping was as familiar to him as breathing – he always felt a bit like Peter Sellers in one of those Inspector Clouseau films. He could almost hear *The Pink Panther* theme tune playing in the background as he checked that the path was all clear.

Mind you, he thought with a silent grunt, this whole case was becoming like something from a farce. Here he was, shivering, wet and miserable, sneaking around a bloody cowshed of all things. It was a far cry from his usual beat of tracking dirty politicians, ferreting around in public records and sitting outside buildings in the relative warmth and comfort of his car, fighting off boredom and just waiting for something – anything – to happen.

Going around to the front of the farm building, dodging yet more stinging nettles lying in wait for the bare exposed bits of his legs, where his socks and trouser-leg didn't quite connect, the first thing he noticed was that the yellow police crime scene tapes were now gone.

He wasn't surprised. He'd been holed up in a spinney all day yesterday with his best pair of binoculars, and had seen the last of the SOCO team leave. He'd had an uncomfortable feeling that the woman copper who seemed to be in charge of the case had spotted him climbing the gate leading to the field on the opposite side of the spinney earlier that day, but if she had, she'd not been interested enough to send anyone out to scout around. She'd probably thought he was a journo.

He just hoped that she didn't make another call to the farm any time soon. The last thing he needed was to get his collar felt now.

He pushed open the clammy steel-grey corrugated door and winced as it screeched on rusty runners. Inside, the place was deserted, with only the unmistakable whiff of cow left behind. He stared around somewhat blankly, not really sure what he was doing here. The place would have been gone over with a fine tooth comb by the experts, so there'd be no fleas left for him to find.

Perhaps he just wanted to get a feel of the place. He poked around, trying to imagine the scene. The dead girl, dressed bizarrely in a wedding dress. The shuffling of the disturbed cows. The police lights, the chatter of the various people called out to the scene of unexpected, illicit death.

Gregory Innes didn't consider himself to be a sensitive man. Hell, in his line of work, how could he be? Nor was he particularly introspective, although he was always vaguely aware that life had done him down, right from the cradle. And he knew for a fact that the damned world didn't consider that it owed him a living, and the feeling was fully reciprocated. So, it wasn't surprising that he didn't consider that he owed Julia Reynolds a damned thing either.

He was out for number one. Always had been, and always would be.

The doctor for instance. Now he might just prove to be a valuable source of income in the future. He was sure he wouldn't want anyone, police, media, and certainly not the medical council, to know just what *he'd* thought of Julia Reynolds.

Still, as he stood in that bleak, bare and cold place, Gregory felt himself shiver, unusually touched by some kind of pity. She'd been so young and beautiful after all, and too stupid to know that life was an even bigger bitch than herself. But she'd found out all right, and Gregory thought he might just know who'd taught her.

The problem was, he didn't know for *sure*. But if he could only find a scrap of proof, even if only circumstantial proof, he could be on easy street for once. Well, *easier* street, then. Nobody in this affair was a millionaire, after all.

He tensed suddenly, hearing the sound of a motor. He cursed, slipped to the door, saw the farmer, Owen Wallis's more up-market Range Rover heading his way and understood at once that there was no way he was going to get away without being spotted.

He slipped through the open door and headed across the muddy ground towards the hedge as fast as his spindly legs would carry him. His running technique might not be pretty, but it was effective. He heard an outraged 'Oi!' coming from behind him and then he was back through the hedge, hardly noticing the scratches this time round, and running downhill, arms cartwheeling comically as he quickly veered out of control. He hit the bottom of the slope still running, however, and managed to stay on his feet, the adrenaline rush making him feel like laughing once more.

Inspector Clouseau strikes again!

Theo Greenwood indicated an overstuffed leather chair in a billiard-table shade of green and smiled briefly. 'Please, have a seat. Can I get you anything? Tea, coffee, a cold drink, or something stronger?'

Hillary smiled back and shook her head. 'No, I'm fine thanks. Sergeant?'

Janine also shook her head, well aware that the older man was trying desperately not to look at her breasts. It wasn't that she was dressed in any way provocatively. She tended to wear the clothes her mother insisted on buying her for birthdays and Christmases to work, on the sound basis that it was the only place they were fit for. Consequently, she was wearing a demure white blouse, under a hand-knitted slate-grey cardigan with a complicated rib-pattern. Her mother, a dedicated knitter, could always be relied upon in that department.

'You've come about that poor dead girl, yes?' Theo Greenwood said, sitting down in a similar green chair, and gazing at them across the width of a massive, mahogany desk. They were in his 'den' at the Hayrick Inn.

Hillary had been reluctantly impressed by the older, near-Elizabethan part of the Hayrick, but much less so by the 'sympathetic' conversions at the back. The old stable blocks had, of course, long since been converted into bedrooms, and although the accommodation block had been built in matching stone, and had newly planted creepers already blazing in red glory around door lintels and mullioned windows, it had none of the charm of the original coaching inn. But from the moment she'd stepped into the hotel's lobby, she could tell it was successful. Part of the reason for that had to be due to its prime location on the old Oxford to Banbury road. Legend had it that back in the eighteenth century, the local highwayman, Claude Duvall, had regularly robbed the patrons of their valuables, but one glance at a list of charges whilst waiting for the receptionist to inform Theo Greenwood of their presence, had convinced her that good old Claude wasn't the only one who indulged in daylight robbery around here.

Still, she was perfectly willing to concede that the Hayrick had all the facilities conference-goers and tourists could possibly want. For the tourists, it was within comfortable driving distance of Oxford, Warwick Castle, the Cotswolds and Stratford-Upon-Avon. For the conference-goers, it wasn't far, but far enough, from both London and Birmingham, to provide authentic country-house hotel living. The conference rooms no doubt boasted the latest in conferencing satellite links and who knew what else.

She was only surprised that Theo Greenwood had kept a whole room for himself. She suspected he was the kind of man who'd use every available inch of space to its maximum earning potential. On the other hand, she supposed if he had to play the genial host, he needed a showpiece office that looked as if it had been nicked from a turn-of-the-century local squire.

She admired the genuine Victorian green enamel, ebony and ivory inkstand and pen set that held pride of place on the desk, even as she doubted the authenticity of the signed oil over the fireplace. Mind you, she thought the hand-painted Delft tiles surrounding the fireplace were genuine enough, and would probably retail for a small fortune.

'Yes, we've come to talk about Julia Reynolds,' she said now, getting the interview underway. 'But I must say, I'm surprised to hear you talk about her that way. From what we've learned so far, you seemed to have had nothing good to say about her.'

Theo Greenwood shifted uneasily on the chair. He had rather fine, wide grey eyes, but the way they drifted about the room, as if trying to find somewhere to settle, made him look shifty.

Janine, beside her, abruptly crossed her legs, revealing shapely calves, and ankle-length boots of soft butter-coloured suede. Both women noticed the hotel-owner's eyes assess her knees before drifting on to inspect a vase of copper-coloured chrysanthemums on the windowsill to his left.

'Well, yes, I suppose that's fair,' Theo conceded unhappily. 'I mean, I have to admit that we didn't see eye to eye. But the poor girl is dead, and naturally, one doesn't like to be cruel. Not when someone can't fight back.'

Hillary nodded. She had no reason to doubt he was being honest enough, although she could sense that Janine didn't like him. Hillary wasn't so quick to judge. She'd dealt with too many witnesses, over too many years, not to look before leaping. 'What was your problem with Julia, Mr Greenwood?'

'Specifically? I didn't want her to marry my son,' he admitted, bluntly enough. 'Roger's a good boy, but he's young for his age. He was infatuated with her, of that I have no doubt, but I think he was finally beginning to see through her.

For all his *naïveté* when it comes to women, I was pretty sure that he wasn't as serious about her as she thought he was.'

Hillary nodded. 'But some might say that was wishful thinking, Mr Greenwood. From the witnesses we've questioned so far, it seems everyone else thought that they were still very much an item.'

Theo sighed heavily. 'I'm not saying that he wasn't still keen.'

'So what are you saying?'

'That he was beginning to notice things about her, that's all,' Greenwood senior said, flapping his right hand about in a vague gesture of annoyance. 'He'd begun to suspect that she might have feet of clay after all. Too many people were telling him that she was stringing him along, that she had other men on the side, that kind of thing. At first, he wouldn't hear of it, but I think, with so many people telling him the same thing, he was beginning to doubt her. I know for a fact he asked her outright if she had another man.'

Janine scribbled furiously in her notebook, knowing from the itch on her leg that the hotelier was eyeing up her thighs.

Dirty sod.

'So you think he was keeping a careful eye on her?' Hillary clarified, careful to keep her voice neutral. Even so, Mr Greenwood senior caught on quickly.

'Now, wait a minute. I'm not saying Roger was insanely jealous, or anything like that. There was nothing, you know, obsessional or unnatural about him keeping an eye on her. I'm just saying that he was not so besotted as once he was. That's all.'

Hillary decided to backtrack a little and give him time to calm down. 'Tell me about the party. You were at Owen and Wendy Wallises' twenty-fifth anniversary party, yes?'

'That's right.'

'Known them long?'

'No, not really. It's just that Owen and me are trying to sort out some business dealings. In fact, we had a long discussion the night of the party. Wendy wasn't too pleased.' If

Greenwood was sorry about upsetting his hostess's feelings, he certainly didn't show it.

'And did these business dealings have anything to do with Julia Reynolds?' she asked, knowing they couldn't possibly do so, but hoping his indignation might get the better of him. Which it did.

'Good grief, no,' he snorted. 'She was just an itinerant hairdresser, for Pete's sake. No, Owen has some land on the top road, more or less adjacent to this place. I wanted to buy it. I have it in mind to expand, build a leisure park, dig out a big lake perhaps, and stock it with fish, or even set up windsurfing possibilities. You've seen those adverts for lake-side parks I'm sure - bicycling, canoeing, that sort of thing? It would be perfect for the Hayrick, and would mean a lot for local employment.'

Hillary held up a hand to slow him down. 'I'm sure it would, yes.' At the moment, she had no interest in the plans for his empire. 'Mr Greenwood, you were talking to Mr Wallis for some time during the party, which means your son could have left at any time, and you wouldn't have known?'

Theo Greenwood's face suddenly did something remarkable. It puffed up and reddened, his cheeks bulging, his eyes receding and his nose, in some strange way, seeming to elongate. For just a second he did, in fact, look remarkably like a pig. Beside her, she could sense Janine gaping, no doubt thinking the same thing.

'So could anyone else, Inspector Greene,' Theo Greenwood said eventually, his porcine imitation slowly abating. 'The party sprawled all over the lower floor of the house, and out into the garden, too, at one point, in spite of the mist and damp.'

Hillary nodded. 'And just why was it that you disapproved so strongly of Miss Reynolds, Mr Greenwood? Apart from her being a 'mere itinerant hairdresser', was there any other reason why you didn't consider her good enough to marry your son?'

She was verging on rudeness, something Janine didn't hear from her boss often, at least, not when dealing with witnesses. Did it mean she suspected the hotel owner of the murder? She glanced sharply at Theo Greenwood, who was rapidly going pale. Or was the DI just playing him?

'I ... well, I mean ... I know it sounds, in this day and age rather snobbish, I suppose, but ... no. I mean yes. I mean to say, I thought Roger could do far better for himself.'

'And told him so?'

'I made no secret of the fact, certainly,' he said, with pitiful dignity. He picked up an old pen, complete with nib, and fiddled with it unhappily. He was clearly agitated, Janine realized, but that could just be due to having his male ego dented. No man liked to be talked to by a woman as Hillary had just talked to him.

Hillary herself wasn't so sure that that was all there was to it. She was catching the faint but unmistakable whiff of prevarication from Theo Greenwood. Something besides being thought of as a snob was eating away at him, and she wanted to know what it was. Trouble was, she was equally sure that the man wasn't going to simply let it slip. She'd have to find out some other way.

'I see,' she said blandly. 'So, did you speak to her that night at the party? Julia Reynolds, I mean?'

'I did not. I was careful to avoid her. It wouldn't have been beyond her to make a scene. She had no sense of discretion at all. Especially when she'd had too much to drink. As it was I thought ...'

He trailed off, obviously wishing that he'd kept his big mouth shut. Hillary would have bet a month's wages that it wasn't an unfamiliar feeling for him, either. For all his debonair, mine-host, hotel-keeping ways, she didn't think that tact and diplomacy came naturally to Mr Theo Greenwood.

'As it was you thought – what, Mr Greenwood?' Hillary prompted, quickly disabusing him of any idea that good manners would prevent her from pouncing on his mistake.

Hell, she was a detective inspector. Pouncing was one of the few pleasures of her occupation.

'Yes. I was about to say that I thought her choice of costume was typically annoying.'

Hillary nodded. So Mandy Tucker had got it right. Julia had worn the wedding dress to upset Theo Greenwood. And had obviously succeeded. Whether she'd also worn it as a hint to his son, she'd have to wait and see.

'So you did not see her leave the party?'

'I did not,' Theo Greenwood said flatly.

'And you have no idea who might have killed her, or why?'

'No.'

Hillary nodded. 'I'd like to speak to your son now, please, Mr Greenwood.'

'Is that really necessary? He was talking to you people nearly all day yesterday. He's signed a statement.'

'I'm sure he has. But I'm the senior investigating officer, and I'm sure he wouldn't mind. After all, the woman he loved was brutally murdered. I'm sure he'll want to co-operate fully.'

The barely veiled threat had him once again doing his pig impersonation, but after a few splutterings he conceded, with ill-grace, and left the den in search of his son.

'I can see why he put Julia Renolds' back up,' Janine said, the moment the door had closed behind him. 'Fancy having him for a father-in-law! Lecherous old sod.'

'Apparently, that's just what she did fancy,' Hillary pointed out with a smile. 'Having him for a father-in-law, I mean. And you can see why! This place must have had her salivating. Roger is his only son, right?'

Janine quickly checked her notes. 'Yep. The whole lot'll probably go to him. And if this deal to build a leisure park is pulled off, the sky's the limit.'

If. Hillary wondered if the much-touted leisure park was quite the sure thing that Mr Theo Greenwood would have them believe. Despite her earlier indifference about Theo Greenwood's empire, she now made a mental note to get Tommy Lynch to go over the Greenwood financial holdings and check on the upcoming deal with an accountant's magnifying glass. Although all the signs pointed to this being a sexually-motivated killing, she didn't want to leave any stone unturned. An old tutor at police training college said nearly all crimes came down to sex and money.

And there was money here, all right, and Julia Reynolds had been scheming to get her hands on it.

There came a timid tap at the door, and Janine quickly got up to open it. Hillary had expected Theo Greenwood to return with his son and force them to more or less turf him out on his ear, but there was no sign of him as Roger Greenwood came in. Which meant that Daddy wasn't anxious to tangle with the big bad coppers again, and that sent the alarm bells ringing in her head.

Roger Greenwood didn't resemble his father much physically (which must have been a relief to Julia Reynolds) although he had his thick, dark hair. His figure was much taller and thinner however, and he had big, startlingly blue eyes. There were dark rings around them at the moment though, and he walked as if he felt very old. He seemed to be in genuine mourning for Julia, and Hillary decided to be much more gentle than she'd originally intended.

'Please, sit down Mr Greenwood. I'm Detective Inspector Hillary Greene, the senior investigating officer in this case. First, let me tell you how sorry I am for your loss.'

After a moment's hesitation, Roger Greenwood sat in his father's chair, and nodded mutely at her introduction. He looked ill.

'I know this isn't a good time, but I need to ask you some questions about Julia. And the night of the party. All right?'

He nodded mutely. He was wearing a heavy black jumper that was too big for him, giving him an even more vulnerable air. She could feel Janine shifting in her chair, and knew her sergeant was hoping that he wasn't going to cry. Hillary rather hoped he wouldn't too.

'So, how long had you two been going out?'
'Nearly ten months.'
'It was serious then?'
'Yeah, it was.'
'Were you engaged?'

'Not really. I mean, we were talking about it.'

'Oh. You see, we were wondering if she wore the wedding dress as some sort of private joke?' Hillary said softly. 'You know, to tease you? Were you reluctant to propose?'

A ghost of a smile crossed the young man's face, then disappeared. 'No. I mean, I don't think her choice of dress meant anything. She just looked fabulous in it. Julia liked to look stunning. And she was stunning, wasn't she? You saw her?' he demanded eagerly.

Hillary nodded, trying not to remember the state the young hairdresser had been in at the time. Her face empurpled and agonized, her tongue protruding.

'Yes, I could tell she was incredibly beautiful,' Hillary said gently. 'You must have been proud to be seen around with her.'

'I was.'

'But, perhaps, she made you feel a bit insecure as well?' she began to probe carefully. 'We've talked to lots of her friends and acquaintances, who all said she was very vivacious. And popular.'

'I know what you're trying to say,' Roger Greenwood said, with the first trace of spirit since coming into the room. 'You needn't beat about the bush with me. But she wasn't a tart or anything. She was just a normal woman. And when she was with me, she was mine. You know what I mean?'

Hillary did, but couldn't let it go at that, despite the clear agony in the big blue eyes that pleaded with her to do just that. It was her job to press.

'I think so. But one of her friends was sure that Julia had another boyfriend, at the same time as yourself.'

Roger Greenwood leaned back against the chair slowly, and Hillary could almost see the fight going out of him.

'She might have done,' he admitted miserably. 'But she said no.'

'You didn't believe her?'

'I believed her when she said she loved me, when she told me I was the only one she wanted.'

The unspoken words hovered, almost a physical reality, in the air between them.

'But you really knew she had someone else?'

He shrugged helplessly. 'I didn't *know*. Not for sure. Sometimes I was convinced of it. Other times....' again he shrugged.

'Perhaps that's why you couldn't bring yourself to propose? Because you knew she'd say yes, but not for the reasons you wanted. Am I right?' Hillary asked delicately.

Roger smiled. 'I knew Julia liked my money, if that's what you're getting at. Or rather Dad's money. But why shouldn't she? She was a beautiful woman, and beautiful women are entitled to things, aren't they? I mean, everybody says they're not, but in the real world, everyone just knows that they are. Look at celebs.'

Hillary considered this rather confused speech, and realized he'd probably hit the nail right on the head. Everyone said that looks didn't matter. But then everyone said that money wasn't everything. To an awful lot of people, however, that was just so much bullshit.

'So you loved her in spite of her faults?' she said simply.

Roger looked at the older policewoman in surprise. 'You understand? You really understand.'

Hillary nodded. 'I think so, yes.' She was often amazed at what people were prepared to put up with, especially from those they loved. Or needed. 'Tell me what happened that night at the party. Did you ask Julia to leave the farmhouse with you at any time?'

'No. No, I didn't. We were dancing for the first hour or so, then we got something to eat. She'd had a few drinks from the bar – she liked those mixers, you know, in the bottles. But then, I just lost sight of her.' He hesitated for just a moment. Should he tell them about catching her eavesdropping at the door to the Wallises' library, when his father and the farmer had retired there to discuss business?

No, he couldn't do that. They might get the wrong idea about her. *He* knew she was just being curious. But they might not realize that it meant nothing at all. Julia just always liked to know things, that was all. And she'd always said his dad needed watching.

'I thought she might have gone to the loo, so I hung around with some of the younger guys there for a bit,' he went on instead, with a small shrug. It couldn't, after all, be important. 'But she never showed up again. I was just wondering if someone had pissed her off, and she'd left in a huff, when Michael Wallis came back and said … said … about the cowshed. I'm sorry. I can't say anymore.' His voice, which had been cracking steadily throughout this recital, suddenly broke. He began to sob.

Hillary reached into her handbag for a tissue and handed it over. She waited.

Janine studied her boots.

Eventually, the harrowing sounds ceased, and Hillary decided to call it a day. 'Mr Greenwood, would you mind if we took the clothes and the shoes you were wearing that night for forensic examination? If, as you claim, you never went to the cowshed that night, this will help with elimination purposes.'

Roger nodded, wiping his wet eyes with the back of his hand. 'Sure, I'll go get them.'

Hillary nodded to Janine to accompany him. Not that she suspected he was going to do anything stupid, like run the shoes under the tap or anything. Still, you never knew.

She paced about uneasily while they were gone, knowing that, logically, Roger Greenwood should be top of her list of suspects. He was the current boyfriend, suspected infidelity, and was on the scene (or as near as damn it) at the time of her murder. It was almost certainly a sex-crime, so what the hell was the problem?

Well, the problem was, her gut simply didn't like Roger Greenwood for the killing. In fact, her radar told her that of the two men she'd questioned this afternoon, it was Greenwood Senior who had secrets he wanted kept hidden.

Still, they'd see what forensics came up with on the shoes. The preliminary reports so far had picked up no trace of Roger

Greenwood's presence in the cowshed, which was why they were only now taking away his clothes for more direct tests. No fibres, no hair, no DNA and no fingerprints had meant that they'd probably not have been able to get a warrant for his clothes if she'd applied for one, which was why she'd been glad he'd volunteered them.

Once Janine had rejoined her with the evidence bags, they took their leave of the grieving boyfriend and stepped outside into the car-park.

A variety of baccate shrubs, well groomed and tended, blazed with cheerful autumnal cheer. A blackbird, busy trying to prise a worm from a well-tended lawn, ignored them as they trooped past. Yellow, orange and copper-toned trees sighed in a high wind, the sky that clear bright autumnal blue that wouldn't last.

'Check the photographs of the party that Tommy should have by now, and make sure that Greenwood gave you the right clothes and shoes,' Hillary reminded her sergeant automatically as they made their way to the car, ignoring the way Janine rolled her eyes.

The blonde sergeant dumped the evidence bags on the back seat and slid in behind the wheel. Although they'd come in Hillary's ancient Volkswagen, she was driving. It was the usual protocol for the junior officer to drive. She just wished Hillary didn't keep reminding her of the obvious. Did she look like a grandmother in need of being taught how to suck eggs?

Janine longed for the day when she could delegate the scut work to others, and wondered if she should give Mel a hint that she was ready to move up. She needed his recommendation if she was to apply for Boards.

Perhaps she'd wait until they were in some lovely country hotel, rather like the Hayrick, and then suggest it. When they were tucked up in some ancient four-poster bed, all sweaty and sticky. He'd be in a good mood by then.

She'd make sure of that!

Tommy couldn't believe his luck, but there it was, right on camera. A purple Mini.

It had been another of the constables doing the house to house who'd told him about Kirtlington's recently installed sleeping policemen and the speed camera. Tommy had taken a trip down to Traffic, not really believing that the car he was looking for would actually have been filmed. Which just goes to show – you should never bet against lady luck. He quickly jotted down the number plate, let his fingers do the walking across Traffic's computer keyboard, and within seconds, up popped a name.

Registered owner, Mrs Vivian Orne, from Nuneaton.

chapter six

Whilst Hillary and Janine had been out at the Hayrick Inn questioning the Greenwoods, Tommy, after his brief and rare moment of triumph over the matter of the purple Mini, spent the rest of the day re-interviewing some of the party-goers. He knew Hillary would probably want Janine to go with him to Nuneaton, for although he'd run Vivian Orne through the computers and found no evidence of a criminal record, and despite the fact that she would almost certainly turn out to have nothing whatsoever to do with the case, protocol still had to be followed.

But the interviews yielded nothing new. Nobody had seen Roger Greenwood, Michael Wallis, or any other male, treating Julia Reynolds with aggression or unwanted attention. And since it was the twenty-fifth wedding anniversary of fairly staid, well-to-do people, there hadn't even been much hanky-panky or naughty snortings of things illegal. It had, in short, been a rather dull, nice-mannered party.

At least he was coming to the end of them now. Tommy looked up to see a twenty-something man, dressed casually in jeans and shirt, walk in to the interview-room. He checked his list, and looked up. 'Mr Bellamy? Charles Bellamy?'

'Charlie, yeah.'

Tommy automatically ticked the name off the list. 'Please, sit down. You're a friend of Mr Roger Greenwood?'

'That's right.'

'Thank you for coming in.'

Charlie Bellamy shrugged. 'I don't mind. I mean, it's murder, right? You have to do what you can. Mind you, I don't know what I can do to help.'

'How did you come to be invited to the party, Mr Bellamy?'

'I work for the Wallises. I'm their gardener. Nothing fancy, mind, it's only me, but they like the garden to look good, and there's enough of it to keep me employed full time. It's what I went to horticultural college for.'

Tommy nodded, trying to look impressed. 'And you're also a friend of Roger Greenwood?' he pressed.

'Yeah, since primary school.'

'So you knew Julia?'

'Yeah. Not well. I mean, she was younger than I was, and so we didn't socialize or nothing. But even if we had, I doubt she'd have given me much of a second look. I wouldn't have rated.'

Tommy looked up from his notebook. Had he detected a touch of bitterness there?

'Oh?'

Charlie Bellamy had one of those friendly faces with red cheeks and the fit, compact body of someone who did a physical job, five days a week. He would easily have had the strength necessary to strangle a young and equally healthy woman.

Now Charlie grinned. 'I can see what you're thinking, mate, and you're only half right. Yes, I suppose I felt a bit resentful that Roger's bird didn't even deign to notice my existence, but no, it never really worried me. For a start, she was my mate's bird, so I wouldn't have looked at her twice anyway. But besides that, she was definitely not my type. She was much too hard for my liking, know what I mean? I like 'em cuddly and not overly bright.'

Tommy nodded absently. Like Hillary, he too had been building up a mental image of their victim, and this description of Julia tallied with what others had been saying about her.

'Did your friend know how you felt? About Julia, I mean?'

Charlie shrugged. 'I dunno. I never came out and said,

"Hey, Rog, I think that Julia is a right hard cow". I mean, that's not the way you talk to a mate, is it?'

'No. But if things were getting serious, I mean, if you thought he was about to propose to her, you might have said something then? Nobody likes to see a mate head for the rocks, right?' Tommy raised an eyebrow in question. After all, if there had been some sort of bust up between friends, it's possible Charlie might have felt miffed, and blamed the rift on the girlfriend. Such things had happened before.

Charlie Bellamy seemed to give this question some serious thought before finally shaking his head. 'Nah. First off, I think it's always best to keep your nose out of other people's lives. And secondly, I don't think old Rog actually was going to propose. I think his old man being so anti had finally begun to make him think again.'

'Really?' Tommy said sceptically. 'It's been my experience that when a parent sticks his oar in, the son is more likely to dig in his heels and carry on regardless.'

Charlie laughed, and nodded. 'I know what you mean. But Rog isn't like that. For a start, his old man is loaded, see, and getting more loaded by the minute, and Rog isn't stupid. He knows which side his bread's buttered all right. He wouldn't want to get disinherited or nothing. And besides all that, I think he wasn't quite so keen on Julia as he was in the beginning. You know, it was beginning to cool off some. At least on Rog's part. I think Julia was still keen to get him down the aisle though.'

Tommy nodded. Bellamy sounded sincere. 'The night of the party, did you and Roger meet up?'

'Sure. Had a few drinks. I was on shandies, Rog was sticking mostly to beer. Nothing heavy. He wasn't drunk or nothing.'

'And Julia?'

'Oh she was knocking back those fancy drinks in bottles. Alco-pops or whatever. She could get really rat-arsed, but most people wouldn't notice. She wasn't one of those who got maudlin, or really loud. I reckon she was well on her way to being sozzled, though.'

'And you didn't see Roger leave with her? Go out into the garden for some fresh air?'

'No. And frankly, mate, I think you're barking up the wrong tree. Don't get me wrong or nothing, I read the papers too. I know when some bird gets killed, you have to look real long and hard at her old man. But Rog just ain't the sort to go and do something like that. And, yeah, I bet the friends and families of killers say that all the time too, but....' He shrugged helplessly.

Tommy felt like joining him. He tried to get some sort of timeline going on Roger Greenwood's night at the party, but, like all the others, Charlie had only the vaguest sense of time. He could only say as far as he knew, Roger had been 'around' throughout the entire evening. Tommy finally shook his hand and let him go.

Janine was in the interview-room adjacent, this time questioning the friends of the victim.

'It's Miss Morley, right? Phillipa Morley?' she spoke now to the latest in a long line, trying not to look impressed in any way. But the fact was, this girl was almost as stunning as Julia Reynolds had been, but in a dark, exotic way. She had the mocha skin that bespoke a mixed parentage, and the long, tightly curled, raven-black hair that looked so stunning *en masse*. Add to that almond-shaped and coloured eyes coupled with an instinctive sense of fashion, and you had a recipe that would set many male hearts pounding.

Janine sincerely doubted that Julia Reynolds had ever regarded *this* woman as a friend. A potential rival, perhaps. The competition for sure and one who had to be constantly watched at all times. But a friend? Not on your Nelly.

'It's Pip,' Phillipa Morley said at once. And smiled charmingly, revealing dazzlingly white teeth. Janine smiled briefly. According to her notes, Pip Morley worked in Summertown in a travel agency. Had Julia cultivated her friendship in the hope of cheap holiday deals, Janine wondered cattily?

'You knew Julia well?'

'Oh yes. But we weren't close. Julia's best friend was Mandy Tucker.'

Janine nodded. 'So, have you any idea who might have wanted to kill Julia, Pip?'

'No. She had a boyfriend, but I never saw him as the dangerous type. Besides, I think he was beginning to cool a little.'

'This is Roger Greenwood we're talking about here?'

'The rich man's son, yeah,' Pip grinned. 'Julia liked to brag about him. And at first it was obvious that she had him really hooked. He was like a little panting puppy dog.'

'But not any more?'

'No. At least, I didn't think so. Of course, Julia didn't see it.'

'And you didn't mention it?'

Pip laughed. 'I should say not. Nobody ever rained on Julia's parade, not unless they wanted to get flattened.'

Janine nodded. 'You didn't like her?'

Pip Morley shifted restlessly on her seat. 'It's not that. I didn't *dislike* her, I just understood her, that's all. She wanted the best, and was beautiful enough to get it. I could respect that, in a way. It's just not my way, and Julia knew it.'

'So how would you rate Roger Greenwood as a potential killer?' Janine asked, genuinely curious to get another woman's honest opinion.

'I'd have rated him very low, frankly,' Pip said at once. 'I never got any bad vibes off him and, like I said, I think he was well past the stage when he could get ragingly jealous. Besides, he always struck me as being something of a pragmatist, and I know from Julia that his father was dead set against her. Roger always struck me as being too wary, too careful of himself, to do anything really out of line. Know what I mean?'

Janine, unaware as yet that Tommy was getting almost exactly the same reading of Roger Greenwood's character in the next interview-room, simply nodded.

'So, do you know anyone who *might* be the strangling type?'

'Only her bit of rough,' Pip said promptly.

And Janine nearly fell off the chair. 'Sorry?'

'Leo Mann.'

Janine blinked. She'd heard that name before. Leo Mann. Mann. Of course. Leo, 'The Man' Mann. Big-time loser. Thug. General purpose, up-for-hire bully boy. She took a deep breath, wondering for some obscure reason, if Pip Morley was having her on. 'Let's make sure I've got this right,' she said carefully. 'Julia Reynolds was seeing Leo Mann?'

'Sure. On and off,' Pip admitted casually. 'I think she liked the glamour of having a boyfriend on the wrong side of the law. She used him a bit like an accessory, you know - the ultimate thug on her arm, whenever she wanted to go clubbing.'

Janine smiled. 'Sounds like you knew Julia very well indeed.'

Pip shrugged. 'At first I thought she was crazy. Leo Mann gives me the creeps. But she'd been seeing him for months and months, and I never saw her with a black eye, so I suppose she kept him under control. Knowing Julia, I suspect she did, anyway. Still, not my cup of tea.' And Pip shuddered.

Janine could hardly believe her luck. Their vic had been two-timing Leo Mann. You could almost say the case was solved.

She rushed Pip Morley through the rest of the interview at double-speed, then all but skipped upstairs. She should have clocked off her shift over an hour ago, but like all cops, barely bothered to register the overtime. She'd never get paid for it anyway. You just worked to solve the cases so that it looked good on your CV when promotion opportunities came a-knocking. That was one good thing about working with Hillary Greene, Janine acknowledged, she always made sure credit was given where it was due. Not like some dinosaurs, who took the credit for everything. She was thus very careful to report to Hillary Greene directly with her latest offering.

Hillary, who was already shrugging into her jacket ready to go home, listened carefully. Tommy, not to be outdone, remembered the purple Mini, and made his own modest report.

'OK Janine, first thing tomorrow, pull in Leo Mann,' Hillary ordered. 'But do your homework first. See if any of his previous trouble has involved violence against women.' She had a nagging idea that it didn't, although her memory wasn't as reliable as it had once been. If Frank Ross had been there she'd have asked him, but Ross, much to everyone's relief, always left on the dot when his shift was over. But Leo 'The Man', was just the sort of low-life scum Frank would know well.

She could see Janine was fizzing, and wouldn't have dreamed of giving someone else the follow-up interview, or even taking it for herself. She just had a hunch her sergeant might be in for a disappointment, that was all. Still, them was the knocks.

'Then I want you both to get off to Nuneaton to interview this Vivian Orne woman. She doesn't sound very promising, but the purple Mini needs to be crossed off the list. Tommy, you're sure from the speed camera photo that it was a woman driving, not her husband?'

'It looked like it to me, guv,' Tommy confirmed, and Hillary nodded glumly.

Her phone began to trill and she sighed heavily. Another few minutes and she'd have been safely out the door. She picked it up, hoping for a simply enquiry or wrong number.

No such luck.

'Hello, DI Greene? Owen Wallis here. Look, I thought I'd better tell you. I found some strange bloke hanging around the cowshed this afternoon. He ran off when I challenged him.'

Hillary gave a mental groan. 'I'd better come over then,' she said dully. She glanced outside, noting that although it wasn't yet fully dark, it soon would be. She hung up and briefly explained to Janine and Tommy. Janine was already applying some lipstick, ready to leave, and looking bored.

Tommy asked hopefully, 'Want me to come, guv?' A moonlight walk out in the countryside with Hillary would be just what the doctor ordered.

'No, it's all right Tommy. You slide off.' She was sure he had a girlfriend waiting for him somewhere. It was only pitiful old maiden DIs like herself who had nothing to go home for, and no one to go home to. Briefly she wondered if she should get a cat. But the way her luck seemed to be running lately, the poor thing would probably end up drowned in the cut, and mourning over a soggy moggy wasn't her idea of fun.

Janine yawned. 'Well, I'm off to change into my party frock.'

Hillary blinked, then nodded. Of course. It was the promotion party for Marcus Donleavy tonight. All the gang were going, which meant she'd have to put in an appearance as well. Thankfully, Puff the Tragic Wagon started first go in spite of the cold and damp, and she was soon on her way out into the sticks. If she hurried, she wouldn't miss too much of Marcus's party.

It was near dark when she arrived and Owen Wallis was already waiting in the Range Rover. Hillary, unasked, climbed in beside him.

'Like I said, he was up in the cowshed. Took off like a rocket when he heard the Range Rover coming,' the farmer said by way of greeting. He must have had eyes like an owl, for he set off up the track without turning the headlights on, and Hillary clung on to the side of her seat nervously.

'Can you describe him?' she asked.

'Tall, lanky-looking bloke. Light-coloured sandy hair. Not old, not from the way he ran, but I wouldn't say he was really young either.'

Hillary nodded. That sounded like the man she'd seen before, the one who'd seemed so awkward climbing the gate. If the man who'd killed Julia was the type of sicko who liked to revisit his hunting grounds, perhaps pick up some kind of souvenir from the scene, then the sort of behaviour their mysterious friend was exhibiting would fit the pattern perfectly. On the other hand, it could just be Mr Bloggins, working for the *Daily Scrunge*, looking to milk the story for another byline.

By now they'd reached the cowshed. It looked dark, smelly, and sounded full of cows. Owen Wallis turned off the engine.

'Well, he won't be here now,' she said pragmatically, climbing out and looking around, her mind mentally ticking off the pros and cons. 'But if you wanted to keep an eye on things, perhaps wait for a chance to have another look around, where would you hole up?' she asked the farmer.

Owen Wallis give her a startled glance, then slowly looked around and eventually nodded uphill. 'Well, in the spinney, I reckon,' he said at last.

Hillary regarded the small copse of trees without any enthusiasm. The field between her and it had recently been ploughed. And she still needed to get back for Marcus's party. Oh what the hell, she muttered under her breath. If she got back in her car and arrived early at the shindig, she'd only eat too much. And her hips definitely wouldn't thank her for that.

'Well, might as well take a quick look around since I'm here. Don't suppose you have a torch?' she asked, without much hope.

But Owen Wallis came up trumps. She supposed farmers were a bit like boy scouts when it came to surviving in the countryside. She took the long, reassuringly heavy, black, rubber-handled torch from him and trudged off. Owen Wallis, after a moment's hesitation, set off after her. She supposed his innate sense of gallantry was kicking in. Either that, or he didn't want her traipsing over his fields, helping herself to his turnips. (Perhaps he'd heard her stomach rumbling?)

She stumbled only once, over some weeds that caught around her ankle, and only Owen Wallis's strong grip prevented her from ending up face-first in the mud. Or in something far worse.

They made the edge of the spinney a few minutes later, where she peered uselessly into the trees, feeling a bit daft. Chummy was long gone. Besides, it was really dark inside, and she was definitely not about to go rooting about in there. 'Look,' she began to explain quietly, then nearly jumped out of her skin as something inside the trees suddenly blundered up out of cover and thrashed off to the left. Even then she was still thinking pheasant, or maybe deer, fox or other form of wildlife. It wasn't until her torch beam picked out the undeniably human form running like the clappers for the far edge of the small spinney that she realized what had happened.

'Bloody hell, he really *was* holed up here,' she yelled, her voice sounding comically aggrieved. 'Let's get him!' she hollered, her blood up and for a moment forgetting that it was just herself and the farmer here, and that she didn't, in fact, have a battalion of gung-ho bobbies behind her for backup. The next moment she realized the true situation, and wished bitterly that she'd accepted Tommy's offer to accompany her after all. This would have been right up his alley. As it was, she was stymied.

But she hadn't reckoned on the fury of an irate farmer when faced with a trespasser.

'I'll cut him off this side,' Owen Wallis yelled, dashing behind her and away to the left. 'You take the far end,' he called back over his shoulder.

Hillary barely had time to yell, 'No, Mr Wallis, please,' before the farmer disappeared into the gloom. Great, this was just what she needed. If Wallis got injured, she could just see Mel's face. Not to mention the new super's. And not to mention the headlines: 'Member of the public wounded aiding female detective inspector.' Or something even more hideous.

And Wallis would probably sue the shit out of Thames Valley as well.

Hillary eyed the spinney glumly, weighing up her best chances of getting out of this with her skin intact. No way was she going to go blundering in there, holding a torch and providing an attacker with an easy means of spotting her exact location. She'd lost count of the number of times that she'd watched scary films or thrillers where the heroine did just that. It always made her want to spit.

She tried to fight back the stomach-churning thought that the watcher in the woods might have a knife. Or even a gun – a shotgun maybe. If so, Owen Wallis might be dead before she even got to him. The thought was enough to make her set off counter-clockwise, turning off the torch and stumbling a bit in the darkness before her night vision was restored. Common sense told her that the man in the woods would surely change direction. He wouldn't want to go back towards the farm, because his instinct would be to head for deeper countryside. But which way?

The trouble was, she had no clear idea of the geography around here. She paused, listening, and heard only the sound of an approaching train. There was obviously a railway line close by. She skirted the trees, listening anxiously for the sounds of hostilities, but could hear nothing but her own quickened, nervous breathing.

She felt slightly sick. Once again, she wished Tommy Lynch was with her.

She moved back into the ploughed field, half-crouched in spite of her protesting back and straining calf-muscles, and made her way to the far end of the spinney, where she hunkered down and considered her position.

She was fairly sure at this point that Owen Wallis was all right. He certainly hadn't shouted for help. She tried to take some comfort in the thought that whoever was in the spinney was probably more afraid than she was. Unless, of course, he was a psychopath who didn't do fear. In which case he was probably salivating at the thought of strangling someone else: her for instance.

Hillary shook her head. No sense thinking like that. She shifted her weight from one foot to the other, trying to prevent pins and needles, then saw movement between the trees and peered hard. Yes! It was definitely a human shape.

The thing was – was it Owen Wallis or the watcher?

'There he goes, there, stop him!' The shout was obviously from the outraged farmer, some yards further back, and Hillary jumped, stood up, dropped the torch, and raced after the fleeing figure, now way off to her left.

Hillary knew many officers worked out at the gym, took martial arts courses, did marathons and swimathons for charity and what not, but she was not one of them. And boy, did her body remind her of it now. Within a few hundred yards of the fleeing figure she could already feel the beginnings of stitch. And although she was wearing sensible lace-up flatties, they weren't exactly trainers, and the wet ground was heavy going. Her breath began to sound like a steam engine labouring up a hill.

She could hear Owen Wallis cursing somewhere behind her, making the lumbering sounds of an outraged bull elephant. She hoped she didn't sound quite *that* bad and had to fight the urge to giggle. It was nerves, of course, but even knowing that didn't stop her giving a sudden grunt of laughter.

The figure in front of her finally cleared the ploughed ground, plunged through a hedge and disappeared. Hillary desperately put on a last-ditch burst of speed, hit the same gap in the edge, and found herself yelping in pain.

Thistles, lots of thistles, tended to have that effect.

She heard a curious 'pinging' sound up ahead, followed by a yelp of pain that was definitely not her own, and, thus encouraged, plunged forward straight into a barbed-wire fence. She heard the same 'pinging' sound as before and swore long and hard as the wire cut fabric, flesh and blood.

Her flesh and blood, dammit.

She managed to get disentangled and squeezed through. As she did so, she heard a slithering sound a little further along, and took off towards it, only to find herself abruptly running pell-mell down a steep gradient, covered in what felt like gravel. She let rip with a surprised shout and instinctively dug in her heels, leaned back to try and stop herself from going face forward, and sat down abruptly on her backside. Stinging nettles and sharp stones kissed her hands and wrists as she scrabbled about for purchase, for now she could hear a roaring, truly terrifying noise.

And too late, far too late, realized what it was.

There was light – a sudden bright circle of light that lit up the bare branches of trees and the shingle in front of her, like something out of an alien abduction movie. And, turning her blood to ice, came the unmistakable sound of a train's warning siren blowing urgently.

She was all but on the railway track now, and an express train was heading straight for her.

She leaned back against the wet prickly earth, tucking her legs up under her protectively as the train roared by. Rectangles of light from the train's windows passed by in a blur, faces and scenarios rushing by. A man reading a paper, a little girl looking out and staring at her with big eyes, her little red mouth pursed in an 'O' of astonishment. An old lady, looking equally surprised.

As well she might.

Hillary knew that long-shanks must have managed to get across the line before the train had arrived, and knew she'd be in no condition to take up the chase once the train had gone by. Her heart was going like she'd been popping speed all day, and she had to keep swallowing hard to fight down the urge to throw up. Her sides hurt, she stung all over and, as far as near-death experiences went, this one you could keep.

'Sod this for a game of soldiers,' she muttered as the last, lighted carriage sped by and the train disappeared around a bend in the track.

Above her, she heard Owen Wallis arrive at the edge of the embankment and could imagine him peering down the incline. 'Hey! Hey! Is everything all right down there?'

'Yeah, it's all right,' Hillary yelled back. 'But I lost him.'

She leaned forward, resting her forearms atop her bent knees, and took long, calming breaths. She could feel herself shaking, and was vaguely aware of Owen Wallis clambering clumsily down to sit beside her, the top of his arm just pressing slightly against hers. She found his silent presence oddly comforting. For a moment, the two of them simply sat there and watched the moon shine benevolently on the railway lines. Then the farmer said bluntly, 'Well, sod it.'

Hillary couldn't have said it better herself.

chapter seven

Jerome Raleigh looked up as someone knocked at the door to his office, then slowly rose as Chief Superintendent Marcus Donleavy entered. 'Sir,' Jerome said neutrally, his face showing neither dismay nor anticipation at having the newly promoted officer return to his old haunts only a day after his celebratory party.

'Don't panic,' Marcus said, with a brief grin. 'I've only come to see if you've got any last minute queries, then I'm off.'

Jerome nodded to a chair and hoped the chief superintendent would be as good as his word. Marcus Donleavy was nobody's fool, and Jerome sure as hell didn't want him looking over his shoulder in the months to come.

'Thanks, but everything seems to be running smoothly,' Jerome assured him.

'You've talked to all your staff?' Marcus asked casually.

'Yes, finished yesterday. No surprises. Except, perhaps one?'

Marcus lifted one silver eyebrow and then grinned again. 'Let me guess. Why haven't I managed to get rid of Frank Ross yet?'

Jerome spread his hands wordlessly.

'For many reasons,' Marcus began. 'For a start, he was a great pal of Ronnie Greene, and when the shit hit the fan about his corruption, sacking another known crony would only have given the press and knockers even more ammunition.'

Jerome nodded, hoping his superior officer couldn't see just how interested he was in what Donleavy had to say about

Frank Ross, and was careful to keep his tone strictly light. 'But surely, even before it all came out, he must have been a pain in the neck?'

Marcus nodded. 'Oh yes. And other points south. This is where the second reason comes in. In spite of it all, Frank Ross has got one of the best system of narks in the squad. He's old time. He was on the beat forever. Grew up amongst the scum. He understands them in a way that the new up-and-comers never will. It comes in handy. No two ways about it.'

Jerome thought about it for a few moments, understanding what Donleavy wasn't saying, as well as what he was. In a pitched battle with hooligans, you'd want the surprisingly benign-looking Frank Ross firmly on your side. And when you needed to put the wind up someone, it would be Frank Ross you sent out on the errand. Nasty yes, and in an ideal world, the likes of Frank Ross wouldn't ever be needed. But Jerome Raleigh knew – and knew very well – that the police didn't operate in anything approaching an ideal world. And nothing he was hearing sounded alarm bells. In point of fact, he was more sure now than ever that cultivating Frank Ross would be a good idea.

'Sticking with that particular team,' Jerome continued smoothly, 'Tommy Lynch seemed promising. He was bright, still eager, and willing to learn.'

'Yes, we normally put those we think have real potential with DI Greene for a while. She's good at training them up.'

'Did I detect some tension between the other sergeant, the good-looking blonde woman, and Philip Mallow?'

Marcus sighed. 'I wouldn't be surprised. Mel's a good man, as you'll see. But he has a bit of a weakness when it comes to women.'

'That could be awkward.'

'Hillary certainly finds it so,' Marcus mused. 'But she can cope.'

'You rate her,' Jerome said simply. 'I was surprised she wasn't at your party last night. Did she have something else on?' If so, why wasn't I informed, he added silently.

'Only if you want to count playing chicken with an Inter-City Express,' Marcus said drily, and quickly explained the events of the previous evening, as related to him by Hillary. Jerome listened silently, without interrupting. 'Apparently,' Marcus finished, 'this farmer got a really good look at the suspect as he came barrelling out of the woods and all but rammed into him. It was a full moon, and Hillary said he seemed confident that he'd be able to identify him again. So she brought Farmer Jones straight back here and oiked the resident artist out of it, to do both an identikit drawing, and a straightforward sketch. She's asked for the results to be run in today's local papers. She might get a nibble.'

'Was she hurt?'

'Hillary?' Marcus said, sounding slightly surprised. 'No. At least, she didn't say. Mind you, she isn't the sort to go looking for sympathy. I expect she got the usual spate of cuts and bruises. Probably scraped some skin off various parts when she slid down the railway track. That sort of thing.'

'Bloody lucky she didn't fall onto the lines. Then we'd be having a very different conversation,' Jerome said mildly.

Marcus shot him a look. 'She's not gung-ho, if that's what you're after,' he said, after a thoughtful pause. 'On the other hand, if an opportunity presents itself, she'll always go for it.'

Jerome nodded. He'd have to remember that.

Marcus sighed and got to his feet. He hoped the new man from the Met was going to work out. But at the moment, he wouldn't lay bets either way.

Janine Tyler leaned across the scratched, nicotine-stained interview table and shook her head sadly. 'Oh, come on, Leo,' she said scornfully. 'You're really trying to tell me that your woman was putting it about with another bloke, and you didn't give a monkey's? Do I look as if I was born yesterday?'

'Nah, darling, you look much better than any squalling new-born brat,' Leo 'The Man' Mann assured her, with what she supposed was meant to pass for charm.

Janine sighed heavily. 'Spare me, Leo. Let's get back to Julia

Reynolds shall we? You obviously have a penchant for beautiful women. Julia was quite a looker, wasn't she? A real catch for the likes of you. No offence.'

'None taken, darlin', Leo Mann grinned lasciviously. 'And you can offend me any time you like.' His rap-sheet gave his age as twenty-four but he hardly looked eighteen. He was skinny, with a blond skin-head cut, tattoos, nose and eyebrow-piercing, the lot. He was dressed in an old Grateful Dead T-shirt, grungy with age, and denims that looked as if they could get up and walk, all by themselves. He was wearing a lot of silver jewellery. Not gold. Silver. Janine found it faintly fascinating.

Silver. As the Yanks would say – go figure.

'Mind you, she wasn't so very beautiful when we last saw her,' Janine carried on thoughtfully. 'Her face was all purple-red, her tongue sticking out. She looked gross.'

Leo Mann shifted his bony backside on the seat and looked, for the first time since they'd hauled him in for interview, faintly uneasy. 'Poor cow,' he said flatly. 'But I didn't do nothing to her. And you can keep me in here till kingdom come, and you won't get me to say I did, 'cause I didn't. See?'

'Come on, Leo, you know as well as I do that you're handy with your fists. I've got the charge sheet right here to prove it,' she went on impatiently.

Leo Mann leaned forward. He had the words LOVE tattooed on both sets of knuckles. Not LOVE on one and HATE on the other. Again she found the idiosyncrasy faintly fascinating. She only lifted her eyes from the pale-blue letters when he began to speak.

'And do you see on any of these here charge sheets,' – he tapped hard on the pieces of paper littered across the table – 'where it says I knocked about a woman?'

This time it was Janine who shifted unhappily on her seat. Because, of course, Leo Mann knew as well as she did, that he had no previous for aggro to women.

'I love me mum,' Leo said, and nodded. 'My old man scarpered when I were ten. Mum brought me up. She wouldn't have no messing about when it came to knocking women about. Now then,' he added, tapping a fingertip on the table pointedly once more, before leaning back in his chair and crossing his skinny tattooed arms across his skinny chest.

Janine sighed, and started all over again.

Hillary smiled grimly as Graham Vaughan handed her a cup of tea. The cup and saucer (no mugs in Graham's office) looked to her to be genuine Spode. She'd met Graham through a friend of hers, Tania Lay, way back in the uni days. The solicitor hadn't been out of the closet then, and was pretending to date a female friend of Tania's. Now he'd been openly living with an architect from Stoke-on-Trent for nearly ten years. 'How is Brian nowadays?' Hillary asked.

'Still trying to make shopping precincts look attractive,' Graham said, rolling his eyes.

'Rather him than me! So, what time are the enemy due?' she asked wearily.

'Thomas Palmer is the man we're dealing with. His solicitor is a chap called Mike Pearce. I don't know him, or his rep.'

'And this Palmer is determined to try and grab all of Ronnie's assets?'

'Only the ones he knows about,' Graham said with a laugh, and a very shrewd look at his client. Hillary felt her stomach clench and hoped her poker face was intact.

'Come on, Graham, not you as well. You know as well as I do how thorough an internal investigation team is.' She took a sip of tea. 'Besides, you know better than most, that even if Ronnie *had* stashed it somewhere, I'd be the last person he'd want to see get their hands on it. He'd be damned sure to hide it where I couldn't find it.'

Graham nodded. That was true. He'd known Hillary and – perforce – Ronnie, for years. A true marriage made in perfidy.

Hillary let out her breath very carefully. Graham was, in all respects, a very cultivated, charming, literate and gentle man, but he had all the instincts of a vulture. He could smell carrion from miles away.

She wondered, briefly, what he'd do if she told him that she might, in fact, have figured out where Ronnie had hidden his ill-gotten gains. She had the name of the bank in the Cayman islands (or thought she did). She had a list of numbers she'd found concealed in a book belonging to her late husband. All she needed was to get on the internet, go through the bank security checks and then there'd be no doubts left.

And there, she suspected, was the heart of the problem. Because once she knew for sure where Ronnie's loot was, she would be forced to make a decision about it one way or another. To come down on the side of the angels – or the opposition.

And she simply didn't trust herself. Now how sad was that?

'Here they are,' Graham said, leaning forward to answer his secretary's buzz. 'Show them right in.'

Abruptly, Hillary pushed all thoughts of her moral dilemma behind her and remained seated as two men were shown into the room.

'Mr Pearce?' Graham rose and shook hands with one of the two men. At only five feet six, most people seemed to tower over Graham, which often gave them a totally false sense of superiority. She quickly turned her attention to the other man though, the local branch leader of ESAA, and found the animal rights activist was already looking straight at her. He was tall, fit, healthy and middle-aged. His grey gaze was steady. Hillary barely lifted her lips in a slight smile. He smiled back, just as slightly.

'Please, take a seat. We all know why we're here,' Graham said. 'Tea?' He started to pour before either of them could decline or accept. 'Now, do you have anything to add to your last letter to me, Mr Pearce?' he asked, mildly.

'Mike, please. And no – the position of my client is still as it was then.'

'An extremely unreasonable one, if I may say so,' Graham put in gently.

'We don't think so,' Mike Pearce came back at once.

'But I'm sure a judge *will* think so,' Graham said persistently. 'Let us review the facts.'

Hillary listened as the two solicitors went over the old ground. She thought Graham had the better argument - but then she was biased. She sipped her tea and studied the ESAA man instead. Why not? He was making no secret of openly studying *her*.

'Did you approve of your husband's illegal activities, Detective Inspector Greene?' Tom Palmer finally asked, making Graham stop mid-flow.

'I hardly think that's an appropriate question, Mr Palmer,' Graham chided, as if telling a naughty boy not to pull the wings off a butterfly and Mike Pearce too laid a warning finger on the back of his client's hand. Hillary saw that Graham had noticed the gesture, and hid a smile.

'Do you approve of blackmail, Mr Palmer?' Hillary asked sweetly.

Graham coughed. 'Hillary, please!'

Hillary shrugged. Tom Palmer's face hardened. 'I was hoping you were going to be reasonable about this, DI Greene,' he said flatly.

'Did you?' Hillary asked, sounding puzzled. 'Why?'

Graham quickly hid a smile behind his raised tea cup. He knew what was going on here all right. The opposition had called for this meeting to give them a chance to sound out their adversary. They were hoping to discover a nervous woman, wary of opening up the whole Ronnie Greene can of worms again, and were quickly and very neatly being handed their heads back on a platter.

Graham Vaughan could simply have told them they'd be wasting their time trying intimidation or cajoling tactics on Hillary Greene. But it was much more fun this way.

'Your husband was a crook, DI Greene,' Tom Palmer said flatly, and both Graham and Hillary noticed that this time Mike Pearce did nothing to rein his client in. In fact, both solicitors were now watching their client with all the avid attention of tennis aficionados with tickets to the centre court at Wimbledon.

'So he was,' Hillary said simply. 'But I'm not.'

Tom Palmer smiled. 'But that's not what we're here to determine, is it?'

'Then why bring it up?' Hillary asked reasonably. She looked relaxed in her chair, and took another sip of tea. It was really good stuff.

Mike Pearce, sensing his client was losing the round, coughed discreetly. 'Perhaps we should get down to details. I think we can all agree that Mr Ronnie Greene amassed a fortune via the exploitation and suffering of animals. And I think nobody disputes the fact that the only real asset to be uncovered belonging to Mr Greene, namely the house at 24 Wittington Road, Kidlington, Oxfordshire, was paid for from the illicit earnings—'

'Indeed, we do dispute it,' Graham put in, before the other could finish. 'My client had a joint mortgage arrangement with her husband, and paid for half of it from her legitimate earnings as a well-respected and still-serving police officer of Thames Valley Constabulary. As all the paperwork will show.'

And so it went on.

Hillary smiled slightly at Tom Palmer over the top of her tea cup and turned her mind back to more important things. How was Janine doing with Leo 'The Man' Mann? It would be nice to think when she got back to HQ there'd be a confession, all neatly typed up and signed, waiting for her. But she had grave doubts.

And just what was the story with Jerome Raleigh? By now, the whole station should know everything there was to know about the man, from why he'd moved from the Met, why he hadn't married, was he gay, who did he have the gen on, why there'd been a delay in his transfer, and what kind of music he preferred, right down to the name of his pet budgie.

But nobody seemed to know dick.

And that, in itself, was enough to scare the living daylights out of Hillary. In the office, as on the street, she liked to know who she was dealing with. She liked to keep up with the current state of office politics too, just so that she could keep well out of the way of it and avoid taking any knives to the back. Having an enigma for a boss wasn't a state of affairs inclined to promote dreamless and restful slumber at night.

'I'm sorry you feel that way,' she heard Graham make winding down noises, and put down her empty cup on the table. She saw Tom Palmer look at her curiously, and realized the other man must have guessed that she'd zoned out. Good. That would tell him just how ineffective his war of attrition on her nerves had been.

'So, we'll see you in court, Mr Palmer?' Hillary said, rising, and holding out her hand. Only when it had been taken and rather bemusedly shaken, did she add, 'and please, give my love to ESAA. The last time I had any dealing with animal rights fanatics was when I helped Sergeant Sam Waterstone send one of them down for the murder of a security guard at an animal lab.'

Graham Vaughan coughed into his hand like a startled turkey. It was his way, Hillary knew, of disguising his rather high-pitched giggle.

'So, how did it go with 'The Man'?' she asked, as soon as she'd returned to the office and spotted Janine hunched dejectedly over her computer terminal. 'Has he got much to say for himself?' She sat down at her own desk and checked her watch, feeling guilty at the hour and half she'd just taken off work.

'Not yet, boss,' Janine said grimly. 'Trouble is, I've got no real ammo to lob at him. None of his priors are for violence against women. And he sticks to it that he didn't care that Julia was sleeping with Roger Greenwood.'

'He give an alibi for the time she was murdered?'

'No,' Janine said, her eyes resuming some of their old fire. 'He says it's none of our business.'

'Ah. A comedian,' Hillary muttered. 'How long's he been cooling his heels?'

'About an hour. I took an early lunch.'

'Where's Tommy?'

'At the lab. Oh, the results came back on Roger

Greenwood's clothing. Nothing conclusive. There were microscopic traces of cowshit on his shoes, but then there would have been on anyone's walking up the road to the farmhouse. There were fibres of Julia Reynold's white wedding dress on his clothes, but then there would have been. They'd been dancing together and what not.'

Hillary sighed. Great. 'So we can't rule him in, can't rule him out,' she grumbled.

Janine shrugged helplessly. Sometimes them was the breaks. With the advent of clever forensic science docu-crime dramas on the television, the general public had been fooled into thinking that science, DNA, and clever gizmos and gadgets could just hand you the identity of a killer, more or less on a plate. Cops and scientists knew better. As did barristers. And defence barristers knew it better than any one else.

'OK. Let's have another go at Mr Mann,' Hillary said wearily. 'Then you and Tommy had better get off to Nuneaton.' Although the way the day was going, she didn't expect miracles from their purple Mini lady either.

Leo Mann grinned as they came in. 'Two lovelies for the price of one. Must be my lucky day.'

Hillary grinned at him openly. 'Ah, a ladies' man. I do like that. You'd be surprised how many ingrates and Neanderthals we have to deal with in here every day. Right, Sergeant?'

Janine grunted and Leo Mann grinned, showing slightly yellow teeth. 'Don Juan, at your service.' He half-bowed over the table.

Janine rolled her eyes. 'Oh, please!'

'So, tell me about Julia,' Hillary said simply.

'Ah, too good for the likes of me,' Leo said, totally ignoring Janine now, who was left feeling abruptly lost. It was as if her DI and the scumbag she'd been interviewing all morning had taken one look at each other and found they were both Masons, or something. Where the hell did this instant rapport come from?

'I knew she was only stringing me along for the sake of

variety,' Leo said now, with a winsome grin. 'But, what the hell? It meant I could walk into the local boozer with a stunner like Julia on my arm, and all my mates would be treating me like the next best thing since sliced bread for months to come – trying to get me to give them the secret of pulling a stunner. Get me?'

Hillary did. 'She was worth the hassle. Yeah, I get it. The fancy term for it is quid pro quo. So you knew all along she had a fiancé? And really didn't care?'

Leo shrugged. 'Good luck to her, I say. The boy was loaded. You could see why she was anxious to get him down the aisle. And why not? Julia was like one of them birds from that telly series, you know, about them chicks married to footballers. She deserved the good life.'

'Even so. It had to have been a bit damaging to the old ego?'

'Nah, not really. I gave her what fancy-boy couldn't. She liked me.' Something wistful, a touch of pain perhaps, fleetingly touched Leo Mann's multi-pierced face, and Hillary sighed.

'Men often kill the women they love, Leo,' she pointed out softly.

'Yeah. But I didn't kill Julia.'

'So why don't you tell us where you were the night she was killed?'

'Don't have to, darling,' Leo said, waving a playful finger in front of her face. He was rather enjoying this interview. The older bird was something to look at in a way. Reminded him of those actresses in the old black-and-white movies his mother used to love watching. All curves and class.

'Let me guess. Out ram-raiding were you? Breaking into some warehouse? Lifting videos?'

Leo grinned. 'I do like a woman who understands me.' He laughed modestly, and Hillary couldn't help but grin back. Sometimes villains brought out the softer side of her nature. Not often, but sometimes.

'I try my best to understand all my customers, Mr Mann,' she said, then let her face fall. 'The thing is, Leo, I have to do my best by Julia, too. She's the one who's dead. And someone killed her. Don't you *want* to help me out?'

Leo frowned, leaned forward, then fiddled with one of the silver rings looped through his eyebrow. 'I hear where you're coming from, but I ain't a nark.'

'No. But you were Julia's lover. She was your bird, and someone strangled her to death. Surely she deserves some loyalty from you?'

Janine felt her jaw drop open. She couldn't believe this. Hillary Greene was playing the poor sap like Vanessa Mae played the violin. She'd have him blubbering into his tea next.

'I don't know who killed her,' Leo Mann said at last, his voice suspiciously thick with repressed emotion. 'But if I was you, I'd look at the men she was shagging.'

'We have been,' Hillary said crisply. She didn't want him blubbing either. 'But although there had been many men in her past, there was only you and Roger Greenwood in her present.'

'It's not Roger Greenwood I was thinking of so much,' Leo said reluctantly. 'Talk to his old man.'

'We already know Theo Greenwood didn't want her for a daughter-in-law,' Janine put in, but Hillary held up her hand. For a second, she simply stared at Leo Mann, and then slowly shook her head in disgust. 'I missed it,' she said sadly. Damn, she must be getting old.

Leo Mann grinned, then shrugged. 'They kept it very quiet,' he said consolingly. 'I often wondered if Theo Greenwood didn't bung her some of the old readies, now and then, just to help her keep her mouth shut.'

Janine's eyes rounded as she finally caught on. Julia Reynolds had been doing the double – boffing the old man *and* the son. The father must have been both green with jealousy and rage, and sick with fear and spite. Hell! No wonder Theo Greenwood didn't want to see their vic walk up the aisle with his precious son!

'This is probably going to be a waste of time,' Janine grumbled, as they pulled up outside a neat house in one of

Nuneaton's better 'burbs. 'Let's just hope she's in,' she muttered, ringing the doorbell and glancing around. A nice garden, but looking a bit neglected perhaps? She was almost quivering with impatience. Hell, they should be back at base, grilling Greenwood senior, not out here, questioning housewives. But what Hillary wanted, Hillary got.

The door opened, and a tall, gaunt-featured brunette stared back at them. 'Yes?' she said blankly. Her gaze, Janine noticed, was fixed at some point over her left shoulder.

'Mrs Vivian Orne?' Janine held up her ID, as did Tommy. 'Thames Valley Police, Mrs Orne. Nothing to worry about, we just need to ask you a few questions.'

'You'd better come in then,' Vivian Orne said dully. As she stood back to let them pass, Janine shot Tommy a quick, frowning look. It wasn't very often they were received with such a lack of emotion, and for a wild moment she wondered if they might be on to something here after all. 'Just through there,' Vivian Orne waved vaguely to an open doorway. 'Would you like a cup of tea?'

'No, thanks,' Tommy said immediately. There was something about the way she'd asked the question that made him wonder whether she even knew where the kitchen was, let alone what a kettle was for. He looked again at Janine, the question in his eyes. Was she on something? Ludes, maybe?

Janine gave a quick shrug back and went into the living-room. It was pleasant enough but needed dusting. On a mantelpiece was a picture of a young boy of maybe eight or so. In front of it a candle burned.

'Please, sit down.' Vivian Orne indicated the sofa, then moved to one of the big armchairs grouped around a mock fireplace.

Janine brought out her notebook. 'It's about what you did three nights ago, Mrs Orne. The middle of the week. Your car was photographed in a small village called Kirtlington. We need to know what you were doing there.'

Vivian Orne blinked. 'Was I speeding? Sorry.' She stared at the carpet for a moment that then stretched itself into half a minute. Still she said nothing. Janine coughed. 'Kirtlington, Mrs Orne. What were you doing there?' she prompted.

'I've no idea,' Vivian Orne said, surprisingly. 'I mean, I didn't intend to go there. I was driving back from visiting my mother you see, and there was an accident on the motorway, according to the radio, so I got off and tried to make it through on the country roads. But I think I got a little lost. I remember pulling off to the side of the road at one point to check the map, but I'm pretty hopeless at that sort of thing. Sorry,' she said again.

Tommy was staring at the lit candle in front of the picture of the boy. He was thinking of a woman on tranquillizers. He was thinking about the lack of emotion. The undusted living-room. He tried desperately to catch Janine's eye.

But Janine wasn't looking at him. 'Does the name Julia Reynolds mean anything to you, Mrs Orne?' she asked crisply.

Vivian Orne was staring at the carpet again. Slowly she looked up. 'What? No. Sorry.' She shook her head.

Tommy coughed loudly, waited until Janine glanced at him curiously, then deliberately turned his gaze back to the candle. Janine followed the direction of his look and frowned, not getting it.

Tommy sighed. 'I think that's all we need for now, Mrs Orne,' he said gently, risking Janine's ire. She did, in fact, shoot him a furious glance but rose reluctantly to her feet as Tommy did the same. She knew better than to argue in front of a witness. But what was the silly sod playing at?

Vivian Orne showed them out listlessly, not even bothering to ask what it was all about. And Janine didn't like that. Why no curiosity? It wasn't natural. She waited until they'd walked back to the car before rounding on Tommy.

'What the bloody hell's got into you? Couldn't you tell something was a bit off in there?'

'Yeah, I could,' Tommy said flatly. 'Their kid's just died.'

Janine, her mouth already open to let rip, found the words drying up on her tongue. Suddenly, she understood the picture, the candle. The shrine. 'Oh shit,' she said. That would explain the lethargy and the lack of interest all right. What did it matter if the cops came calling when your kid was dead?

Janine shook her head wordlessly, slipped behind the wheel, and made a brief call back to headquarters. She told Hillary that the purple Mini situation was a non-starter, and that they were headed back to base.

Beside her, Tommy said nothing.

chapter eight

Carole Morton pushed open her front door, bent to pick up the mail and a copy of the local paper, and headed for the kitchen. She switched on the kettle, fed her cat, and began rifling through the envelopes, finding nothing but the usual bills and advertisements. At least there were none of those demanding forms from the Inland Revenue; not that her little bit of alimony, coupled with her part-time job as a receptionist at the local health centre ever paid her enough to land her in hot water with Her Majesty's Inspector of Taxes.

She made her tea, went through to the small, warm living room, and settled down with the paper. Muffet, her beautiful white and ginger spayed feline, jumped onto her lap with a chirruping sound of contentment, turned in a neat circle and settled down.

Carole took a sip from the mug and idly turned to page two to run her eyes down the letters column, and abruptly found herself looking at one of those police artist's drawings you sometimes saw in the paper. She wondered idly what he'd done. Rapist perhaps? She stared anew at the picture, and then had one of those earth-moving-beneath-your-feet moments that put your heart in your mouth and punched a sick fist into your stomach.

She knew him.

Slowly, with a slightly shaking hand, she put her mug down on the coffee table and began to stroke Muffet's silky fur in a subconscious desire for comfort. The cat began to purr in appreciation, although her mistress hardly noticed. With a dry mouth, Carole quickly read the article, but it told her less than nothing. The police at Thames Valley Headquarters in Kidlington would like to hear from any member of the public who knew this man. He was said to be between twenty-five and forty, which fited, but the description of the clothes he was last seen wearing meant nothing to her.

Carole slowly reached for her tea again and began to drink, her hand shaking. She was beginning to lose that momentary feeling of having stepped into the Twilight Zone, but whilst the sharpness of shock was beginning to fade, it was leaving behind it a very real aftertaste of apprehension.

Should she telephone the police? That was the logical thing, the *right* thing to do, and there was a local number to contact. But what if she was wrong? Or simply mistaken? After all, she'd only seen the man once, and that had been, what, a month ago? Maybe not quite that. Yes, she could definitely be wrong about it. But the more she gazed at the sketch, the more sure she was that she wasn't wrong.

If only she knew what he'd done!

Carole watched more than her fair share of television of a night, and knew all about those films where innocent members of the public 'helped police with their inquiries' and became prime suspects themselves, or were framed, or got chased by maniacs. Of course, that was just the television. She knew *that*. Even so, reprisals by gangs and such like, really did happen in real life. She knew that, too. People being too afraid to talk in case their houses got burnt down, or their pets got killed. She began to stroke Muffet just a little more quickly. The cat stretched and clawed, and purred louder.

But that was usually about teenagers, hooligans, drug dealers, all that sort of thing. This man, well, he looked so normal. And when she'd seen him at the health centre, he hadn't seemed in any way dangerous. But then again, you never knew did you? Perhaps the police only wanted to talk to him as a witness or something. The article didn't actually say he was a wanted man, exactly. Just that the police needed to talk to him.

All her life, she'd done the right thing – had even obeyed her parents as a teenager. She'd certainly never been in any trouble with the law, and considered herself to be a good neighbour and an upstanding citizen. Her instinct was to ring the number and get it over with. She knew herself well enough to know she'd only fret if she didn't.

Then again, she'd always been innately cautious as well. It paid to be careful. Finally, she decided to wait and show the newspaper to Betty tomorrow. She'd been working the same day, and although it had been Carole who'd spoken to him, Betty had a good memory for faces. If Betty thought it was the same man, she'd definitely call.

Feeling better for having come to a decision now, Carole turned the next page of the newspaper and began to read about the upcoming attractions at the Oxford Playhouse. Pity you had to wait until Christmas time for a good panto.

Muffet heaved a sorrowful sigh as all the vigorous stroking came to a sudden end, and yawned widely.

Tommy looked up at the house number to make sure he had it right, and then nodded to himself. It was a nice place, only a bungalow, but a large and old one. It had lovely gardens too, bursting with autumnal colour. There was some money here, and no mistake. He only hoped there'd be no grieving parents behind *this* door.

Tommy rather liked having a rural beat. He enjoyed driving through the small Oxfordshire villages, and often found himself admiring thatched cottages, converted mills and such like, and wishing he and Jean could afford such a place. Of course, they never would. But still, he could take picnics on village greens, feed friendly ducks, and walk along canals and river-banks whenever the fancy took him. Now he glanced around at the village of Upper Heyford and wondered how often that row of terraced, rose-bedecked cottages had been photographed for calendars and postcards, or been snapped to adorn tourist pamphlets.

The door in front of him swung open and the woman

inside stared out at him curiously. She was dressed in a white, wrap-over dress, four-inch high heels and was smoking avidly. She had wild-looking wavy blonde hair, more make-up than Joan Crawford on a bad day, and looked to be approaching sixty.

Tommy gulped. 'Mrs Finchley? Vera Finchley?' he asked, holding up his ID. 'Detective Constable Lynch, ma'am. It's nothing to be alarmed about, I just wondered if I could have a little chat?'

Tommy never knew how women were going to react. And from the briefing Hillary had given him, this one was also a possible lush, which only added to the variables. He only hoped – oh how he hoped – that she wouldn't come on to him.

'Police? Well, I suppose you'd better come in then,' she said, her voice showing no signs of slurring. Mind you, with dedicated drunks, that meant nothing.

Tommy smiled his thanks and walked in. Mrs Finchley led him down a short corridor and into a large and spacious living-room, overlooking the back of the garden, and a field of peacefully grazing sheep. A panoramic view of the valley stretched away to Lower Heyford, a mile down the road, and to Steeple Aston, at the top end of the valley. With the trees turning colour, it was a simply stunning vista.

'So, what's up? There hasn't been a car crash has there? My husband's all right?'

'Oh yes, ma'am. It's nothing of that nature,' Tommy said quickly, wondering if he should sit down or wait to be asked. 'It's about Julia Reynolds.'

At this, Vera Finchley's face began to crumble. 'Oh poor Julia. I heard about that.' Her voice wobbled, then seemed to right itself. 'I think I'll have a drink. Can I get you something, Constable?' Tommy quickly shook his head. 'Well, I'll have just a dash,' Vera Finchley said, pouring out nearly a half-bottle of vodka into a tall straight glass. She added lime segments from a dish, and ice. It looked like a very elegant drink. Tommy had no doubt that had he drunk it, it would have had him under the table in nought-to-sixty seconds flat.

He got out his notebook. 'I understand Julia did your hair for you, Mrs Finchley? Was she a good hair stylist?'

Vera Finchley took a hefty gulp then slid into a chair, waving a hand vaguely about for him to also sit. 'Of course,' she said, and self-consciously touched her errant locks. 'Don't you think so?'

Tommy agreed quickly. The truth was, he hadn't seen such rampant blonde hair on a woman since the days when Farrah Fawcett made the windblown look popular. 'And when she was here, you liked to chat, I suppose?' he nudged her along hopefully.

'Oh, all the time. She was getting married you know. To that millionaire's son – the one who owns that fancy hotel up on the main road. Full of it she was. Told me she wanted to go to one of those fancy ocean islands on her honeymoon.'

Her glass, Tommy noticed aghast, was almost half empty, and yet he had no clear picture of her drinking from it. How did dedicated drunks manage that? He decided to hurry up the questions before she became comatose.

'And you talked to her about your life. Your husband?'

'Max?' Vera Finchley snorted inelegantly and loudly, making Tommy jump. 'What would I want to talk about Max for? Boring old fart, he is.'

Tommy nodded, and this time caught her out taking a swig. He knew neither Hillary nor Janine (and certainly not Frank Ross) would ever hesitate about taking advantage of a drunk witness if it meant getting results, but Tommy felt vaguely ashamed of himself as he let her take yet another swig before carrying on.

'Oh? That's strange. A friend of Julia's said you'd told her something a bit racy about your husband. We were wondering what that was.'

'Huh?' Vera looked up from the clear but vanishing liquid in her glass and stared at Tommy flatly. She looked, suddenly, very sober indeed. 'Racy? Max? You're having a laugh. Besides, what interest would Julia have in Max?' she asked suspiciously.

'I wasn't suggesting anything like that, Mrs Finchley,' Tommy said reassuringly. 'In fact, we rather gathered that you told Julia your husband had been involved in some high-risk business venture.'

He couldn't, after all, come right out and say that Mrs Finchley had all but said that her husband was a crook. But a sly appeal to the old ego might just open reluctant lips.

Vera Finchley's lips pinched closed and Tommy sighed. 'We understand that some businessmen, whilst not exactly breaking the law, can be very aggressive when it comes to making money. I can't say as I blame them. If you have the brains for it, why not?' He smiled disarmingly.

At least, he thought he smiled disarmingly. From the look on Vera Finchley's face, however, you'd have thought he'd just done a Rottweiler impersonation.

'Sorry, don't know what you mean,' Vera said, sitting up straight and slamming her drink down hard and dead centre on the nearby occasional table.

'Oh? You never told Julia Reynolds that Mr Finchley was doing some clever, maybe underhanded business deal?'

'Don't be daft. He don't work for the Bank of England you know.' Vera suddenly gave a loud snort. Tommy wondered if it was her version of laughter. 'All this,' – she waved a hand at the bungalow and the gorgeous view – 'is down to me. My side of the family did all right.' She nodded vigorously, then went promptly to sleep.

Tommy blinked, wondering if she was all right. Her head had lolled back on the chair, her lower jaw swung open and she gave a sudden, violent snore. Tommy decided that whoever it was that said discretion was the better part of valour, most definitely knew his onions from his turnips, and scrammed while the going was good.

Hillary decided to treat herself to a late lunch at HQ's local pub, and was perusing the menu, trying to talk herself out of the scampi and chips and into the herb omelette with salad, when she felt someone slide into the booth beside her.

Detective Inspector Mike Regis grinned back at her. 'Hello, long time no see. I didn't expect to see you in here.'

Mike Regis worked Vice, and had been called in on the Dave Pitman inquiry, which Hillary had solved, in spite of being sidelined. But she'd never held a grudge against Mike Regis – it wasn't his fault that Mel had pulled rank on her, and Regis *had* been instrumental in shutting down a drugs distribution ring on the same case. He'd also helped her in her last murder case as well. Moreover, she'd sensed, right from the first, that they thought the same way and seemed destined to get on like a house and fire, and perhaps, who knew, maybe just start a little fire of their own. Pity he had turned out to be married. An even greater pity that she'd only found out about it by overhearing gossip, instead of from the man himself.

'Eating?' she asked succinctly.

'Just finished. Me and Tanner had business with Luke Fletcher.'

Hillary whistled silently. Luke Fletcher was quite easily the biggest thorn in Thames Valley's collective backside. Drug dealer, pimp, extortioner, and almost certainly a murderer, although nothing would stick. 'And how was he? Really pleased to see you, I'm sure.'

Mike Regis grinned, the crows' feet appearing attractively around his dark-green eyes. 'Oh he was, he was.' He paused as a waitress came over, and Hillary gave her order for omelette and salad. He pushed a hand through his thinning dark-brown hair and leaned back against his chair. 'Reason I was glad to see you, is this,' he said, and reaching into a briefcase by the side of his chair, shuffled some papers around, and came out with a thin folder in a plain beige cover.

Hillary raised an eyebrow. As far as she knew, she wasn't working on any cases that might overlap with Vice. And if she were, why this hole-in-the-corner exchange?

Curious, and wary, Hillary opened the folder and began to read. She managed to stop her mouth falling open, but only just. Inside, was a rap-sheet on one Mr Thomas Palmer, founder member of the Oxford branch of ESAA. Her eyes widened as she took in the fraud charges in his youth, and opened even wider at the obtaining-money-with-menaces stretch he'd done only four years ago. Graham would be very pleased with this. Very pleased indeed. Even if he couldn't get a member of ESAA's past misdeeds legally introduced into any civil court action, she knew he had ways and means of ensuring that judges and other people who needed to know discovered the truth about such naughty goings on. Totally illegal, of course, and downright unethical, which was why Hillary, as a serving police officer, would have nothing to do with it. She'd just fax the whole lot over to him and then forget all about it, like a good little girl.

'Thanks,' she said flatly, when she'd read it through. She closed the folder and slipped it into her own, voluminous bag then leaned back as the waitress returned with her dinner. The omelette steamed appetizingly with heat, and the salad looked crisp and fresh and green, the tomatoes juicy. Very healthy and good for her. Damn it, she wished it were scampi and chips.

But her thighs and hips were thanking her. They'd bloody better be. She reached for the salad cream and splodged it on, then sighed and took a bite. Eventually, she had to ask. Just as Mike Regis, damn him, had known she would. 'And just how did you know those charming people at ESAA were giving me grief?'

Regis grinned and shrugged. 'Oh, through a friend of a friend. He knows Palmer's solicitor. Don't ask.'

Hillary wasn't about to. Usually when somebody did you a favour, you not only looked the gift horse well and truly in the mouth, you checked its fetlocks, mane and chest too while you were at it. Not to mention keeping a wary look out for mange, foot rot and fleas. Well, you did, if you were a serving copper.

But Hillary trusted Mike Regis. Well, when it came to things like this, anyway.

'Thanks,' she said again, and meant it. Suddenly, she had a lot more confidence in the outcome of the up-coming civil battle to keep her hands on her own property. 'So, how's …

what's her name? Your wife?' Hillary said flatly, and saw Mike Regis's eyes narrow.

'Laura? She's fine. Didn't know you knew her,' he said, just as flatly.

Hillary speared some egg and chewed. 'I didn't. Didn't know *of* her, either,' she added, carefully.

'So that's why you blew me off in the canteen that day,' Regis said candidly. 'I did wonder.'

It was typical of him not to offer a useless apology. And now that the ball was firmly back in her court, she supposed she could play it coy, but what was the point? They were all grown ups here, and unless she'd seriously misread Mike Regis (and she didn't think she had) he'd appreciate the cards-on-the-table approach.

'Look, Mike, let's be frank. When we first met, I liked you right off. I felt we could get on. And we worked the Pitman case together well. I didn't think I was kidding myself when I thought you might be interested in starting something a bit more personal than simply jogging along as workmates, did I?'

Mike Regis, who was watching her closely, shook his head. 'No, you didn't get it wrong,' he admitted quietly. He'd become very still in his chair, and Hillary was aware that the ends of her fingertips had started to tingle. She took a deep, calming breath.

'OK. So you wouldn't have been wrong if you'd got around to thinking that maybe I was willing to give it a go,' she admitted honestly. 'But when I found out you were married, that was it. You have to know the scuttlebutt about Ronnie. The man was about as faithful as Don Juan with a harem full of nymphomaniacs. I've been the 'wronged wife' too many damned times to ever play the other woman to some other poor unsuspecting cow. It's as simple as that.'

She forked a tomato and ate it, waiting calmly. She watched him thinking, weighing his words, and found herself half interested and half dreading what he had to say in response.

'I understand all that,' Regis said at last. 'It just didn't occur to me that you didn't know the rest. Everyone else does. Or so I assume.'

'The rest?'

'Laura and I will be filing for divorce. We were only waiting until Sylvie – our daughter – was old enough to hack it. Our marriage has been over, like, for ever. Hell, she's been seeing this chartered accountant bloke for nearly eight years. I'll be moving out as soon as I can get another place.'

Hillary nodded. 'Well, when you have, and when the decree nisi comes in, if you're still interested, let me know.' It sounded hard and bold, but Hillary knew he was already reading between the lines, something that was confirmed by his next words.

'You think I might be handing you the old married man's mantra? The "my wife doesn't understand me, and we're going to get divorced as soon as the kids are older?" speech?' Mike said harshly. Then he laughed. 'Yeah, well, can't say as I blame you. I just thought you might have given me the benefit of the doubt. Hell, it doesn't matter.'

He slid out of the booth and headed for the door, where she finally noticed his sergeant, the silent and all-knowing DS Colin Tanner, waiting patiently for him.

Hillary watched him go and smiled bleakly. What if he didn't come back? What if, a year down the road, she heard that the newly and amicably divorced Mike Regis was seen out and about with a new woman? Someone who'd actually trusted him?

Hillary grinned. She couldn't help it. Life was a bugger, but you had to laugh, right?

She shook her head, paid for her meal and left the pub.

Walking back to HQ, she tried to talk herself into believing that she'd just done the right thing. Let's face it, she thought grimly, apart from anything else, Mike Regis was such a bloody good copper that if they *had* got together, he'd have eventually sniffed out the fact that she knew where Ronnie had stashed his dosh. Then he'd nab her. Of that she had no doubts whatsoever, simply because, were the situation reversed, she'd sure as hell nab *him*.

So, all things considered, Romeo and Juliet they definitely weren't.

Back at HQ, Dr Steven Partridge caught her as he was leaving. Today he was dressed in something that the actor who played Hercule Poirot might wear. She could swear she could even smell pomade on his hair. She wondered, not for the first time, what the doc's wife made of her husband's sartorial love affair with himself.

'Ah, Hillary, glad I caught you. I've left the reports on your desk. Your bride in the cowshed. I've done the autopsy – and by the way, thanks for sending DS Ross. His comments as I cut and diced were, as ever, riveting.'

Hillary grimaced. Hadn't she told Janine to go? She'd have to have a word with her sergeant. 'Sorry, Doc, but Frank's like a toxic substance. I have to spread him around evenly, giving everyone their fair share of misery, because if I leave him concentrated in one place too long, people start dropping like flies.'

Steven Partridge smiled bleakly. 'So it was just my turn with the poisoned cherub then? That's a relief. For a moment, I thought I'd somehow found my way onto your shit list.'

'As if you could. So, give me the highlights.'

'Strangled, as you thought, and manual strangulation at that. She was definitely drunk, although probably not falling down drunk. She put up a bit of a fight, and there *were* traces of skin and blood under her fingernails, I'm glad to say. DS Janine Tyler and Tommy Lynch were hitting the computers for a DNA match as I left. They seemed excited, bless them.'

Hillary grunted. That was all well and good, if their boy had previous form, and had his DNA in the system. But she had the feeling this was a one off. 'Well, it means I can start to get our list of suspects in to donate DNA, if they feel so inclined,' she mused thoughtfully.

'And if they don't, you'll turn your beady little eye onto them faster than a speeding bullet?'

Hillary laughed. 'Oh, a lot faster than that, Doc. A lot faster than that!'

Upstairs, Tommy confirmed that so far they'd had no luck with a DNA hit. But the computer could run for hours yet. He also filled her in more fully on Vivian Orne, and the reasons behind the very short interview.

'Oh, and by the way, I had a word with Mrs Finchley,' Tommy said. 'She's definitely got a drink problem, and when I mentioned that Julia might have hinted that Mr Max Finchley was a crook, she certainly reacted as if I'd struck a nerve.'

Hillary nodded 'OK, get on to the husband then. Check him out. Maybe shadow him for a day or two, see if you pick up anything interesting.'

'Right, guv,' Tommy said, delighted. He always liked following people around. It made him feel like one of those private eyes in American thrillers.

chapter nine

Hillary slowly read through the full post-mortem report, and then the forensics they had so far. Apart from the DNA samples scraped from under Julia Reynolds' fingernails, they had practically nothing to go on. Doc Partridge had said her blood alcohol level meant she was more or less drunk, but there had been nothing, ostensibly, about Julia Reynolds' behaviour at the party which should have led to her being manually strangled.

A stranger then? An outsider? Again, the problem remained. How had she been lured to the cowshed in that gorgeous dress? The dress hadn't been torn or ripped, her shoes showed no signs of scuff marks. Julia's arms were not bruised, so it was unlikely she'd been forcibly dragged or manhandled into that shed. She'd gone willingly. And probably, from what they'd pieced together so far of her character, to meet a man.

The question was – which man?

'Guv, for you. Wendy Wallis,' Tommy said, breaking into her morose thoughts and waving the receiver at her.

'Mrs Wallis? DI Greene. Is there something I can do for you?'

'Well, yes. Well, no, not for me personally. I have a friend here with me, Sharon Gunnell. This is very awkward over the telephone, so I was wondering if it was possible, I mean convenient, for you to come over and talk to us? Sharon and myself, perhaps now or quite soon?'

'Of course,' Hillary said smoothly. 'I'll be there in twenty minutes or so.' She hung up, glanced at Tommy, then mentally shook her head. She doubted turning up with a big constable in tow would be ideal for worming information out of two, already nervous, women. 'Mrs Wallis has a friend who needs to speak to me,' Hillary said, and glanced across at Janine. 'Doing anything vital?'

Janine grimaced. 'No, boss,' she admitted, grabbing her coat. As she did so, she glanced at her closed desk drawer, where the brochure for the weekend break in the New Forest lay concealed. Had she done the right thing in booking it and paying the deposit? At least there was no way Mel could back out of it now. And the little inn in the village of Burley sounded ideal. Remote, pretty, just the place for two trysting coppers to make whoopee.

She was still smiling to herself as she followed Hillary out, making Frank Ross, just coming in after a very late and very long lunch, do a comical double-take. He slouched his way over to his desk, already feeling out of sorts. Whenever somebody else was happy, he wasn't. It was one of the few principles by which he led his life.

'I bet Mel must be feeling chipper. The happy hooker is beaming like a cat that's just had a canary sandwich.' Tommy pretended not to hear. 'Do you think the chief and our Janine are gonna tie the knot then? Wouldn't put it past the stupid bastard.'

Tommy sighed heavily.

'And I reckon, despite what the guv says, that new super is as bent as a corkscrew.'

Tommy turned off the computer and grabbed his coat. 'Got a suspect to tail,' he said briefly, just to let Ross know he wasn't the only one who could do hands-on coppering. Besides, if he stayed, he might just deck the prat.

'He'll spot you a mile off, you bastard,' Frank Ross muttered, just far enough under his breath for Tommy not to hear, as he watched the constable leave.

Hillary Greene had given Frank the task of finding out what Leo 'The Man' Mann had really been up to on the night of the vic's murder. So far, he'd put out feelers with all his narks, and was due to meet another in the pub in an hour. He supposed he could put in some paperwork. Then again, the nark might be early, and he wouldn't want to miss him, would he? Frank Ross grinned to himself and contemplated his fifth pint of the day. And felt, for some reason, a lot happier about life in general.

Sharon Gunnell looked distinctly apprehensive.

'Thank you for coming, Inspector Greene. This is Sharon Gunnell, the friend I was telling you about.' Mrs Wallis made the introductions calmly.

Hillary saw Janine take her notebook out and half hide it behind her handbag, and gave a mental nod of approval. People tended to dry up when their every word looked as if it were being written down.

'You see, the thing is, Sharon realized, after she'd given her statement to the police the night of the party, that she'd forgotten to mention something.' It was Wendy Wallis who took up the baton, which was fine with her. Hillary knew full damned well that Sharon Gunnell hadn't forgotten a thing, but had kept her mouth deliberately shut simply because she didn't want to get involved. It was often the way with witnesses. The trouble was, conscience had a nasty habit of being a right pain in the bum about things like that, until in the end it was just far easier on the nerves to spill it. Not very public-spirited maybe, but then Hillary had never been one to rail against human nature. What was the point? At least the witnesses had come through in the end. So she simply smiled and nodded and played the agony aunt.

'That's often the way,' she said, careful to keep her voice sympathetic. 'What a witness will recall just minutes after learning about a murder, and, say a few days later, is surprising. I expect that's what happened here, isn't it?' she finished, turning firmly to Sharon Gunnell with a gentle smile and no-nonsense air of expectancy.

Sharon was one of those stick-thin women who seemed to live on their nerves. She smiled, showing uneven, tobacco-stained teeth and fiddled with a strand of long, dark-brown hair. 'Yes, that's exactly right,' she said, relieved to be given a gracious out, and so unexpectedly soon. 'But I don't expect it's important. I mean, I might have called you all the way out here for nothing.'

Yeah, right lady, Janine thought, with an inner snort. And I'm Mary Poppins.

'So, what was it that you wanted to tell us, Mrs Gunnell?' Hillary nursed her along patiently. 'I assure you it will be in confidence.' Unless, of course, she had to testify to it in a court of law. But Hillary wasn't about to go there yet. Not with one as skittish as this.

'Well, it was about eleven-thirty or so. I know it was around then, because Bill, my husband, started to make those I-want-to-go signs, and I thought it was way too early when I checked the clock and saw the time. I could hardly leave my best friend's silver wedding anniversary party before midnight, could I?' she said, with a quick grin at her friend. Wendy Wallis nodded back encouragingly. 'So it was only a little while later that I saw him leave. Mr Greenwood. The father, I mean, not the son.'

'Theo Greenwood?' Hillary said, wanting it perfectly clear.

'Yes. I was in the kitchen, washing a wine stain off my skirt. Some idiot had knocked into me holding a glass. Luckily it was white wine, not red, or it would have been ruined. Anyway,' she hurried on, 'I looked out the kitchen window, which was open to let in some fresh air, and that's when I saw him.'

Hillary nodded. 'You saw him where, exactly?'

'Crossing the lawn, between those two rose beds you have out back,' Sharon said, suddenly turning to speak to her friend.

'I can show you if you like,' Wendy said helpfully, and Hillary held up a hand.

'Later, thank you. For the moment, Mrs Gunnell, just tell us what you saw.'

'Well, that was it really,' Sharon said. 'Mr Greenwood – I knew him by sight, because he and Owen had disappeared off to the study to talk business and Wendy pointed him out to me, because she was hopping mad about it, and who can blame her in the middle of the party and all? So I knew who he was. Well, anyway, he walked down the garden path, across the lawn, and out through the side gate onto the lane outside. The reason it stuck in my mind later was because of the way he walked.'

Hillary blinked, and heard Janine's pen, which had been busily scraping across the page of her notebook suddenly stall. Obviously they'd both been caught out by Sharon Gunnell's words. The way he walked, Hillary repeated mentally to herself. What? Had he waddled; done a Max Wall impersonation; what?

'Was he limping?' she suddenly asked sharply, as a thought occurred to her. If Julia Reynolds had managed to get a good backwards kick and land a blow on her assailant's shin before she succumbed, it might be possible that her attacker would have a limp.

'Oh no. Nothing like that,' Sharon sounded almost shocked. 'I just meant that he wasn't mooching about. You know, like you do at a party. You go outside to have a ciggie, or get some air, or just have a rest from the loud music and you just sort of wander about. But he wasn't doing that. He walked straight across the grass like he knew where he was going. As if he had somewhere specific in mind. Do you see?' she added timidly, glancing from all three women and wondering if she'd just made some kind of a fool of herself.

Hillary nodded. 'Yes. Yes, I do see. Did you see him come back?'

'Oh no. I washed my skirt off and went back inside to make sure Bill wasn't trying to say his goodbyes on the sly. He'd do that. Then, of course, I'd have had no choice but to say goodbye too, and it was such a lovely party. Oh!' She put a hand to her mouth as she suddenly realized that, for one of the guests at least, it had been anything but.

'I see. Well, thank you, Mrs Gunnell, you've been very helpful,' Hillary said.

Wendy Wallis rose, too, relief plainly written all over her face. 'You understand, Inspector,' she said firmly, 'we're not saying that Mr Greenwood did anything improper. Nor are we trying to imply that he was in any way, well, implicated in what happened.'

And he was, after all, the man who might be willing to give her husband umpteen pounds sterling for some acres of his land, Hillary added silently and more cynically. 'I can reassure you that we don't jump to conclusions, Mrs Wallis,' she said vaguely, and, with Sharon Gunnell's relieved goodbyes ringing in their ears, stepped outside and walked towards the car.

Janine slid, without asking, behind the driver's wheel as Hillary slammed the car door shut and reached behind her for the seat belt.

'The Hayrick Inn, boss?' Janine asked, rhetorically.

Hillary sighed and nodded without much enthusiasm. Truth to tell, she'd rather have a bit more under her belt before confronting Mr Theo Greenwood. So far, they only had Leo Mann's word for it that Julia Reynolds had been playing the old horizontal tango with him. And so what if a member of the party saw him walking through the gardens at around the time Julia was killed? A good defence lawyer would treat such hearsay and vague suspicions with much derision.

But then again, Theo Greenwood wasn't a barrister, and might just let something slip if they rattled him hard enough. She couldn't afford not try it, anyway.

Theo Greenwood wasn't happy to see them. The Hayrick Inn, Hillary was surprised to see, did a roaring trade in 'traditional afternoon tea', catching a lot of the overflow of American tourists doing the Oxford-Stratford-Cotswold scene. She was careful to report in at reception and keep herself well out of public view, since people like Theo Greenwood had a nasty habit of knowing people who knew the chief constable. And too many unnecessary black spots against your name could get you a reputation as a troublemaker, whether it was warranted or not. And with a new super on the scene, it didn't pay to take unnecessary chances. So she had no objection to Mr Greenwood ushering them out of sight and into his impressive office once more.

'I must say, Inspector Greene, I wasn't expecting you back so soon. I take it there was nothing amiss on my son's clothes and shoes? He was told he could come and pick them up tomorrow?'

Hillary nodded, settling herself down comfortably in the proffered chair and thus letting the hotel owner know that they were in for a long haul. 'No, nothing untoward, sir,' she said ambiguously. 'It was yourself we wanted a word with, not Roger.'

Janine wondered if the hotelier looked just a shade jaundiced? She rather thought he might.

'Me?' Theo said, and gave a rather false laugh. He must have heard the hollow ring in it himself, for he suddenly rose and walked briskly to the drinks cabinet. 'Can I get you anything?'

'Not for me, thank you, sir,' Hillary said, and Janine murmured similar polite refusals. They let him get a drink, surprisingly a simple soda and ice, and then settle back down again. 'Can you tell us how long your sexual relationship with Julia Reynolds lasted, Mr Greenwood?' Hillary began with deceptive mildness.

Yes, definitely jaundice, Janine thought with a hidden smile. With just a touch of magenta and, around the gills, a smidgen of green.

Theo Greenwood swallowed hard once or twice, then put down his glass of soda with a commendably steady hand. 'I see,' he said heavily. 'I wondered if you'd get on to that.' He leaned back in his chair and sighed. 'It was last year. I met Julia at a party. We hit it off straight away. For a much younger woman than myself, she was surprisingly mature.'

'She didn't mind that you were married? Or didn't you tell her?' Hillary put in, still in that mildly curious voice that even Janine found grating. Her DI's studied indifference made even her teeth itch, so what it did to the subject being interviewed she couldn't tell.

Theo Greenwood flushed an ugly shade of red, and once again his resemblance to a pig suddenly shone through. 'No, I ... er, didn't as a matter of fact. Never said so in as many words, that is. But I'm sure she guessed,' he added gruffly.

'Who ended it, Mr Greenwood? Or was it still going on, perhaps?' Hillary mused.

'Of course it wasn't! She was seeing my son. What kind of perverted mind have you got?' Theo sputtered.

Hillary smiled sweetly. 'Oh, when you deal regularly with pornographers, paedophiles, rapists, victims of incest, and what have you, you tend to lose any surprise at the depths to which human nature will sink, Mr Greenwood,' she said, calmly. 'So, I take it you were not both seeing Miss Reynolds at the same time then?'

Theo Greenwood, thoroughly disconcerted, as Hillary had intended, shook his head. 'No. We weren't.'

'So who ended the affair between you?'

Greenwood reached for his soda. 'She did,' he admitted quietly, trying not to notice the way the pretty blonde sergeant grinned over her notebook.

'She did,' Hillary repeated softly. 'Did that make you mad, Mr Greenwood?'

'What? No. Sad more like. I liked Julia. She was like a breath of spring. She was funny. I was sad that she broke it off.'

'Oh,' Hillary said flatly. 'Now I'm confused. I thought you said before that you didn't like Julia Reynolds. That you thought she wasn't good enough for your son. I got the distinct impression that you thought a nobody hairstylist from the sticks wasn't the sort of daughter-in-law you wanted. Now you tell me she was a breath of spring. Which is true Mr Greenwood? We like to get these details straight, you see. On a murder inquiry especially.'

Theo swallowed hard once again. 'I, look here, I can ... All right, you've got me.'

Janine felt her heart give a sudden lurch, and she looked up in amazement. Surely he wasn't going to just confess, right here and now? She'd heard of cases where a suspect just crumbled and gave it all up, apparently out of the blue, but she hadn't expected to see it happen for herself.

Hillary, who'd seen far more and believed even less, could have told her not to get so excited.

'I'm a bit of a snob,' Theo Greenwood confessed, miserably. 'I was flattered when Julia and I got together, and I would have carried on having an affair, well, *ad infinitum* I suppose, if she'd have had me. But when I found out, after she'd ditched me, that she'd taken up with Roger! Well, I saw red. I didn't like it. It felt all … wrong. Dirty. Unnatural somehow. But Roger wouldn't give her up and…. well, obviously, I couldn't tell him why she wasn't good enough for him, could I?' he appealed to them, hands spread helplessly.

You bloody hypocrite, Janine thought savagely.

Hillary merely shrugged. 'So you saw red. By your own admission, you were very angry. Angry enough to kill her?'

Theo paled still further. 'No. NO! Besides, she chucked me last year and took up with Roger. If I was going to snap or do something crazy, I'd have done it then. Not waited nearly a year, wouldn't I?' he flung out with equal measures of desperation and triumph.

'Maybe yes, maybe no, Mr Greenwood,' Hillary said, again with that weary indifference, as if speaking to a backward child. 'People kill for all different reasons and at different times. Some people explode in a moment of rage, others fester and plan and continually put the evil moment off, until something, a word, a gesture, maybe even something as simple as suddenly being in the right place at the right time, finally sets them off and – bang. You have a strangled girl on your hands.'

'Well, that's not the way it was,' Theo said wildly, looking from Janine to Hillary and back again. 'I swear. I never went anywhere near that cowshed.'

'So just where did you go when you left the party at eleven-thirty that night, Mr Greenwood?' Hillary asked simply.

The older man blanched. 'What? What do you mean? I didn't go anywhere.'

'That won't do, you know,' Hillary chided. 'You were seen leaving the party. You left, walking across the back lawn between the two rose beds the Wallises have in their garden, and out into the lane. Where did you go, Mr Greenwood?'

Both Janine and Hillary could see that their knowledge of the accuracy of his route that night had shaken him. 'I went to my car to get some cigars,' he said at last, sounding more bewildered now than anything else. 'Owen Wallis and myself had just agreed, in principle, to him selling me some land. I wanted to celebrate. Ask him. He'll remember me giving him a cigar. They're very fine cigars, although in the end, he turned it down. The man doesn't smoke.'

Hillary said nothing. In truth, there was nothing she *could* say. If Owen Wallis did indeed confirm that Theo Greenwood had offered him a cigar at around 11.45 that night, then that was that. And somehow, Hillary got the feeling that Owen Wallis was going to up and do just that.

'You haven't got any plans for a foreign holiday in the near future, have you, Mr Greenwood?' she asked, rising to her feet.

'No, I haven't.' The relief in Theo Greenwood's voice and face was palpable as he suddenly realized the ordeal was over. 'And if I was, I'd cancel it, before you ask.' He even managed a smile.

Outside, Janine muttered something in disgust under her breath. Then added more audibly, 'Back to the farm, boss?'

Back to the farm.

Frank Ross looked up as Hillary and Janine trooped in, faces as long as wet weekends. Now that was *much* better. That was how things should be. Now the laws of the universe were back in their proper working order.

Time to show them how real policing worked.

'Guv, I've found out where our pal Leo Mann was on the night of the killing. He and some pals of his were out forcing cash machines. It's got Mann's MO all over it, plus we've got a positive sighting of him in Summertown that night, around the time the girl got it. I reckon it's enough to rule Mann out.'

'Oh great. Another dead end,' Janine snarled. First Owen Wallis confirms what Theo Greenwood had said about going out for the cigars and now this. She wasn't best pleased when Hillary told her to go with Frank and bring in Mann and have a chat with the sergeant in charge of the robbery. She left, muttering under her breath.

Frank Ross trudged off behind her, wondering gleefully if the blonde wonder was going to complain to lover boy that Hillary Greene kept giving her all the crap jobs. And he wondered, even more gleefully, just what Mel would do about it.

Hillary sat down at her desk, wondered if she dared get off home on time for once, then wondered what would be the point if she did? All she had to go back to was an empty narrow boat and a Dick Francis novel that might, or might not, hold the key to Ronnie's dirty dosh. She'd be better off thinking up new lines of inquiries for her team tomorrow. Unless they came up with some new leads, they were buggered. Already the first forty-eight hours were over and, as everyone knew, the majority of cases that were going to get solved, were already solved by then.

She sighed and reached for the first of Tommy's reports.

chapter ten

Gregory Innes turned into a small cul-de-sac on Nuneaton's northernmost boundary and cut the engine. Now this was more like it. Houses, shops, streets, gardens. No barbed wire fences, cowshit or railway embankments here. Even now it made him break out in a cold sweat when he remembered being chased by that mad farmer and that crazy female cop.

Detective Inspector Hillary Greene.

Since she'd chased him, almost into the path of an oncoming train, Gregory had been learning all about DI Greene, and what he'd learned hadn't exactly filled him with joy and inner serenity. Word had it, around those in the know, that she had a good nose on her and all the leniency of a pit bull on downers. And a good copper's nose was the last thing he wanted poking around in his business – especially now that he'd finally struck paydirt.

He slid his lanky frame out of his rusting second-hand Volvo, and once again checked out the house. The first time he'd come here, nearly three months ago now, he hadn't paid it all that much attention, except to ascertain that anyone living here could afford to pay for his services. Mock-Tudor in style. Good garden, clean windows. There had to be a reasonable amount of money here sure, but not, he supposed glumly, huge gobs of it. Which was just typical of his luck. A perfect blackmail opportunity had come his way, but how much would they really be good for?

Vivian Orne, the wife, was an aerobics and dance-class

instructor as well as part-owner of a local gym. She brought in enough readies to help pay the mortgage on this place, run a nice new Mini and put her kids into a good school, but she was not exactly Rockefeller. Likewise her hubby was the proud owner of a garage that also sold second-hand cars. A nice little earner, no doubt. Perhaps he could ask for two thousand a month? They'd cough up that much, surely? After all, they had their own lives to think about – not to mention the happiness of their one remaining kid, the little girl he'd seen the last time he'd been here.

He could take a nice holiday for a change. Play the gee-gee's maybe. Kick back and relax a bit. Wait a few months, then up it to three thousand. And there was still the doctor. He'd be good for another thousand a month easy. Probably more. He'd have to check around and see how much GPs earned. All his life, Gregory had been a grifter, with nothing coming easy. It was time he had a slice of the pie. Nervous, but determined, he walked up the garden path and rang the doorbell.

Tommy watched Max Finchley shrugging into his heavy black duffel coat. He was parked by the construction site of what was soon to provide both underground and high-level parking for the city of Oxford's long-suffering motorists. At the moment, it looked more like a bombsite than a building site, and Tommy re-read nervously the placard on the chain-link fencing warning members of the public that detonations would be happening tomorrow at 10.15.

That would probably gather a crowd.

Tommy, who still had memories of Molotov cocktails at public riots, couldn't see the fascination in explosions and fire himself.

He lifted his binoculars and focused them once more on his mark. Funny, he'd never expected Max Finchley to be a construction worker. Remembering Vera Finchley drinking her expensive vodka in her big and impressive bungalow, he had been expecting her husband to be some kind of executive.

Tommy noted in his book the time Max Finchley clocked off

and watched a steady stream of workers – brickies, carpenters, demolition guys, scaffolders, steel workers – all head for the main gates.

Max Finchley was about five foot ten, Tommy reckoned, mid-forties and going bald. And was a possible crook. Well, Tommy snorted, in this line of work, notorious for scams, what *couldn't* he have been getting up to? How many times had he been called on to sites just like this by irate and incensed site-managers. 'Buggers will take anything not nailed down' had been the general complaint. But surely this sort of thing wouldn't be enough to provide a motive for murder? Julia Reynolds knowing Max Finchley was a tea-leaf wasn't a strangling offence, surely?

He frowned as Max Finchley picked up his lunch box, one of those old fashioned, black tin boxes with an arched hinged lid, and got in line to filter out. And something, some little jarring note that wasn't big enough to register fully-formed in his mind, but was enough to niggle, nonetheless, made him sit up and take notice.

But what the hell was it?

He watched like a hawk, but all the man was doing was shuffling in line, waiting to get past the watchman on the gate. Nothing.

He sighed, then reached into his glove compartment and, not for the first time, drew out the small jewellers' box inside and opened it. He stared down morosely at the small, star-shaped diamond, sure that Jean would like it. A solid-minded Baptist herself, just like Tommy's mother Mercy, Jean knew the value of things. She'd be pleased with it, he was sure.

They'd been going steady for over four years now, and there'd been nobody else for Tommy and, he was certain, not for Jean either. Marriage was the next logical step. He wanted kids and he wanted to see his mother made happy, holding a grandson or granddaughter in her arms. So why the hell had he been hanging on to this diamond for almost a month now?

He shook his head, knowing why, and snapped the lid shut

just in time to see Max Finchley walk towards his car in a makeshift parking area on the far side of the site.

Tommy was careful not to be seen as he followed Finchley's nondescript Ford Mondeo through Oxford's hideous rush-hour and out into the open countryside. When he was sure he was only heading back home to Upper Heyford, Tommy dropped back and returned to HQ. He would be back, bright and early, to get on Max's tail when he returned to work next morning. Perhaps then he could spot whatever it was that was bothering him.

Hillary had just got off the phone, when a uniform from downstairs stuck his head around the door and told her that they had a member of the public downstairs wanting to speak to the officer in charge of the Julia Reynolds' murder inquiry.

'Off the street?' Hillary asked, picking up her notebook.

'Phoned the number in the *Oxford Mail*, guv, about the police artist's sketch of the bloke you chased. They directed her here.'

Hillary nodded. She knew by now that her 'heroics' of the other night would be all over the station. As usual, opinions would be mixed. There were those who held fast to the belief that only those holding the ranks of sergeant and below had any business being out and about in the field in the first place. The likes of DIs should be kept chained safely behind their desks, where they couldn't do so much damage. Then there'd be the young and eager beavers who'd joined up just so that they *could* indulge in midnight chases across open fields, who would be green with envy. Then there were the more seasoned coppers, who'd just be glad she hadn't got hurt – and rather her than them.

The young officer who followed her down to the interview-room was one of the envious ones. 'Word has it, guv, you nearly got sliced-and-diced by the inter-city?'

Hillary laughed. 'Very damn nearly, Constable. Take my advice – if you're ever going to chase suspects in the dark, take along a seeing-eye dog, and make sure the bugger goes in front.'

He was still grinning about that as he opened the door to interview room three, slipped inside, and then closed it behind him. He took up position by the door and waited, po-faced.

Carole Morton looked at him nervously then straightened up visibly as Hillary took a seat opposite. 'Hello. It's Mrs Morton, isn't it?' Hillary asked, glancing down at the piece of paper the constable had given her, which bore the witness's name, address and contact number. 'I'm Detective Inspector Hillary Greene. I hear you contacted us about the artist's drawing of a man we'd like to question. Do you know him?'

'Yes. Well, not to know his name. I've seen him before.'

Hillary nodded. Not ideal, but at least she seemed positive. 'You got a good look at this man? In daylight?'

'Oh yes, that's right. I showed the paper to Betty, and she remembered him, too.'

'Betty?'

'She works with me on reception. At the health centre in Oxham.'

'Ah,' Hillary nodded. Oxham was a large village between Oxford and Middleton Stoney, which was still able to boast a village shop, complete with a functional post office, as well as a thriving health centre that catered for locals from up to five villages away in any direction. In point of fact, unless her memory was playing her false, it was where Julia Reynolds herself had been registered as a patient.

'This man, he's a patient there?' Hillary asked.

'Oh no. He came in, it must have been early last month some time, and asked to see Dr Crowder. He hadn't got an appointment, and I tried to explain that before he could see any of the doctors he needed to be registered as patient, but he was insistent. Said that it wasn't a medical matter anyway but something else, something personal, and that he'd wait until the doctor had finished his morning surgery. As I said, he was most insistent, but polite enough, so I couldn't see the harm in it. And he was as good as his word. He sat there in the waiting-room for over an hour.'

'He didn't give you a name, I suppose?'

'Not that I can remember, no.'

'I see,' Hillary said philosophically. 'And then what happened?'

'Well, when Dr Crowder had seen his last patient, I went in and told him about the man, and he told me to send him in. He was there for about – I don't know. Ten minutes or so. Then he left. I haven't seen him since.'

'But you're sure it's him, the man in the paper?' Hillary asked, making notes as she went.

'Yes. Well, as sure as I can be. I mean, a drawing's not as good as a photograph, is it, but it's certainly a good likeness.'

'Do you think you'd be able to pick this man out of a line-up of say, six or eight men, Mrs Morton?'

Carole Morton took a deep breath. 'Yes. I think I could. And Betty as well.'

Hillary nodded. She'd obviously had to screw herself up to come here, but having done so, Hillary couldn't see her backing out now. 'Well, I hope that won't be necessary. At the moment, we have no evidence that this man has committed any crime, but we do need to speak to him. So you've nothing to worry about, and you've been very helpful. Thank you. We'll be in touch if we need you again.'

Carole Morton looked surprised and perhaps just a shade disappointed that it was all over so soon, and had been rather a banal and run-of-the-mill affair after all. Hillary imagined she'd have thought her interview with the police would be a much more interesting experience.

After she'd gone, Hillary remained seated in the now empty interview room, tapping her pen thoughtfully. So, the mystery man had been to see a local doctor. But not on a medical matter. Curious. She walked out into the main lobby and back up to her desk, quickly checking the Reynolds file. Yes! Not only was she registered at Oxham, but Dr Crowder was also Julia's doctor.

She quickly checked her watch. Nearly 5.30. What time did doctors clock off nowadays? She went outside, surprised to find Tommy Lynch crossing the car-park. 'Guv,' he said, spotting her and doing a quick detour to intercept. He told her about his surveillance of Max Finchley and his gut instinct that there was something 'off'.

Hillary nodded. 'Better keep on it then,' she said flatly, then added, 'You off, or do you have time for another interview?'

Tommy, of course, had time.

On the way to Oxham, she filled him in on the nibble they'd got on the man who had been hanging around Three Oaks Farm.

'Beginning to sound less and less like a journo after a follow-up, doesn't it?' Tommy said. 'Especially as this puts him in the area nearly a month before Julia was murdered.'

Hillary nodded. So far, they'd been working on the assumption that the Julia Reynolds killing had been an opportunistic crime. A sudden rush of blood to the head and wham. But what if it had been well thought out and meticulously planned, the seeds of it going back maybe a month or even longer?

Still, it was hard to see what Julia's doctor would have to do with anything. She'd noted in the file that he'd been interviewed as part of the routine, but nothing useful had come of it.

She was somewhat relieved to see the health centre still open, but even before she was halfway to the reception desk, the grey-haired woman behind the glass partition was already telling her that the doctors were finished seeing patients for the night.

Hillary pulled out her ID and introduced herself and Tommy. 'I was hoping to have quick word with a Dr Crowder? Is he in?'

The receptionist, now a little flustered, buzzed them through. 'Straight down the corridor, turn left, and first on the right.'

Hillary nodded, passing posters giving dire warnings about all manner of dread diseases, and was glad to reach her destination. There a sign on a door told her she'd found the rooms of Dr Lincoln Crowder. A host of letters followed his name. Sounded as if he was the chief of the Indians. She knocked and entered, Tommy coming in awkwardly behind her. The room was small, and already he seemed to fill it.

Dr Crowder, a small, grey-haired, precise-looking man, leaned back in his swivel chair and looked at them with curious eyes.

Hillary sat in the chair indicated. 'I'm currently heading a murder investigation, Dr Crowder,' she began crisply and calmly. She'd quickly learned that when it came to talking to well-educated and professional people who had every reason to consider themselves well up on the totem pole, they responded better to something that caught their attention. She saw that she'd succeeded by the way Dr Lincoln Crowder slowly put down the pen he'd been holding, and turned his swivel chair around a little more to face her.

'Yes? We're talking about Julia Reynolds, I imagine?'

Hillary nodded. Not a hard guess to make, under the circumstances. She didn't think a country doctor had that many patients murdered.

'I spoke to an officer some days ago.'

'I know, but we have some further questions, Doctor. About a month ago, a man came to see you. He wasn't a patient,' she added quickly, before the doctor could begin to tell her what he could and couldn't discuss. She quickly passed over a copy of the identikit drawing. 'You may have seen a copy of this before, in the *Oxford Mail*, Dr Crowder?'

'I don't take it,' the medico said at once, and took the leaflet. He stared at it for a good few seconds, but Hillary had no doubts at all that he recognized the man. She felt, rather than saw, him stiffen. He seemed to draw in on himself slightly, reminding her of the way a hedgehog will curl into a prickly ball at the approach of danger.

'You recognize the man?' she asked needlessly. Hillary watched him closely, seeing the way his face closed over. From the way his eyes flickered, she could tell his mind was racing. What did they know? What should he tell them? How much?

'You seem to be on the horns of a dilemma, Doctor,' Hillary said, willing to go halfway, whilst at the same time letting him know that she wasn't going to be messed about. 'But as I said, this is a murder inquiry, and you are obliged to co-operate. Now, do you know this man?'

'Yes. His name is Gregory Innes. I only met him once. As you say he isn't a patient, and didn't consult me on a medical matter.'

'Can you tell me what he did consult you about?'

'I'm afraid not.'

Hillary allowed her voice to drop a notch. 'Doctor, let's be clear about this. You have just said this man wasn't a patient, so confidentiality isn't an issue.'

Dr Crowder held up a hand, stopping her. 'But I'm afraid it is. Mr Innes himself isn't a patient, but what we discussed *did* affect a patient, and it's that patient I can't possibly discuss.'

'Julia Reynolds?' she asked sharply. 'Did this Mr Innes want to discuss Julia Reynolds?'

Doctor Crowder looked her squarely in the eye. 'The patient we discussed was not Julia Reynolds,' he said firmly and clearly.

Hillary sat back in her chair, a little stumped. Something about the precise wording of the doctor's response set off alarm bells. She'd met his kind before. They always answered questions perfectly truthfully, but not necessarily honestly. The patient they discussed was not Julia Reynolds. But she wasn't willing to bet that Julia Reynolds name hadn't been mentioned.

'I'm not sure I understand,' she began slowly. 'If you can't discuss patient details with me, how is it that you could apparently discuss patient details with Mr Innes?'

Dr Crowder began to look unhappy. 'That was different. Mr Innes had permission, written permission, which I verified by telephone, from the patient concerned.'

So it definitely wasn't Julia Reynolds then. Neither of her parents had mentioned anything about Julia being in contact with her doctor recently.

'He was acting on behalf of a patient?' Hillary asked, desperately searching for some clarification. She was sure she was on to something here, but trying to winkle out just what it was was more frustrating then trying to scratch an unreachable itch. 'He was a doctor himself?'

'No.'

He said this so abruptly that Hillary knew she'd just touched a nerve.

'Do you know exactly what his profession was, Doctor?'

Lincoln Crowder ran a finger along the top of his lip. He was sweating, Hillary realized, and doubted that this was a man who sweated much. It made Hillary wonder, rather uneasily, what a medical doctor could have to feel so uneasy about.

'He was a licensed private investigator,' Doctor Crowder said finally. And Hillary bit back a groan.

Oh great. That was just what she needed.

'And I'm afraid that's all I can tell you, Inspector,' Dr Crowder said. 'I simply can't discuss what our business was.'

'Do you have an address for him?' Hillary asked, reluctantly getting to her feet, but loath to let it go at that.

'No. He showed me his card, but I was more interested in verifying the letter he brought with him from the patient concerned, than in noting down his office details.'

Tommy, silent and watchful by the door, got a sudden jolt of *déjà vu*. As with Max Finchley just an hour or so ago, he had the sudden but undeniable feeling that something else was going on. Something he wasn't seeing. He could tell that Hillary felt it too.

'I seem to recall he was from Birmingham. Maybe Walsall. Somewhere like that. The Midlands. But I really don't know for sure.' Doctor Crowder firmly opened the door and stood to one side, and Hillary nodded, biting back the childish urge to tell him that she'd been chucked out of better places than this.

Back in the car, Tommy turned in the driver's seat, ignoring the way the wheel dug into his chest, and looked across at her. 'He was hiding something, guv,' he said.

Hillary nodded. 'Without a doubt. But what?' And did it

really affect the Julia Reynolds murder case, or was she just being side-tracked?

'Tommy, first thing tomorrow, I want you and Janine to find out all you can about Gregory Innes. If he's got a licence he'll be in the system. And put out feelers. PIs come in all sorts, from the fairly bog-standard and basically decent, to the downright dirty. I want to know what his rep is.'

'Could be he was hired by a jealous wife, guv. Our vic had a way with men, didn't she?'

Hillary nodded. It had been one of the first things she'd thought of. 'But if so, what's Doc Crowder got to do with it? Why not just follow Julia, get his snaps of her doing the naughty, and pick up the pay check? Besides, he was talking to the doc over a month ago, and not, according to our learned medical friend, about Julia Reynolds at all. And what was he doing hanging around Three Oaks Farm?' Hillary muttered, more to herself than to Tommy. 'That's what really gets me.'

'Perhaps he fancied solving the Julia Reynolds murder himself, guv?' Tommy speculated. 'It would be a feather in his cap, that's for sure, and good publicity. This thing with the doc could be related to another case, and it's nothing more than a coincidence that Crowder was the vic's GP.'

'Maybe,' Hillary said. Maybe not. One thing was for certain. She was looking forward to meeting Mr Gregory Innes.

If only to ask him what the hell he thought he was doing dodging trains and playing silly buggers with detective inspectors.

chapter eleven

DI Mike Regis watched Thomas Palmer park his navy-blue Alfa Romeo and climb out. The ESAA man looked carefully up and down either side of the road, then glanced up nervously as a woman across the way opened her front door to deposit two empty milk bottles on the doorstep. Palmer ducked his head down and headed quickly for the gate of number 39. Definitely a man with something to hide.

People who were obviously up to no good always intrigued DI Regis. Not for the first time, though, he wondered what the hell he was playing at with this particular specimen. It wasn't as if Hillary Greene had *asked* for any favours. Nor could she have made it any clearer just what variety of pond life she considered him to be. So what exactly did he hope to gain from all of this?

His dark-green eyes narrowed as a rather attractive brunette dressed in a powder blue lacy nightie and matching floating peignoir, ushered Palmer quickly inside. It was like watching something out of a naughty French film, circa 1950. He called a pal in dispatch, who quickly ran down the name of the residents – a Mr Malcolm Newcombe and spouse, Rebecca Margaret. Malcolm Newcombe. The name rang a vague bell, and he wasted a few minutes going through his mental list of known villains and punters, before finally giving a muffled grunt of victory. Malcolm Newcombe wasn't a crook, but he *was* the master of a local hunt. If it was still in operation, that is. Mike, back in his uniform days, had been present during an anti-hunt demonstration, when Malcolm Newcombe had been dragged from his horse and had later vehemently pressed charges of assault against his attacker, a normally mild-mannered mother of three, who ran her own herbalist shop in Cowley.

Mike began to grin. He couldn't help it.

Now what would those nice animal lovers at ESAA say if they knew their esteemed chairman was having it away with the wife of a local fox hunter? He'd have to come back with a camera. A few candid snapshots and Hillary would have some nice ammunition in her arsenal when it came time to go to court. Palmer, frantic to keep the knowledge of his affair from the others in his little coterie, might even find some way of scuppering the court case in order to keep them in the dark. You never knew your luck.

Mike sighed and switched on the engine. He was being daft, no two ways about it. He pulled out into the traffic and headed downtown. Hillary had made it perfectly clear that she wasn't interested. If he was honest, he was only going to follow up on the Thomas Palmer thing so that he could pop the little gem into her lap and then give her the finger, just as she'd given him.

Very grown-up.

An impatient honk behind him made him realize that the traffic light he'd stopped for had turned green and he pulled away guiltily, wondering who the hell he was supposed to be kidding.

Roger Greenwood looked up as one of the guys from across his hall of residence banged on his door.

'Rog, phone for you.'

He thrust aside the textbook he was reading on certain tax relief systems in place for the benefit of landlords, and trooped out into the hallway. He was in his final year at college, a BA in business studies within his grasp. He saw the student who'd called him, glance at him curiously as he closed the door to his own room, no doubt still mentally cursing the fact that he'd been given the room nearest the hall phone.

Roger wasn't stupid. He knew that news of his girlfriend's

murder had quickly done the rounds, making him the target of the latest juicy gossip, but it had been his own decision to return to college so soon. He'd thought it might help take his mind off things, about Julia and his dad, but now he wondered if he'd made a mistake after all. Nearly half the people around him wondered if he was a killer but were far too polite to say so, whilst the other half wanted to ask him what it felt like to have a loved-one butchered, but daren't.

Oh yeah, and the bleeding hearts kept trying to get him to go into therapy. It was driving him up the wall.

He was dreading Julia's funeral, and could only hope that, once it was all over and done with, his life would get back to normal. The trouble was, he didn't believe it would happen. Nothing in his life felt normal now, and he couldn't envisage a time when it might.

He lifted the receiver, which was dangling heavily from its twisted cord and put it to his ear. 'Yeah?'

'Roger Greenwood?'

'Yeah.'

It was a woman's voice, hesitant and breathy. He wondered if it was a crank call. He'd already had a few items of hate mail, the usual kind of sick stuff, which he'd quickly binned. He was on the point of hanging up, when the woman spoke again.

'Look, how much would it be worth to you to know who wanted your girlfriend dead?'

Roger blinked. He'd been tensed for the usual 'you're going to hang, you murdering male fascist bastard' diatribe, and the simple question floored him.

'What? What do you mean?' he heard himself ask stupidly.

'I know who wanted her dead, see. And he was there, at the party, so he had the opportunity. If you want to know, give me a call. Got a pen?'

Roger hadn't. 'Hold on,' he said desperately, still feeling totally off balance, and jogged back to his room for a notebook and pen. When he got back he half expected to hear the dial tone, but she was still there.

He jotted down the number she gave him. He recognized the first two digits as being local. Someone in Steeple Barton, or Kirtlington? He was sure he didn't recognize the voice, so it was not a near neighbour, at least.

'Look, is this a hoax?' he demanded, not sure what he wanted the answer to be.

'No. But I want money.'

'Oh, piss off,' Roger snapped, and slammed the phone down with hands that shook. Just another vulture. Just someone else who wanted to feed off Julia. People had always been doing that when she was alive. Now, even when she was dead, they still couldn't leave her alone.

Oh yes, he knew what they were saying about her.

He walked back to his room, sat down in front of his textbooks and stared out of the window grimly. But after a while, he carefully folded the slip of paper with the telephone number into the pages of his book.

Hillary looked up from her seat in interview room four as Janine and Tommy ushered in Gregory Innes. When she'd got in and found both of them had arrived well before her, and had collated a fairly impressive dossier on the PI already, she'd been impressed, and had said so. So when the man himself walked in, trying to look comfortable and at ease, she already knew the basics.

Gregory Innes had been born to average working-class parents in Birmingham. He'd gone to one of the local schools, then a nearby college of further education to do a business studies course. He'd worked at various jobs, was currently renting a distinctly average house in a distinctly average suburb in Solihull, was divorced with no kids, and had been working as a self-employed PI for the last eight years. According to his local nick, he'd never been in any serious trouble with the law per se, but one old-timer sergeant had said that he wouldn't be surprised if the PI wasn't above a bit of petty crime now and then. But nothing had stuck.

As Gregory took a seat, Hillary noted the off-the-rack slacks, the parka he'd probably bought in a going-out-of-business sale five or six years ago, the tired and wary eyes, the bad hair cut. This was the kind of man who, if asked, would say he'd never had the breaks. Luck had always gone to the next guy standing in line at the bus queue. He was the kind who thought nobody loved him (and if his parents were deceased, he was probably right) and who would justify any behaviour on the premise that if he didn't look after number one, who would?

A loser, in other words. A disgruntled, nearing middle-aged, lonely, sad, little man.

'Mr Innes, we meet again,' she said with a small smile. 'Please, sit down. I got you a tea, milk and one sugar, all right?'

'Thanks,' Gregory Innes said, picking up the plastic cup offered and taking a sip. 'But you're mistaken, Chief Inspector ...?' He raised an eyebrow, and Hillary smiled again. So he wanted to play silly buggers, did he? She knew all about the old trick of using a title just above the one you knew someone actually held. It forced them into correcting you and admitting a lesser status and thus, supposedly, putting you at an immediate psychological advantage. Oh please! Just who did he think he was dealing with? Tweedledum?

'My name's Hillary Greene,' Hillary said neatly. 'And we met the night I chased you off the property of one Mr Owen Wallis.'

Gregory Innes shook his head. 'I'm sorry, I don't have the faintest idea what you're talking about.' He took a nervous gulp of lukewarm tea and tried to look faintly puzzled.

'No?' Hillary sighed heavily. Perhaps he thought he was dealing with Tweedledumber?

'Sergeant Tyler, would you please phone Mr Wallis and tell him we have the man he saw clearly the other night, the one who almost fell over him, and we'd like him to come in and identify him. While you're at it, ask him if he'd like to press charges of trespass and criminal damage and—'

'All right, all right,' Gregory Innes said, holding out a hand with a gesture of defeat and a hopefully woebegone smile. 'No need to get so official, is there?'

Janine, who'd half-risen from her chair, sat back down again. She noticed the PI's gaze kept skipping across to Tommy Lynch, then back again, and had him pegged as a closet racist. Either that, or he suspected the big black constable was there to beat him up. Janine could have reassured him that things like that never happened nowadays, and certainly not on Hillary Greene's watch, but why bother? She hated giving a sucker an even break. It was something of a philosophy with her.

'So, you admit you were there,' Hillary said flatly.

'Yeah, I was there,' Gregory agreed. 'But I was only watching the place. I'm not a burglar, and I wasn't scouting out a house to rob, you know. Nothing like that.'

He was as nervous as a kitten at Crufts, Hillary mused, and wondered exactly what he'd been up to to make him feel so antsy in the presence of a roomful of coppers.

'And why exactly were you scouting out the cowsheds, Mr Innes?' she asked politely.

Gregory shifted in his seat and, to give himself time to think, drained the plastic cup of tea before pushing it to one side restlessly. He didn't like this female cop. And not only because of their moonlight chase playing dodgems with the trains, either. Gregory had had plenty of dealings with the fuzz in his time, and usually they were willing to cut him some slack in return for the odd snippet of information. After all, he wasn't exactly a criminal – not a really hard bastard or anything. He'd never slapped around a little old lady for her pension, or smashed a broken bottle in someone's face. So it was only right he didn't get hassled.

'Look, I was hoping to pull in a bit of business, all right? I knew a girl had been killed, and I thought there might be a bit of something in it for me. You know, members of the victim's families sometimes like to hire a PI. It makes 'em feel as if they're doing something positive themselves. Maybe even post a reward.'

Janine felt her nose wrinkle in distaste. What a Prince Charming.

'So if Sergeant Tyler were to contact the Reynolds, they'd have heard of you, would they?' Hillary asked mildly, and knew from the way Gregory Innes smiled, his bony shoulders relaxing against the chair, that he'd already covered himself.

'Sure they will have,' he said. 'They declined, at the time, but I thought it worth while checking out anyway.'

Hillary nodded at Janine, who left to do the telephoning, but Hillary already knew what she'd find. Whatever else he was, Gregory Innes was too smart to be caught out in a lie that could be so easily disproved.

Gregory was glad now that his usual policy of covering his own arse at all times was once again paying off.

'So why, if you had legitimate reasons for nosing into an official police inquiry,' Hillary said, neatly turning the screw in another direction, 'did you leg it in such a spectacular fashion?'

Gregory flushed. He knew the battle-axe wouldn't like PIs nosing about on her territory, and wouldn't put it past her to slap some sort of bogus charge on him if he wasn't careful. Obstruction of justice maybe. 'Well, you know how it is,' he said hopefully.

'Tell me,' Hillary said bluntly.

'Well, like you said, I suppose, strictly speaking, I was trespassing,' Gregory was forced to admit. 'Although I wasn't doing any harm to old Farmer Jones's fields or cows or nothing. I didn't trample no corn or leave any gates undone, and I do think it would be unfair to have me up for that. I was only trying to see if I could do anything to help after all.'

Hillary sighed. Before long he'd be whining how nobody understood him, and life had always been unfair to poor little him and his pet dog Towser.

Janine returned with a quick shake of her head. As she'd thought - Innes *had* checked with the Reynolds. She was only glad the grieving parents hadn't been conned into hiring him.

'How well did you know Julia Reynolds?' Hillary asked. But if she was hoping for a knee-jerk reaction, she was disappointed.

'Didn't know her from Adam. Or Eve,' Gregory corrected, with what he no doubt thought of as a winsome smile.

'So let me get this straight,' Hillary said. 'You just thought you'd latch on to the tail end of a murder inquiry and see what you could come up with? Even though nobody had hired you?' She let the scepticism she felt leach clearly into her voice.

Gregory again shifted unhappily about on his seat. He knew how lame it all sounded, but he wasn't going to blow it now. 'That's right. I've got a living to earn.'

'Yes. With Birmingham, the second biggest city in the UK right on your doorstep, I'd have thought there'd have been more than enough dirt and tragedy there for you to grub around in, Mr Innes. Why come to a small Oxfordshire village?'

Gregory flushed. 'There's no law against me seeking work outside my catchment area, so to speak, is there?' he demanded belligerently.

'Did someone teach you that in PI school, Mr Innes?' Hillary asked, patently amused now.

Gregory flushed. Sarky cow.

'All right. So you say you don't know Julia Reynolds, and you just happened to cast your net this way. Tell me about Dr Lincoln Crowder.'

Gregory felt the chair underneath him give a lurch. Or at least it felt like it had. Janine watched the colour seep out of Prince Charming's face, and hid a grin. She had to hand it to Hillary, the DI knew how to land a good sucker-punch along with the best of them.

'Who?' Gregory finally managed to croak.

Hillary slowly leaned forward on the table, resting her elbows in front of her and leaning her chin on her cupped hands. It had the effect of putting her face on a level with the PI's and only inches apart. 'Dr Lincoln Crowder.' She repeated each syllable clearly and succinctly. 'And, Mr Innes, please don't bother to lie to me, I won't be at all happy about it.'

Gregory flushed again. Shit, what was she? Mystic Meg or something? How much more did the bitch actually know?

'Sorry, don't seem to recall the name,' he said with an over-the-top apologetic shrug.

Hillary sighed. 'Then let me refresh your memory, Mr Innes. Dr Crowder works in one of our local health centres. You went to see him, about three to four weeks ago. What did you discuss?'

Gregory Innes scratched his head. 'I did?'

Hillary sighed heavily. 'Janine, go and fetch Dr Crowder here please. And then Mr Wallis. I'd like to urge Mr Wallis to press charges, and I'm sure Dr Crowder will be able to remember what he discussed with Mr Innes here.'

Once again Janine half-rose, and once again, Gregory Innes suddenly had a miraculous breakthrough with his memory. At the same time, Hillary scribbled something on a note, and passed it to Tommy who read it, nodded, and left.

'Oh, *that* Dr Crowder. Yes, I remember now,' Gregory said, wondering uneasily what it was she'd got the big bugger doing. 'Oh it had nothing to do with Julia Reynolds. How could it?' Gregory said, suddenly beaming. 'This was, as you said, about a month ago now. No, that was about another case entirely.'

Hillary nodded placidly. 'What case exactly?'

'Oh I can't possibly discuss cases,' Gregory said, then added quickly, 'except in very general terms, of course,' as Hillary's face tightened ominously.

'General terms will do,' Hillary smiled. 'For now.'

Innes nodded. 'Well, as I seem to recall, it was to do with an inquiry I was making into paternity. The CSA were having difficulty with one of its runaway dads, and the mother called me in. Seems daddy-o was claiming the sprog wasn't his, and she needed DNA testing to confirm that it was. One of Dr Crowder's patients, obviously. I was there strictly in the course of legitimate business.'

And, Hillary thought grimly, fighting back a quick stab of anger, this little shit-heel knew as well as she did that Crowder was hardly likely to breach patient confidentiality without a fight, and warrants and legal writs up the wazoo. Which was no doubt what Innes was counting on.

Hillary frowned. Wait a minute though. Crowder had told

her that the PI had brought with him written permission from a patient to discuss his or her case. But exactly which patient would that be? According to Innes's story, the would-be father would hardly be likely to give his own doctor permission to bandy about samples of his DNA, would he? The trouble was, she couldn't see how any of this fitted in with the Julia Reynolds case anyway.

'So, is that all, Inspector Greene?' Innes asked, sensing that now might be a good time to chance his arm and see if he could wriggle out of here. He'd obviously given the cops something to think about. But nothing, he was fairly sure, that could disrupt his own nice little arrangement.

Behind him, he heard the door open and glanced around to see that the big black constable had returned.

'For the moment, Mr Innes,' Hillary said softly. 'For the moment.'

She sensed both Janine and Tommy's disappointment as the PI walked out, giving a cocky little swagger as he went past Tommy. The moment the door shut behind him, Janine snorted. 'What a scuzz bucket.'

Hillary smiled at the Americanism.

'He's lying, right?' Tommy said, just to make sure.

'Oh yes,' Hillary mused. 'Porkies of immense size and density.' The real question was, though, what was he lying *about* exactly?

'He's not trying to get himself hired by the Reynolds that's for sure, boss,' Janine said. 'When I talked to them on the phone, they were quite adamant that they wanted nothing to do with him. Mr Reynolds seems to be quite a good judge of character and had him sussed right from the get go. He all but threw Innes out on his ear.'

Hillary nodded. 'Good for him.'

So, the PI had nothing to do with Julia Reynolds' family, and claimed to know nothing about her before her death. And there was no obvious way to tie Julia Reynolds' killing in with a visit to her doctor by a PI more than a month before she was strangled in a cowshed.

'Janine, I want you to find out all you can about Dr Crowder. See if he has any skeletons in his cupboard that we should know about.'

'Boss,' Janine said, gathering her things together and slipping out.

'The DNA came back as a no-match with any known villain, right, Tommy?' Hillary mused, following suit and getting her stuff stowed away.

Tommy, by the door, nodded. 'The skin scrapings under the vic's fingernails, you mean? No, guv, no match.'

'So our perp hasn't got a record.' She pointed to the empty plastic cup of tea. 'Tommy, take this to the lab. Ask for a comparison with the saliva to the DNA the vic had under her nails.' It was not exactly standard procedure, but sometimes it paid to cut corners.

Trouble was, that could take time, and she had the rather distressing feeling that this case was getting away from her. Fast.

Tommy grinned. 'Right, guv.' He no doubt hoped that it would put the PI in the frame. But, as they walked back upstairs, Hillary had very little confidence that they'd be a match. That the PI was up to something went without saying. That he was an avaricious and lying little toe-rag also went without saying. But that was still a long way from being the sort to strangle a girl in a cowshed.

She spent an hour re-reading forensics, paying special attention to the 'results pending' notations, then reached for the phone to get her favourite technician on the line.

'Liz, it's Hillary Greene. About the Reynolds case. That's one of yours, right?'

'Right, how's it going?' Liz's cheerful voice faded as she grabbed some relevant documents then came back to the phone. 'Got it here. What do you need?'

'Pending. Anything in yet?'

She heard rustlings on the other end of the line. 'Let's see. OK, we identified fibres from an anorak, found on the wedding dress, and we've tracked them down to a specific kind ... hang on. Oh, not much use, I'm afraid. Sold by the thousands, all over the UK. Three years old, too.'

Hillary groaned. No luck there then.

'The shoe size - yep, a size eight confirmed, but again, sold by the gazillions. Bog-standard trainer.'

Hillary frowned. A size eight wasn't big. So they weren't looking for a tall, or particularly big man. Unless of course, the sneaker footprint had been left there by a passing walker sheltering from the rain, or by one of the local villagers who'd popped in to say hello to the cows; maybe the wife of the cowman, or one of their teenage kids, or any other Tom, Dick or Harry who might have passed through the cowshed within a few days of Julia's murder.

'You're depressing me, Liz,' Hillary warned, and heard the other girl laugh.

'Sorry. Oh, hang on, this might cheer you up. Then again, perhaps not. We identified those traces of powder in the vic's hair. It's face powder, women's cosmetic face powder, fairly common or garden too, but it's not the same kind the vic was wearing. She had on one of those expensive liquid-that-turns to powder kind. This other stuff was a Max Factor product, fairly old powder, I'd say, and for a woman with dark hair, rather than for a fair-skinned blonde.'

Hillary sighed. 'OK. I suppose I'll be getting the full report soon?'

Liz chortled. 'In your dreams, girl,' and hung up.

Hillary, who hadn't been called a girl in a long time, hung up with a grin.

Face powder.

Could Julia's killer have been a woman? It seemed very unlikely on the face of it. But the size eight sneaker could belong to a tallish, well-set-up woman. More likely, though, the face powder had come from whoever it was who had done Julia's hair that night.

She called Mandy Tucker and asked who did Julia's hair on special occasions.

'There was a girl who used to work in a fancy salon in Summertown that she knew. It might be her. I'll ring back the moment I find out,' Mandy promised.

Hillary thanked her and hung up.

It would probably turn out to be nothing, but in this game, you never knew.

chapter twelve

Frank Ross, driving too fast down an A-road, finished his packet of cheese and onion crisps and tossed the empty packet down beside him. There it joined all the other debris that had accumulated in the passenger-side foot well of his ancient Ford Fiesta over the past few months and gave a faint rustle, making him glance down and almost rear-end the minibus driving in front.

Like most of the rest of the world, Frank wanted to buy a new car. He wanted to move out of his crummy flat above a noisy shop and move into something decent. He wanted enough money to go to Amsterdam whenever he wanted and maybe play a few hands in a little illegal casino he knew out Stepney way. He wanted, in fact, to get his hands on his old pal, Ronnie Greene's, money.

If he only he knew where the cunning old bastard had hidden it, life could be good once more. He'd heard all the rumours that Ronnie had made an absolute fortune from his illegal animal parts smuggling, but he was almost sure that they were more due to legend than reality. And, after all, he should know. Ronnie had cut him in on the odd deal or two – when he'd needed an extra set of hands or pair of eyes. So he knew for a fact that his pal had made the odd thousand out of it here and there, but he couldn't have been raking in hundreds of thousands, like everyone said, surely? Ronnie was a hard bastard, but he wouldn't gyp a mate.

Here Frank pondered. Others, he knew, would think he was

mad to believe it, that Ronnie would sell his grandmother's body to Burke and Hare had they been about, and there was some truth to that, to be sure. On the other hand, he and Ronnie were of the old school. They'd been tight. Hell, Ronnie had even once saved his neck during a football riot gone bad, when he'd been cornered by four Millwall supporters high on booze and adrenaline.

Frank was almost convinced Ronnie would have cut him in for half. Almost. But not quite. After all, being loyal to a mate's memory was one thing, being a bloody fool was another.

Ronnie had always been cleverer than himself, that Frank had always known and accepted. Well, in certain ways, anyway. Like in how to handle money, for instance. So, whilst he, Frank, had been pissing away his extra dosh on trips to Amsterdam, playing the gee-gees and other such delights, he wouldn't have been at all surprised if Ronnie hadn't been putting his money away into some clever nice little earner that would now, years later, have accrued a big interest bonus on top.

If only he could figure out where it was.

It was driving him nuts.

But now that the internal investigation was all over and done with and the dust settled, it would be a good time to nose around and try and find the still undiscovered dosh.

Nobody would be watching him now, right?

He knew for sure Hillary bloody Greene had no idea where it was. For a start, Ronnie had been adamant that he wasn't going to let his soon-to-be-ex-wife get her mitts on it, and had more than once hinted that he'd left the secret of it with Gary, his son by his first marriage, just in case. And secondly Frank was half-convinced that if Hillary Greene *had* found it, she'd have turned it in by now.

It was the sort of thing the silly cow would do.

But that didn't put him much further forward. He couldn't exactly come right out and ask Gary about it. Suppose the boy had already have found it and stashed it, for a start. He wasn't likely to tell good ol' Frank Ross, his dad's best buddy, where it was, let alone cut him in on it, was he?

He cursed as Gregory Innes's car turned right at an orange traffic light, and gritted his teeth as he was forced to go through on red. He only hoped that some eager beaver bastard in a panda didn't pull him over for a talking to. It would be the ultimate humiliation.

He'd been doing the crossword puzzle at his desk when that smug git Tommy Lynch had given him a handwritten note from the guv, telling him to tail the PI when he left the police station. It was nearing the end of the shift, which meant he'd probably be riding around all night following some Sam Spade wannabe through sodding Birmingham, and sod any chance of overtime. He knew from his file, Innes was raised in Leamington Spa but now lived in Solihull. And if there was one place Frank despised above all others, it was bloody Birmingham.

He saw the PI's sandy-coloured head check his rear-view mirror as a car horn tooted at Frank, no doubt pissed off at nearly being hit, back at the traffic light. Frank cursed again. It had been a while since he'd done a tail in a car. Contrary to police drama series and murder mystery novels, the police rarely did work like this. It was nearly all paperwork, research, interviews, keeping narks happy, the occasional rough stuff and then more paperwork.

But he was damned if he was going to lose a tail on a snotty PI. A bloody private dick, of all things. Also, contrary to the world of entertainment, PIs were few and far between in the real world, and this was the first time Frank could recall ever running across one. And a poor species they were, if Gregory Innes was an example. Frank, as a loser himself, had no trouble spotting others of his ilk.

He swore again as Innes hit the motorway heading north and accelerated away. His car had slightly more guts than his own, and Frank hoped the Fiesta wouldn't konk out on him.

For a half hour the pissed-off sergeant kept a steady gap between them, then almost lost him when he suddenly pulled a lane change and took an exit. And not the exit to Solihull, either, he was almost sure. Wasn't it too early for that – and too far east? Geography wasn't his strong point, and he felt the sweat pop out on his forehead. It was clear the PI knew he was being tailed, and Frank had his reputation to think off. Knowing in his heart of hearts that the bitch from Thrupp could out-think him, and the bastard Tommy Lynch could out-computer him, and Janine Tyler could out-blonde and out-sex him, Frank had always known that his own particular strong point was his army of narks, his rep as a good man in a punch-up and his old-fashioned street-wise skills.

To lose his tail on a PI would be something he would never live down.

He hunched over the wheel, his shoulder blades tense. His chins wobbled as Innes went twice around a roundabout, and then shot off towards his old hunting grounds of Leamington Spa.

Where Frank promptly lost him.

It was obvious the PI knew the side streets, the one-way systems, the traffic light patterns and all that jazz. But it was a bus, a blue and cream double decker that he used to shake his tail. And not even Frank was stupid enough to argue with a double decker bus. He pulled up at the side of the road and snarled and cursed and felt like getting out and kicking the shit out of his car. Or, better yet, some purse-snatcher or random mugger of old ladies who just happened to chance by.

But the respectable citizens of Leamington Spa seemed in no mood to oblige him, and only a young mum pushing a toddler in a pushchair watched as a fat man, who looked a bit like Winnie the Pooh in a foul mood, spat into the gutter.

She tut-tutted under her breath and wondered why there was never a policeman around when you wanted one.

Janine knocked on Mel's office door and pushed it open as he called to her to come in. He was dressed in his usual dark suit, his handsome face rather tired and lined. She knew what was ragging him, of course: the arrival of Jerome Raleigh.

Still, she knew how to help him get over that! She moved to his desk, smiling at the way he watched her hips swivelling and then, with a small 'tah-dah' put the brochure for the hotel on his desk.

'What's this?'

'I've booked us in for the weekend. Next weekend after next, that is. It'll be perfect. We can watch the ponies, feed the squirrels, take advantage of the spa, and chill out.' She walked around the back of his chair and looped her arms over his shoulders, letting her hands wander under his jacket, all the while keeping a careful eye on the door. She kissed his ear. 'It'll be great, I promise.'

Mel felt his stomach clench as her hand rubbed across his lower abdomen, and he reached forward and dragged her hand back up. 'Not here, for Pete's sake. What if the brass came by?'

Janine sighed. 'I was keeping watch. You should live dangerously some time, Mel,' she chided, straightening up and moving back around the front of his desk. 'You'd like it. You're getting to be too much of an old man.'

Mel winced, then grunted. He was already living dangerously. Hadn't Marcus Donleavy told him that he'd lost out on the promotion, in part because he was shacked up with his young, blonde sergeant. Didn't Janine get it? He couldn't afford to take any more chances, especially with Raleigh, the new boy, looking around and nosing about to see what was what.

She sat down opposite him and crossed her legs outrageously, allowing the skirt she wore to slide up, and shot him a wicked grin. Mel couldn't help but smile back. Of course she got it, he admitted to himself, but she was young. Reckless. She still knew how to take life by the balls and squeeze. He used to do that once. When had he forgotten how?

He pulled the brochure closer to him. The New Forest. It might be nice, this time of year. Provided the weather was good. Then again, if it rained all day, they'd have to stay in bed. He sighed. This was no damned good. He was going to have to tell her that it was over. He was staring fifty in the face.

If he wanted a superintendency, he was going to have to shape up. And that meant telling Janine.

But not just now.

'Let's just hope we get the weekend free,' he said ambiguously.

Janine grinned and nodded, well satisfied, and tossed her head as she walked out the door, letting her long blonde locks swing free. She even gave them a little flip with her hand as she went. She was vamping for fun, of course, but Mel still felt the impact deep in his groin.

He sighed again.

'Guv, nothing from Julia's computers. The tech guys have checked for hidden messages, her e-mails, stuff like that. She was clean.'

Hillary looked up as Tommy put the report on her table. She shrugged. 'It was always a long shot. Still, if our vic had been into blackmail, the computer might have come up with something.'

'I think it was just her men that kept her in clover, guv,' Tommy said. 'Her jewellery was all good quality stuff, and the real thing. This report from that jeweller in Bicester' – he leaned across with another folder – 'shows Theo Greenwood in particular spent a small fortune on her.'

A uniform had trawled the local jewellery shops to trace the jewellery, and from the copies of the receipts, Hillary could see what Tommy meant. £1,420 on a pair of diamond and Ceylon sapphire earrings. And that was just the start of many such gifts.

'I wonder she threw him over for the son,' Tommy said.

'Ah, but she couldn't marry Theo Greenwood without him first getting divorced. And the wife could have taken him to the cleaners. But the son and heir was a different matter altogether,' Hillary pointed out.

'You still don't like the boyfriend for it then, guv?' Tommy asked cannily.

Hillary didn't. Not particularly. But was too wise to say so out loud. 'Keep digging, Tommy. And don't forget Max Finchley.'

Tommy promised he wouldn't, and packed up to go home. He wondered where Frank Ross was right now, and hoped it was somewhere cold and draughty.

Frank Ross was parked outside a small row of Victorian houses that had long been converted into dingy-looking offices. Insurance companies, small retailers doing catalogue orders for herbal remedies, a tired-looking opticians and a bespoke tailoring outfitters, of all things, rubbed shoulders with the usual dental surgeries and pet-grooming salons.

And one Innes Investigations Ltd.

When he'd lost the PI, Frank had gone straight to the office, where, nearly an hour later, Innes had finally showed up. It made Frank wonder where he'd been and what he'd been up to in the meantime. He saw Innes glance around as he locked up the car and Frank made no attempt to duck or hide as the PI's gaze skimmed the old Fiesta.

He thought he saw the bastard smile.

Incensed, he waited until the PI, cockily whistling the latest pop tune (the little snot), opened the door to the middle 'villa' and went inside. Frank watched as his sandy-coloured head passed the window on the second floor and guessed the PI's office was on the top, ergo the cheapest floor. He hoped the bastard got leg-ache climbing all those stairs.

Only then did he turn over the ignition and drive slowly down the leafy road. He knew the PI lived close, in a small semi in an estate of identical semis, and he wanted a recce before the PI called it a day. It wasn't in his remit, of course, but when had he ever needed to follow the lead of Ronnie Greene's old woman, when it came to good coppering?

He was careful to park around the back, where council garages were already falling to pieces after only two years. He was doubly careful not to park in a way that blocked anyone's egress, then walked, head down, along the narrow alleyway that ran parallel to the back of the houses. He counted until he was sure he had the back of Innes's house, then cautiously peered through a gap in the tall, roughly built wooden fence, to see if there was a mutt in residence.

Frank had a healthy regard for mutts. (He'd once been taught a proper lesson in humility by a porno-queen's particularly well-trained Lurcher/cross/Doberman.) Unlike humans, they were fearless, couldn't often be bribed, and were totally unreasonable. And the damned things nearly all came equipped with a fine set of gnashers.

But there was no evidence of a mutt in the weedy, sad-looking backyard, and with a bit of a grunt and the application of his fat-insulated shoulder, he quickly broke open the padlocked door in the fencing and was inside. He carefully put the door back into position and looked to either neighbouring house once more, but there was still no sign of life. At this hour, most people would still be at work, contemplating the rush hour to come and what kind of a night it would be on the telly.

He walked to the back of the house and the kitchen door, crouched onto his haunches, and peered through the keyhole. Blackness. He tried the door, but it was, of course, locked. He checked the windows, but none of them were unlatched. He shrugged, bent his elbow to the lower right-hand pane of glass in the door and smashed it. He reached in and turned the key, which he knew must be in the lock, and stepped inside a malodorous kitchen. It smelt a lot like his own.

Unwashed dishes in the sink, open cereal packets on the small table; the smell of mouldy bread and slightly off milk competing with the smells coming from a laundry basket, full to the brim and standing next to a surprisingly clean-looking washing machine.

He moved through into the living room, noting the average-sized TV, and eyeing the reclining chair with envy. Even if it was tatty, and dented from years of elbow-and-head resting, it was something Frank had long since coveted and hadn't yet got around to buying.

He didn't know if the PI kept any files in the house. He

thought it might be a long shot – after all, why rent an office and then use your home for work stuff? On the other hand, if the PI was anything like him, he'd want stuff easily and readily to hand, and it was at least worth risking a bit of B&E in order to make sure.

What Frank really wanted was the gen on the PI's latest case. It stood to reason that that was what had brought him sticking his unwanted nose into Thames Valley's neck of the woods. And Frank badly wanted to know what it was.

Hillary Greene had been having far too many successes recently for his liking, first of all nailing the Pitman case, then solving the killing of that good-looking French tart earlier this year. This time, he wanted to crack the case himself, just so that he could thumb his nose at the lot of 'em.

'Course, if he could find Ronnie's money, and if it was enough to retire on, he'd put in his notice so fast the sods wouldn't know what hit them. They'd soon find out how much work he actually did around the place then.

Frank went to the set of drawers that stood adjacent to a gas fire, but came up with nothing but the usual crud – spare light bulbs, photo albums, balls of string, keys to who-the-hell-knew-what, boxes of pens and paperclips, a box of old toy soldiers and other such paraphernalia. But in the bottom drawer he struck gold with a hefty beige folder. He'd just picked it up, turned it sideways to read the name on the tab – Orne – when he heard a car door slam outside. Right outside. Had he read Tommy's report on his interview with Vivian Orne the name might have rung a bell, but Frank never bothered reading other people's reports.

He looked up in time to see Innes getting out of his car. He swore, stuffed the folder back in the drawer, hot-footed it back to the kitchen, and nipped out the back.

Innes would know he'd been raided, of course, and when he realized that he hadn't actually been burgled out of anything, he'd have a pretty good idea who was to blame. But would he call in a complaint?

Possibly.

He was the kind of shitehawk who'd sue for sure if he'd caught Frank red-handed, of that there was no doubt. But Frank had been careful not to leave prints, and he'd even wiped his feet before stepping inside. There was no way Innes could prove it was him. Besides, Frank was convinced that Innes was dirty about something. And crooks, as a general rule, didn't like to put themselves in the spotlight.

Still, Hillary would be hell to live with if Innes did, in fact, lodge a complaint. As Frank knew only too well, even a suspicion of wrong-doing could blight a cop's career for years afterwards. He was glad he'd parked out of sight of the house, and only began to truly relax once he was on the motorway and heading back to Oxford.

He'd take his time and be careful what he put in his report. Apart from anything else, he had to think of a way to gloss over the fact that he'd lost Innes out near Leamington Spa way, unless he simply left that part out altogether and made up some fairy tale about Innes going straight back to his office. The thing was, lies like that sometimes came back to haunt you.

Still, there was no hurry to put pen to paper. Hillary hardly ever bothered to read his reports anyway. Sometimes he suspected her of giving him jobs to do just for the sheer hell of it, or to get him out of the office.

Not that he minded that.

Frank checked his rear-view mirror all the way home, but there was no sign of the PI tailing *him*.

Now wouldn't that have been a kicker?

Tommy glanced around the pub nervously, but it was as nice as his mate, Pete Thorne, had said it would be. It was a small freehouse, one of those old buildings of some historical merit or other, that could be found scattered throughout many Oxfordshire villages. This one had belonged to a local witch or something. Or maybe it was an alderman. He hadn't really been listening when Pete had raved about it.

All he cared about was that it sounded like the kind of place that Jean would like, and so it turned out. It was the usual low-roofed, heavy-beamed country-cottage affair, with a real fireplace big enough to roast an ox, and currently pushing out the heat via a couple of apple-wood logs. Padded seats with old black wood surrounds hugged the bulging, white-washed walls.

Jean was looking really pretty tonight, Tommy had to admit. Had she guessed what he was about to do? He wouldn't put it past her. Women seemed to know about stuff like that. But perhaps he was just being paranoid. He liked to take Jean out for a meal once in a while – when his pay check magically stretched that far.

He looked across at the woman he'd been dating for most of his adult life, admiring the way the ruby-red dress, (although modest in cut and style, as befitting Jean's Baptist upbringing and inclinations,) nevertheless clung to her skin, highlighting high and nicely rounded breasts, and slender thighs. She was wearing low-cut matching red sandals despite the rain outside, and silver and garnet earrings dangled from her exposed ears. Her hair, a mass of black crimped locks, had been pulled back into some kind of complicated French pleat, interwoven with little red and silver ribbons. Tommy knew that several men, even those accompanied by women of their own, had turned and looked when they'd walked in.

And for once, he didn't think it was the deep ebony of their skin that had been the cause.

'This is nice,' Jean said, glancing up from the menu. Like Tommy, she'd lived all her life in England and, like Tommy, her parents had emigrated from the Bahamas in the fifties. Jean had been educated at the local primary school, then the comprehensive, and had taken a one-year secretarial course after her A-levels, that had netted her a job as a secretary in one of the Oxford colleges. One of the Saint something-or-others. She was the youngest of a big family, and still lived with her mother, a fate Tommy shared.

Well, at least Mercy, his mother, and Mavis Dixon, Jean's mother, would be happy about tonight's outcome. He himself wished he didn't feel quite so sick.

'But isn't it a bit expensive?'

Tommy glanced at the menu and smiled wryly. It was, rather, but then he'd bought plenty of cash.

'Have what you like,' he said sternly. Then added, 'I'm having the prawns magenta, then the beef in ale pie, and pear tart.'

Jean grinned, showing even white teeth, and an unusual dash of recklessness. Usually she counted pennies like an accountant. 'Sounds good. I think I'll go for the crab fritters, then the rack of lamb and, I think, the strawberry shortcake.'

Tommy took the menus to the bar, gave the order, and asked what champagnes they had on offer. He chose the mid-range one and asked for it to be delivered in an ice bucket to the table after the meal.

The landlord, sensing something in the air, grinned and promised he would.

Tommy went back to the table, not quite able to feel his toes. He was feeling a combination of fear, excitement, and resignation.

A bit like he felt when called out to riot duty, in fact.

He asked Jean about her day, listening to tales of the local college gossip, and then reciprocating, being careful to keep it light. Tales of murder and mayhem weren't the ideal conversational gambit over a meal that turned out to be very good indeed.

Tommy wished they weren't sat quite so close to the log fire, or perhaps it wasn't that that was making his palms and upper lip sweat. When he saw the barman approaching with the ice bucket, his pulse rate rocketed.

Jean looked surprised, and then went quite still, as the champagne was delivered. She watched Tommy open it, the cork giving a satisfying pop as he did so, then watched him carefully pour it out into the tall, fluted glasses, spilling not a drop.

When he'd finished all that he sat back down beside her, and reached into his pocket. He opened the jeweller's box, and wondered if the diamond had shrunk in size since the last time he'd checked. He glanced up at Jean, who looked as if he'd just offered her the Koh-i-Noor, so perhaps it hadn't.

He noticed a few diners around them were watching openly now, most with big knowing smiles, and wondered what he'd do if Jean turned him down.

He'd rehearsed this moment any number of times – what man didn't – and had never come up with a satisfactory way of doing it. Sure as hell, getting down on one knee was out. And he wasn't the kind of man who could just come out with flowery words. On the other hand, a simple, 'Jean, will you marry me,' sounded so prosaic.

But when he saw her turn her big black eyes on him, and saw the expectation in them, he suddenly knew he was committed. This, so his mother had drummed into him for many a month now, was the moment every young girl dreamed of; he couldn't blow it for her now: it wouldn't be fair.

He swallowed hard.

Here goes, he thought helplessly, opening his mouth and having no idea what was going to come out. He only hoped it wouldn't be anything stupid or hurtful. Or inadequate.

'Jean, I love you. Ever since we met, I've never thought of loving anyone else.' He stopped. Was that true? Well, yes, in a way. He knew loving Hillary Greene didn't count. It probably wasn't love anyway, not in the true sense of the word. That was more of a fantasy. But when he thought of reality, whenever he thought of marriage and kids, it had always been Jean's face that had leapt into his mind's eye. Hadn't it?

'And I know, sometimes, you have to put up with things from me, my job and all, that would have made other girls give up on me.'

Once again he stopped. That didn't sound right. It sounded too everyday. It needed to be more romantic.

'And I want you to know that I know how good you are. No other woman understands me like you do.'

That was better.

'And, well, I want to marry you.' Too blunt? Well, it was out now. 'Jean, do you want to marry me, too?'

Now that definitely sounded stupid.

But Jean was throwing her arms around him, and kissing him, right there in public, something Mavis her mother would most definitely have frowned on.

Tommy was dimly aware of a scattering of applause around about him, and then Jean was slipping on the engagement ring, and suddenly Tommy realized he was going to get married.

He swallowed hard.

chapter thirteen

Gregory Innes couldn't believe the silly bitch had sent cash through the post. And yet there it was next to his bowl of breakfast cornflakes, along with a credit-card bill, a reminder that his council tax was due, and a plea to subscribe to a footwear catalogue.

He counted out the twenties yet again, still coming up with an even thousand. He supposed he could understand why she wouldn't want her hubby to know what was going on, and so perhaps writing another cheque was out of the question. But even so, sending a thousand smackers via a postman? With the rate of thieving that went on? He'd have to come to a different arrangement than this. Perhaps he'd collect at a pre-arranged spot in person. 'Course, that might be dodgy if she called in the cops. And you never knew with women.

But for now, the sight of all those purple twenty pound notes made even his stale cornflakes taste good. He could go on holiday somewhere – escape the upcoming winter. A month in Portugal maybe. With another £1,000 coming next month, and the month after that, life was looking much rosier. He'd see about raising the ante by another £500 sometime in the new year. Let her get used to paying regularly first. It would mean the kid would have to go without the latest pair of designer jeans, or the hubby would have to cut back on his flying lessons, but that was better than having the cops nosing around.

Yeah, she'd continue to pay up all right.

Gregory fanned his face with the wad, and grinned. He liked reasonable women. The smile faded, however, as he contemplated Detective Inspector Hillary Greene – as unreasonable a woman as it was possible to meet. What had possessed her to chase him across the field like that? Even now he broke out in a sweat whenever he remembered the hot, diesel-smelling rush of wind as the train had thundered by just behind him. What if he'd tripped over the track? Got a shoe stuck? He'd have been hamburger meat, and all because of that crazy bitch of a cop.

Gregory knew for sure that she'd sicced one of her lackeys on to him yesterday, and was damned sure that the fat sod had been the one responsible for the broken window in his back door. He'd have to move the Orne folder, that was for sure. Still, he was fairly sure the cop hadn't read it. He'd left a fine tracing of powdered sugar on the top piece of paper in the file, which had been undisturbed, and he'd also stuck a single strand of his hair on a photocopy of a lab report further in, which hadn't been displaced either. (He'd read of both these methods in an old Ian Fleming novel, and had used it religiously ever since. That this was the first time it had ever proved useful simply didn't occur to him.)

Yes, all in all, things were looking up. And even if the Kidlington cops did get on to Orne, she'd keep her mouth shut. For the sake of her hubby and what was left of her family, if not for the sake of her own neck.

So, there was no reason why a cosy future, padded with thousand-pound nest eggs every month, shouldn't long continue. Especially if he could get the doc to chip in with some readies as well.

But he'd have to find somewhere safe to keep the file in the meantime. Now that that fat geek of a copper knew where to look, how long would it be before he lifted it and read it through from cover to cover? And that file represented months of hard slog. Why should the cops reap the benefit of his graft?

Greg stuffed the notes into his wallet, the rest of the cornflakes into his mouth, and stepped outside. There was a raw wind blowing the promise of hail-ridden rain before it, but luckily, no sign of a dingy Fiesta. Greg got behind the wheel and drove to his bank, keeping a careful eye on his rear-view mirror. Still no Fiesta.

At the bank, he waited in line to deposit the money into his current account, then enquired about a safe deposit box.

He never noticed a white-haired fat man walk in behind him, but then, neither had he noticed the same white haired OAP pull out and join him at the end of his busy residential street – probably because he'd been driving a sporty red Mini.

Frank felt extremely stupid in a white wig and fake beard, and it only made him more than ever determined to nail this cunning bastard of a PI.

One of Frank's narks was a make-up artist at the Oxford Theatre and had been willing to help out, so that at least Frank would look legit. Frank believed the nark had been too scared to say no when leaned on, but in reality Nobby Barnes, the cosmetician, had been simply too thrilled with the idea of seeing whether or not he could actually make the disgusting sergeant look like an honest-to-goodness human being, that he simply hadn't been able to turn down the chance to find out. But even he'd been astonished at his prowess. (If only he'd been able to show his boss the transformation, he was sure he'd get the job as chief make-over artist whenever the production of *Cats* came back to Oxford.)

Now an artfully unrecognizable Frank carefully moved up to within ear-wigging distance of his mark, and felt the back of his neck prickle at the mention of a safe deposit box. He also carefully noted the rather tatty leather briefcase that Gregory Innes clutched protectively to his chest as he followed one of the tellers into a back room.

Frank abruptly veered off to one side, much to the surprise of the man in the queue behind him, made a show of picking up a form at random from the stand by the counter, then stepped outside. His chin itched under the glue sticking his fake beard to his chin, and he wanted to scratch his head, but daren't, in case the wig came off. That bloody poof of a nark had put hair clips all over the place, but it still didn't feel safe to him. Grumpily, he reached for his mobile and jabbed in some numbers.

'Guv, it's Frank. The dick just asked for a safety deposit box at his local bank. I think he's stashing evidence.'

Hillary, on the phone at the other end, instantly felt her hackles rise, and leaned forward, elbows on her desk. It was not like Frank to be so diligent, let along gung-ho. And how did he know Innes was stashing evidence? Come to that, what had happened to the report he was supposed to have dropped off detailing yesterday's activities?

Whenever Frank Ross was up to something – which was fairly often – Hillary's internal radar always went berserk. It was doing a fine hokey-cokey right now, in fact.

On the other hand, the poisoned cherub was probably right. A poverty-stricken PI didn't pay out hard-earned money on a box rental unless he had to. And since he hadn't had to before being interviewed by the Thames Valley Police, she had no doubts that whatever was in that box would be of immense interest to her indeed.

But could she convince a judge of that? They needed a court order to open the box, no two ways about it. On the other hand, this was the brutal murder of a young and beautiful girl she was investigating, and judges, despite wide-ranging opinions to the contrary, were only human.

She racked her brains, trying to think of the softest touch she knew on the judicial bench, and the best time to strike. At least the request would be both simple and to the point and narrow in its dealings. They wanted to examine the contents of a box which had been opened by one Gregory Innes on the morning of the 18th. Nice and simple and no fishing expedition attached. The kind judges liked. She might just be able to swing it.

'OK. Hang tight, I'll see what I can do,' Hillary said, grudgingly.

'Right, guv,' Frank Ross said, and snapped his mobile shut. Hang around here at the bank? In a pig's eye.

He found the public gents and removed all the gunk from his face and head, then found a suitably dirty pub, with no noisy pin ball machines going but with plenty of beer stains on the carpet and unemployed men complaining bitterly over their bitter. He promptly ordered a pint. This was definitely Frank's kind of pub. They didn't have a telephone directory of course, so he had to go and nick one from a phone box.

If he was right, Orne wasn't that common a name.

His mobile's battery was running low, but when he tried to change a twenty pound note for ten pences at the bar, he was quickly informed what he could do with his paper money (not a physical impossibility, but painful and smelly nonetheless) and was forced out yet again into the wide cruel world in search of a bank.

A bank, of all things.

Finally, all settled down with his pile of change and a second pint, Frank began to let his fingers do the walking.

Tommy still couldn't believe he was getting married. He'd carefully picked up Max Finchley's trail when he'd left home for work that morning, and had followed him all the way to the construction site, still not believing he was getting married. Now he was parked in a row of cars and trying to get comfortable.

He could make out Finchley in the crowd because of his bright blue construction helmet, his size, and the rolling gait with which he walked. So far he wasn't doing anything more suspicious than overseeing a cement mixer.

He scrupulously noted the times that Max stopped for tea from his flask and a bite to eat – which was roughly every two hours – and whenever he disappeared into the portacabin office on some admin quest, or visited the loo.

But his mind wasn't on the suspect, but on Jean.

Last night already seemed as if it had happened last month, and to somebody else.

When he'd tried to drop Jean off at her mother's, she'd insisted that he came in with her to spread the good news, which he had, and been thoroughly kissed by an excited Mavis Dixon for his pains. (And somewhat disconcerting *that* had been too.) Then his prospective mother-in-law had immediately set about planning the wedding there and then. Consequently he got home late. Naturally, Mavis had rung up her good friend Mercy in the meantime, which meant that Tommy's mother had been waiting for him with a big grin on her face and suggestions for the wedding of her own – most of which went directly against Mavis's ideas, from the colour of the bridesmaid's dresses right down to the choice of caterer.

The only thing on which the two women seemed to agree was the date – June. A June bride, apparently, had the best luck, or something. So, next June, there'd be a Mrs Tommy Lynch, walking around.

No matter how many times he said that in his head, he couldn't make himself believe it. Was that normal?

He supposed he should have told Janine and Hillary at the office that morning that he'd got engaged, but somehow he hadn't done so. Of course, gossip and the station grapevine would quickly do the job for him, saving him the embarrassment. Still, he wanted to see Hillary's face for himself when she heard.

Tommy snorted at the fantasy that shot immediately through his mind and ran a hand across his eyes. So what if her face did fall? What if a puzzled, hurt look should make her eyes darken. What if his wildest dream actually came true, and she suddenly, in one fell swoop, realized in the best Mills & Boon tradition, that she'd fallen head over heels for her handsome DC, without even knowing it.

What would he do then? Realistically? Call the newly ecstatic Jean, her mum, his mum and all of Jean's friends (who'd know by now) and tell them it had been a mistake?

Yeah, right.

Besides, it would never happen. Hillary, when she did finally learn of it, would be happy enough for him, give a moment's thought to a possible wedding present, and then promptly forget it all.

Tommy sighed and reached for his own thermos. It was

nearly one o'clock, and time for lunch. He glanced inside his orange Tupperware lunchbox and discovered that his mother had made all his favourites – cheese and pickle sandwiches, a slice of coffee and walnut cake, and a couple of kiwi fruits. Now when the hell had she had the chance to bake the cake, Tommy wondered, bemused. He felt like a 6-year old being treated to an ice-cream after scraping his knee.

The cake tasted good though.

Through the chainlink fence, Max Finchley also was chowing down, though from the way he'd been dipping into that big old-fashioned lunch box of his all morning, Tommy wondered what could possibly be left.

He drearily noted the time Max went back to work – on the dot of two – and then, a half-hour later, went off with his lunch box further into the site, where he disappeared into a heavy iron-clad shack. Did the man do nothing but eat? No wonder he looked like a walking barrel.

Tommy leaned back in his seat, and tried not to think about getting married. But that was impossible. Instead he watched Max Finchley return with his lunch box, set it straight down on the ground in front of him, then start to shovel sand into the cement mixer.

Suddenly Tommy sat up straighter. Wait a minute. There was something off again. Something that was niggling him about the man's demeanour. What was it exactly? Tommy tried to pinpoint it. Something about the way he put the lunch box down on the ground so carefully? Come to think of it, why *did* he keep it with him at all times anyway? None of the other construction workers guarded their food so assiduously.

Slowly, Tommy got out of the car, wondering if he should report in. But say what, exactly? He wandered over to the gate, where the man on duty looked up at once and fixed him with a gimlet stare. No doubt a big youth was just the sort of tea-leaf he was paid to watch out for. Tommy found himself reaching for his ID in self-defence before fully realizing what he was doing. Now how was that for a Freudian moment? 'DC Lynch, sir. Is the site foreman around?'

The guard nodded quickly. He was a flabby forty-something, but had sharp eyes and probably sharp ears as well. He also had an Alsatian that was lying at his feet, eyeing Tommy as if he were an interesting lunch option.

'Sure. Wanna have him come out here, or do you want to go in?'

'I'll go to him,' Tommy said. 'He's in the portacabin, right?'

'Yeah.'

The guard watched him go with open curiosity, wondering what gives. Nothing had gone missing from the site as far as he knew. Well, nothing had walked lately. Well, nothing really, *really* valuable.

Tommy walked across the wet, muddy ground, wishing he hadn't got himself into this. He still had no clear idea what he was going to do or what he was going to ask. It was all right for the police manual to talk about using your initiative, – and Tommy, who'd sat the written papers for his sergeant's exams only last month, had actually written a long essay on just this subject – but in real life, how did you know if you were being clever, or were just about to make a damned great big muffin of yourself?

He knocked on the site-manager's door and heard an abrupt summons to come in. He did so, finding himself instantly insulated from the cold wind by a stifling electric fire and the humidity of a constantly boiling kettle. The office had a large desk littered with papers and walls lined with pinboards that were, in turn, covered with maps, specs and lists. It even had a secretary, a rather pretty young redhead who looked up from a typewriter (Tommy hadn't seen an actual typewriter for years) and seemed surprised to see him.

A plaque on the desk identified its owner as one Stan Biggins, Site Foreman.

Once again Tommy dragged out his identification.

'Something up? Anything I can do?' Stan Biggins said at once and stood up. He was a smallish man, aged anywhere between 45 and 65, with iron-grey hair, a bristly moustache, and one of those honest, straightforward faces that probably (just to completely flummox you) housed an honest and straightforward personality. Tommy knew that construction sites and scams often went hand in hand though. And he wasn't at all sure that talking to the foreman was the clever move. But here he was, using his initiative.

'I'm here about one of your employees, sir. A Mr Max Finchley?'

'Max?' Stan said, sounding surprised.

Tommy supposed that Stan was no stranger when it came to dealing with the police, owing to the construction industry's penchant for hiring, as Frank Ross would no doubt oh so delicately put it, low-life navvies. But the foreman was obviously surprised at the mention of Max's name, which told Tommy that whatever it was that Max Finchley was up to, Stan Biggins hadn't caught on to it.

Yet.

'Yes, nothing serious sir. Or at least, nothing definite,' Tommy said, aware that he was breaking out in a bit of sweat. Not only was the office unduly warm, but he was desperately casting around for some sort of gambit which would allow him to back out gracefully. 'I take it you've no complaints about Mr Finchley's work? Known him long have you, sir?'

When in doubt, ask something general.

'Going on ten years, I suppose. Good mixer, not much of a brickie. Got a good head for heights though, and he'll really only start to earn his keep when the scaffolding goes up. What do you want with Max?'

'Oh, I can't say yet, sir,' Tommy said gently. 'That big iron-looking building at the far end of the site,' he said, 'can you tell me what's kept there?' He'd seen Max go there just recently, and it seemed an innocuous thing to ask about.

'Explosives,' Stan said.

Tommy blinked.

'Oh,' he heard himself say.

And then, into his mind, came a picture of Max Finchley carefully, *very carefully*, setting his big, old-fashioned lunch box down on the ground. A tin lunch box with a hinged lid.

A fireproof lunch box.

'Oh,' he said again. And smiled.

Max Finchley looked surprised to see the boss heading his way with a big black man in a cheap suit striding along beside him.

Then he began to look distinctly unhappy.

'Max,' Stan said, shouting a little to be heard over the grating noise of the cement mixer. 'This is DC Lynch. We want to see what's in the lunch box, Max.'

Max Finchley fainted.

He just went pale, opened his mouth a couple of times like a fish, gaped in horror from his boss to Tommy then back again, and then just keeled over.

Tommy wasn't quite quick enough to stop him landing face-first into a puddle of dirty yellow mud. Then again, at least he hadn't fallen into the cement mixer. Now that really would have been a bummer. *Suspect dies in a cement mixer whilst being arrested by police.* Tommy was still imaging the possible headlines as he helped Stan to lift the inert man off the ground.

'Bugger me,' Stan said breathlessly. But whether this comment was meant to indicate the weight of the construction worker, the state of his now filthy clothes, or the fact that he'd fainted in the first place, Tommy wasn't quite sure.

By now others were gathering round.

'He had a heart attack then?' one cheerful Irish voice asked.

'Nah. He didn't clutch his chest,' someone else said. 'They always do that.'

Max Finchley, hanging like a piece of unwanted meat between Tommy and Stan, neither of whom knowing quite what to do with him, suddenly groaned and lifted his head. Hastily they put him back down, and he managed to get his feet under him before looking around groggily.

Tommy, once he was sure that he wasn't going to keel over again, reached down and carefully, very carefully, picked up the lunch box.

'Your office, I think, Mr Biggins,' he said, and Stan nodded, awkwardly patting Max Finchley on the back. Without any protest, the construction worker trooped off between them.

Inside the office, Stan offered to open the box and Tommy let him. Max Finchley, white-faced and wide-eyed, watched this procedure and said nothing. Tommy peered down over Stan's shoulder and blinked.

'That looks like dynamite,' he said, after taking a couple of swallows.

'That's because it *is* dynamite,' Stan agreed grimly. 'I think I'd better go and have a word with Pete.'

Pete, it turned out, was the demolition expert in charge of the dynamite who, when tackled, immediately started to swear, upside and down, that he didn't know nothing about any missing dynamite.

Tommy went back to his car and reached for the radio. 'Guv, it's me, Tommy. I think you'd better come down here.'

Hillary, who'd just nobbled a very nice judge (well, he was nice today,) wasn't in the mood. 'Can't, Tommy. I have to get up to Solihull. Frank's caught a break.'

Now there were words she didn't have to say often.

'Guv, I've caught Max Finchley stealing dynamite,' Tommy said, a shade helplessly. That wasn't something he had to say often, either.

There was a small silence on the other end of the line which indicated that, for once, Hillary Greene had been rendered speechless.

At last there came a heavy sigh. 'OK. Bring everyone in here. Witnesses, everything. And try and be quick.'

'And the dynamite, guv?'

On the other end of the phone line, Hillary blinked. Yeah, dynamite. Just what the hell *did* you do with dynamite? On the one hand it was evidence, but you could hardly keep it stored in the police lock-up. For a start, the sergeant on duty down there would throw a hissy fit.

'Shit! I'll get on to the bomb squad, see what they have to say. Get a uniform down there to sit on the dynamite,' she grinned, in spite of herself, 'not literally, of course. It might hatch. I'll have someone come down and collect it.'

She glanced at her watch and wondered, nervously, what Frank Ross was up to. Left to his own devices for too long, Frank had a habit of getting creative. 'I'll brief Janine on this, and she can handle the interviews. Get back here as fast as you can.'

She wanted to see what was in that safe deposit box.

Janine had just reported back to Hillary that she'd been unable to find anything dodgy about Dr Crowder, either professionally or personally speaking, and that as far as his patients were concerned, he seemed to be a fairly well-liked and respected GP.

The blonde sergeant was still not happy at being forced to lend that poisonous git Frank Ross her car. She was more than just a little sceptical about that story of his about his own motor refusing to start that morning. In fact, she wouldn't put it past him to have been made by the PI yesterday, thus making a change of vehicle imperative. Not that he'd ever admit it, of course. But why didn't the boss lend him *her* car? It was years and years old, so what would it matter if Ross pranged it?

But when Hillary hurriedly filled her in on Tommy's situation and asked her to take it over, she didn't feel inclined to grumble, despite already being out of sorts. Although it meant being kept out of the main loop, the bait was irresistible, mainly because she'd never had a case that involved stolen dynamite before, and it sounded intriguing.

She also knew that the powers that be were only human, and could be relied upon to be intrigued by it too; and catching the word dynamite on a report was bound to snare the eye of the top brass, and bring attention to the officer who'd handled it. (So to speak.)

Tommy, returning to HQ, was thinking nervously about his upcoming Boards. He knew examiners liked to keep up to the minute in their subject matter. What if they asked him what he would do if he was confronted by a suspect, all wired up with explosives in the middle of a busy shopping precinct, who was demanding to speak to the Prime Minister?

Tommy, who had no idea what he'd do in such circumstances, wondered if he wouldn't be happier as a lowly DC all his life. Others stayed at that rank and didn't seem to suffer any ill effects. But then, since he was getting married, and kids usually followed, he'd need the rise in pay that came with making sergeant.

He'd have to start swotting up on hostage-taking procedures he supposed gloomily. And then, knowing his luck, the Boards would ask him what to do with a kidnapped pedigree poodle being held to ransom at a dog show.

Hillary took Tommy with her to Solihull, (thus saving him the trouble of coming up with scenarios to rescue purloined pooches) and he filled her in on the Max Finchley bust as he drove.

'So all you had to go on was the way he handled his lunch box?' she asked incredulously, when he'd finished.

Tommy nodded, beginning to break out in a sweat.

Hillary blew out her a breath in a whoosh. 'Rather you than me, sunshine,' she said with some admiration. 'I'd never have risked my neck on something so iffy.'

Tommy gulped. 'No guv,' he said. He knew it. He just *knew* he'd been wrong. If he ever got the urge to use his initiative again, he'd give him himself a firm kicking in the backside.

'Still, it got you a result, so what do I know?' Hillary added judiciously, watching a raincloud offload its contents onto a nearby field of winter-growing barley.

'By the way, I'm engaged, guv,' Tommy said, keeping his eye firmly on the road, and switching on the windshield wipers.

'Really? Jean, isn't it? A pretty girl. Congratulations, Tommy. When's the big day?'

'June,' Tommy said promptly. And turned on the headlights. For some reason he felt suddenly depressed.

Janine was faintly disappointed with Max Finchley. For a start, the man immediately copped to everything, which took all the fun right out of an interrogation. He told her that the explosives man had been in on it from the beginning and regularly got his cut. He told her that he sold the dynamite on to a man called Reg Harris, a well-known safe-cracker up Witney way, and even sold some of it on the internet.

The bloody internet? Janine was sure you couldn't sell dynamite on the internet.

But Finchley, led to a computer terminal, quickly showed her just how it was done. For a start, you didn't call it dynamite, of course, and you had to spread the right coded words around certain chat rooms. But it could be done all right.

Janine filled nearly two notebooks on Max Finchley's activities, and then another one that covered his perfect alibi for the night of Julia Reynolds' murder.

Apparently, he'd been winning a darts match at his local pub when Julia was being killed. And not just any darts match either but the big one. The cup. As witnessed by any number of regulars, not to mention the losing darts team. Everyone had been only too willing to confirm that Max had left the pub well after closing time, totally drunk and incapable, and in the loving bosom of two equally drunk and incapable friends.

Just to clinch it, Janine, on talking to a stricken (and extremely drunk) Mrs Finchley, was sure that the news of her husband's dynamite pilfering was just that – news. Which meant that she couldn't possibly have passed the details on to her hairdresser.

Thus it was that Max Finchley was officially crossed out of the Julia Reynolds murder case.

Of course, the thief-takers who'd long since wanted to nab Reg Harris the Witney safe-cracker, and even Special Branch, (who had more than a passing interest in Mr Finchley's dynamite-buying internet customers,) had plenty of other cases Mr Max Finchley could move on to.

Janine supposed philosophically that, all in all, it couldn't hurt to have Special Branch owe her a favour or two, and willingly passed him over.

chapter fourteen

Roger Greenwood pushed open the swinging double doors of the main kitchen and looked through into the dining-room. They were still there, all the usual suspects.

The Hayrick Inn dining room was a distinctly pleasant place to eat, with every rafter lovingly maintained, every original floor-tile in place, the table linen a rich and heavy cream, the flowers fresh and changed every day. Even the cutlery was real silver, and assiduously counted after every course. (So far, Roger's father had never had the embarrassment of having to call in the cops over a knife-nicker. But Roger assumed it would only be a matter of time.) The lingering aroma of the chef's special fought with the haze of cigar smoke that hung heavy in the air. A few lingering diners slowly quaffed glasses of decades old port and assorted liqueurs. The Hayrick didn't do passing pub trade.

Increasingly, Roger was finding that he loathed the Hayrick's clientele. The old men with their memberships of posh London clubs, their bespoke tailored suits, and their old sports cars retuned to take unleaded petrol, all seemed to him to be so obsolete he wondered how they kept going. Had no one told them it was the twenty-first century? Still, he supposed that the Hayrick, which had parts of its building going back to before Good Queen Bess, probably wasn't the best place to contemplate the modern era.

At least the yuppies, his father's pet-hate, had all but been made extinct now. Since the boom and bust of the eighties, there seemed to be some sort of uneasy peace amongst the upper echelons. Roger hoped they all choked on their amaretto biscuits and coffee, which was probably not a good attitude for a hotelier's son who still had hopes of taking over the family business when the old man finally retired to Marbella.

Roger noticed that his father, lingering expansively over coffee with a group of civil servant types, was looking particularly pleased with himself today. Smug. As if he'd just done the deal of the century. And since he'd not long since signed a deal, amid much mutual back slapping, with Owen Wallis, Roger supposed that he probably had. Not that he'd seen fit to fill his son in on any of the details.

Still, Roger knew his father's plans for their empire well, thanks to Julia. Julia had almost been able to read the gaffer's mind when it came to things like that, and had often explained things to Roger that he hadn't understood.

Julia. Roger sucked in a harsh breath. His father seemed to have forgotten that Julia was dead. The woman his son had loved had been murdered, not even a week ago, and yet here he still was, empire building. Laughing, living the high life and sipping his bloody Napoleon brandy. Did he not care? Did any of them not care?

Julia had always said that his dad was heartless. Even at the party, when Wallis and his father had disappeared into the den during the anniversary celebrations, Julia had laughingly said that they were probably up to no good, and she'd have to see if she could find out what they were up to.

She'd probably been right. In spite of her youth, she had a way of sniffing out corruption. She despised it as much as he did, and yet, unlike himself, she'd seemed capable of incorporating it into her own world without any apparent sign of guilt.

He wondered if she really had overheard their business talk that night. He wondered, with a real pang, if she'd cared about the backhanders his father must have tossed the farmer's way, along with those already greasing the palms of planning officers and who knew else?

With a snort, Roger let the swing doors close and moved back upstairs. He'd be back at college tomorrow, so if he was going to do something, now was the time.

He reached for the phone number his mysterious caller had left, and dialled. It had to be a home number. Not smart. But then again, the caller probably hadn't been trying to remain particularly anonymous.

'Yeah?' the female voice sounded tired, and oddly slurred. Perhaps she was drunk?

'It's Roger Greenwood. We spoke a while ago. You said you had information on the death of my girlfriend.'

'Yeah. Information. You mean, I know who did it and why. Sure. Ready to pay?'

'How do I know you know anything?' Roger asked helplessly. As the son of a wealthy man, he'd been bought up to suspect scams, to be wary of people trying to separate him from his money.

'Because when you check out the info I give you, you'll find it's right, you dummy. You thick or something?'

Roger blinked. 'I'll give you a hundred.'

There was a harsh bark of laughter and then the buzz of the dial tone. Roger sighed, hung up and redialled.

'Five hundred, and not a penny more. The cops seem to be doing a good job. I could just sit back and wait for them to get on with it,' he said shortly. And this time was prepared to hang up himself. Or so he told himself.

'Sure. OK, five hundred. But I want another five hundred when it pans out. Yeah?'

Roger smiled. Now who was being naïve? The girl sounded young. And still drunk. Or maybe just high.

'If it pans out,' he lied.

'You know that burger joint on the Market Square in Bicester?' the girl asked. 'Meet me there in an hour. And bring cash.'

Roger shrugged as yet again the dial tone buzzed in his ear. So what if he was being conned? He'd only be out five hundred. And wasn't Julia worth that? In fact, wasn't he already feeling guilty that the worst of his grief hadn't been grief at all, but only shock?

Already he'd stopped crying at night. Already he was eating properly again. Already, he was beginning to accept the fact that he'd never see Julia again – and that fact wasn't breaking his heart any more. He didn't love her. Perhaps he never had. He knew that now. Otherwise his life wouldn't feel as if it was still well worth living. Had she not been killed, he knew now that he'd never have married her. And she'd have been right pissed off about it, but that didn't mean he didn't still owe her. That it wasn't still a tragedy.

All that fire and life, gone.

Yeah, he owed her a few hundred quid on a long shot.

And besides all that, he felt, deep down in his bones, that the anonymous girl actually knew something. There was a certain ring of confidence in her voice – a sly I-know-something-you-don't quality that made him hope, even as it grated.

Resolutely, he left the Hayrick and headed for the market town of Bicester, and the nearest ATM.

Frank finally struck lucky just as the pub called closing time at 2.30. Trust him to get stuck with a pub that bothered to close. He drank up and then emptied his bladder in the toilet before stepping out on to the mean streets of Solihull with the name and address of one Mr T.A. Orne scribbled down on a sheet of paper.

Most of the Ornes he'd tried had been out, of course, at this time of day. Those that had been in were either retired, young mothers, the unemployed or malingerers. None had reacted to the name of Gregory Innes, however.

Then he'd exhausted the Birmingham environs and gone on to Nuneaton. There, someone had taken the bait. Not that the woman who'd answered had admitted to knowing Gregory Innes – she hadn't, but the hesitation, the moment of startled silence before the denial had been all that Frank had needed.

Now he glanced at his watch, wondering what to do. Hillary and probably Janine were on their way by now, and the guv had told him to sit tight at the bank. But Frank doubted they'd be here just yet. Besides, what was the harm in checking out Mr T.A. Orne before meeting up with the witch from Thrupp? It would do Ronnie's old lady good for once, to know that Frank Ross wasn't one of her lackey, know-nothing arse-lickers.

If Innes wanted to keep T.A. Orne's existence a secret from the police, then Frank wanted to know what was so all-damned important about him. He couldn't see how it could possibly link-up with the Julia Reynolds' killing, but if that git of a PI wasn't up to something, Frank would eat his hat.

Or, since he didn't own a hat, he'd eat somebody else's.

Whistling tunelessly, Frank crossed over to Janine Tyler's Mini and climbed in. He was rather fat, and the Mini was rather small, but he didn't care. The look on Janine's face when he'd asked to borrow it had been reward enough. Not that she'd agreed, of course, but for once, Hillary had backed him up. There probably hadn't been any cars free in the motor pool anyway.

He could still remember the blonde bimbo's threats about what she'd do to various parts of his anatomy if he should so much as put a scratch on her baby, and he almost contemplated dinging a wing just to see her howl.

But he had an idea Hillary bloody Greene would make him pay for it personally so that Janine wouldn't lose her no-claims bonus, so when he pulled away from the kerb, he did so carefully. He wondered what car he'd buy for himself if he could just get his hands on some of Ronnie's money. He'd already put the word out to friends at Gary Greene's station in Witney to keep an eye on him, and to report back to him if the young constable suddenly started spending way beyond his means.

Not that he thought Ronnie would have raised his son to be so stupid, but you never knew your luck.

Hillary glanced around as she climbed out of the car, which Tommy had parked illegally on a double yellow line right in front of the bank. There was no sign of Janine's red Mini, which meant Frank had either found a legal parking spot (extremely unlikely) or had slouched off somewhere, probably to the nearest pub. (Much more likely.)

Tommy put the official police notice in the car window and locked up. He'd only ever had a parking ticket once, when displaying the sign, and he hoped the traffic wardens around Solihull were copper-friendly. It wasn't always the case.

Inside the bank, Hillary quickly identified herself, was shown into the assistant bank-manager's office, and watched the thirty-something survey the court order anxiously and minutely. After a brief chat with his superior, he led them down reluctantly to an underground vault, and located the box in question.

Because Hillary had no key, he had to use both himself, as if unhappily underlining the breach in etiquette.

Hillary hefted the box on to the table provided, told the unhappy executive she'd call him back when she was finished, and watched him go.

Tommy took the seat opposite her, feeling a brief surge of excitement as Hillary opened the box. Of course, there were no hoards of diamonds, or packs of money, or even a treasure map inside, just a plain, thick, buff-covered folder.

Hillary, though, looked as if she'd just come across the whereabouts to Eldorado, and quickly opened the file and began to read.

Frank parked behind a Reliant Robin car, and stared at it for a few seconds. Did losers still buy these three-wheeled trikes? Apparently so.

The surrounding suburb, though, didn't look like the kind that approved of Reliant Robins. Most of the houses were detached, with big, well-kept gardens, neat fences and hedges, well-maintained paintwork and no loose kerbstones. The residences themselves were that curious kind of mock-Tudor come country-cottage, so beloved of developers. Frank knew he'd never have been able to afford a mortgage on one of these babies if he lived and worked until he was ninety.

Perhaps the Reliant Robin owner had a sense of humour. Or, more likely he was one of those sorts who simply went to pieces on a driving test.

He glanced up at the house he wanted, speculating on Mr T.A. Orne. He must be doing fairly well in the world, or he wouldn't be living here.

So just why did the middle-classes hire PIs nowadays? With divorce so painless and commonplace he doubted it was a domestic issue. If you wanted to know if the missus was sleeping around, just assume that she was. Statistically, you were almost bound to be right.

So what else. Missing kid?

Frank could have used the radio and asked for a computer check, but he didn't have time. Besides, it might alert Hillary to what he was up to, and he didn't want to have his wings clipped just yet.

He hiked up his trousers, which kept slipping past his bulging belly and threatening to drop, and set off up the pavement. He'd have to buy some jeans with a bigger waist, but Frank resented spending money on such fripperies as clothes. Beer, fags, women, betting. But clothes? He supposed he could trawl the charity shops though.

At the neat, wrought-iron garden gate leading to the Orne residence, Frank stopped and considered his options. The straightforward approach never appealed to Frank much. He always assumed everyone was up to something, and for a copper, taking the sneaky approach was second nature anyway. So he pushed open the gate, ignored the front doorbell and trotted around the side. The pretty displays of Michaelmas daisies, late-flowering asters, chrysanthemums and dahlias went unnoticed. As did the man who was standing just inside the open door of a garden shed, listlessly scraping damp earth off a shovel.

Terry Orne was the gardener of the family, although lately it had been more of a chore than a pleasure. Something to get him out of the house, a way to pass the time thinking of other things. Something apart from the fact that his son had died and there had been nothing he could do about it.

After the funeral, taking care of the flowers had meant that Vivian, his wife, would have a steady supply of fresh blooms to take to Barry's grave. His small, small grave.

Terry had been scraping the shovel clean for nearly five minutes now. His wife was inside, maybe crying, maybe sleeping. The doctors had given her pills, but she'd stopped taking them about a week ago.

He was staring sightlessly out the dirty shed window, only half his brain registering the fact that there was a stranger walking carefully alongside his house, looking over at the neighbouring gardens and then up at the neighbouring houses, as if checking nobody was watching.

Burglar.

Terry Orne blinked, suddenly coming back to the garden shed. Back to life and reality.

The man was fat, with a full-moon face, shabby-looking suit, piggy eyes and a surprisingly benevolent look. No, he couldn't be a burglar. Not in broad daylight, surely? But he was up to no good. Of that Terry was sure.

Suddenly, Terry Orne felt a burning tide creep up his throat, making his face burn. Was this the bastard who had phoned yesterday?

He'd come home early from his work at the garage. His right-hand man had assured him that there'd be no problem with the bloke from Walsall who was coming down to inspect their classic Humber. Terry hadn't cared if there had been. What was the point? He no longer had a son to pass the business on to, and he doubted if his daughter would be interested. But from the moment he'd walked into the kitchen, and heard Vivian's tense, fraught voice coming from the lounge, he knew something was up.

Vivian had heard him by then though, and had quickly spoken something and hung up the phone. She had refused to discuss it ever since. He knew it had been a man on the other end of the line, because he'd heard as much before the conversation had been so abruptly terminated.

He wasn't stupid. He knew his wife, and never once

suspected an affair. No, he suspected something far more dangerous.

Vivian was one of those women who never let go. Never gave up. She'd been tireless all through Barry's illness, ever since his leukaemia had been diagnosed two days after his sixth birthday. Whilst he had reeled and lurched from one crisis to another, it had been Vivian who'd dealt with the doctors, Vivian who'd done her own research on the internet when the doctors had begun to give up on their son, Vivian who'd lobbied charities, foreign doctors and hospitals, always badgering for a bone-marrow donor to be found, never giving up hope. It had been Vivian who'd all but arm-wrestled doctors into trying the latest medicines, and had even, on one occasion, raided their bank account to pay for illegally-obtained experimental drugs from America.

And who knew what else she might have been up to since? Terry certainly didn't. Though he guessed that she had become involved in something during those final few weeks of Barry's life, something that now seemed to be coming back to haunt her. But what? Barry was dead, for no bone-marrow donor had been found.

He supposed Vivian could have been talking to some shady character who'd promised her the world back when they still had a living son to try and save, but had then failed to deliver and was now – what? Threatening her? Was he demanding money? Threatening to go to the cops? As the episode with the illegal drugs had shown, Vivian would have gone to any lengths to try and save their son, and Terry was right there with her.

But the world was full of bastards, and he only wished she'd confide in him. It was just that, since losing Barry, the stuffing seemed to have gone right out of her. She'd been too listless to care. It was only on the phone yesterday that the old angry spark had flared briefly back to life, only to die again when she'd spotted her husband watching and listening, and had quickly hung up the phone.

Terry had wanted to kill somebody, there and then. Now he felt the same way again.

Months of rage and frustration were coming to boiling point. Weeks of watching his 8-year-old boy fade to white and die. Nights of wondering when, when, *when*, would that final breath be taken? Visions of his boy's eyes, watching him without blame, without hope, ran together in one stream of never-ending guilt. Barry had never once asked them to save him. It was as if, even at only eight years old, he'd known what it would do to them if he had.

But how could you fight death? What was the point of railing against fate? Against the big question, 'Why Me? Why Us?' there was no come back.

Now, though, here was flesh and blood to pound. Here, Terry Orne was suddenly sure, was the man on the other end of the telephone line. The leech who had somehow got his hooks into his wife.

Terry lifted the clean spade further into the air, the knuckles of the hand that clutched the handle going white with tension. *Come on, you bastard, just a bit further. Do a bit more snooping. Yeah, that's right. Look through the lounge window.*

Was Vivian inside, or was she in the kitchen? Or upstairs?

Soundlessly, Terry Orne stepped from the garden shed and began to make his way to the fat man who was peering into the window, his grubby, chubby hands cupped either side of his eyes, shutting out the light and to let him see in.

There was no privacy in death, Terry Orne had learned. Doctors, prodding, poking, prying. Relatives supporting. Friends commiserating. Undertakers asking what casket you wanted. Now, here, in what should be a quiet time for them both, somebody else was snooping. Butting his ugly head into what should be private.

He didn't know what Vivian was keeping from him. He didn't care. He just wanted it all to stop.

Slowly, carefully, spade raised, Terry Orne got closer to the man violating his home, his wife, his life and his all-important grief.

*

Hillary passed on the last of the sheets to Tommy and slowly leaned back in her chair.

It was all there.

Vivian Orne had first contacted Gregory Innes six months ago. Her son, Barry, was dying from leukaemia, and was desperately in need of a bone-marrow donor. So far, it seemed, no match had been found. But a nurse at Barry's hospital had inadvertently said something that had started the desperate mother wondering.

Had a donor been found after all? A donor who had then proved unwilling to go through with the surgery needed to remove bone marrow? It seemed impossible. Who would refuse to save a little boy's life? Yet the doubt must have been terrible, for she'd gone to Gregory Innes to check it out.

Even Hillary had to admit, the PI had done a thorough job. Of course, the nurse, when approached, had denied hinting at any such thing, and the PI had been met with a stone wall at the hospital. But that hadn't stopped him. Illegal wire taps, an unnamed source within the donor system, and the payment of a £1,000 'finder's fee' by Vivian Orne had led Gregory Innes to one Dr Lincoln Crowder, and a surgery near Oxford.

Reading Innes's report on their conversation, Hillary had at last understood what it was that had worried the health official so much. He had not exactly confirmed that a donor in the Oxford area had been found who would prove a suitable match for the desperately ill Barry Orne, but he hadn't denied it either.

Moreover, Innes had found out that Julia Reynolds had had her appendix out a year before. How had he known that that fact was significant unless the GP had intimated to Innes that it might be? How else had the PI got on to the surgeon, and thence to Julia Reynolds' medical records?

Hillary couldn't find it in her heart to blame Dr. Crowder. As a GP, he'd know all about the heartbreak the Ornes must have been going through. His sympathies would have been with the boy – as were her own. Perhaps he thought that the boy's mother would have more success in persuading Julia

Reynolds to donate her bone-marrow. Obviously, the combined weight of the medical profession had failed.

Yes, she could understand only too well why the doctor had taken such a risk, but no wonder he'd been so scared when the police had come calling.

Innes's files had been very careful to make no mention of how he'd got his hands on Julia Reynolds' medical records. Certainly the copies in the folder were bad photocopies of yet other photocopies, but they were still clear enough to show that Julia Reynolds had indeed been thrown up by the medical register of donors as a high-ratio match to Barry Orne.

And from there on in, it got really ugly.

Doctors had at once contacted Julia Reynolds, told her of the match, and tried to schedule a time for her to go in for the necessary surgery. But Julia, with her phobia of hospitals, needles and illness, had flatly refused, and had continued to refuse, despite all entreaties, until the boy had died, just over two weeks ago.

'Shit, guv,' Tommy said miserably, as he read the last page and looked across at Hillary. 'How could she just let a little kiddie die?'

Hillary shook her head helplessly.

She'd had a friend at college once, with a phobia of swans. *Swans*, of all things. Barbara had known in her head that the big white birds weren't evil. That whenever she walked by a river, they weren't going to come at her, hissing and breaking her bones with their big wings. She explained all this to Hillary once, and even admitted that she could see why others thought them beautiful. But she herself could never see one of the birds without breaking out into a cold sweat. Couldn't walk past one unless it was well out on the water. Just the thought of them reduced her to trembling terror. She'd even thrown up once, when they'd been walking past Magdalen College, and a swan, flying low across the bridge, had suddenly startled her. Hillary had only been able to stand by helplessly while her friend was sick, then lead her, still shaking badly, to the nearest pub and a big, comforting brandy.

So she knew something of the stranglehold phobias had on people; of the illogic of them; of their very real power. Even so. But then again, who was she to judge? If she had a paralysing fear of something, how did she know that she would have the strength to overcome it?

No. *She* might not have reason to judge, Hillary thought grimly, but what of the boy's parents? If Innes had gone back to them with the name of the donor, what judgement might *they* have felt entitled to bring down on her?

She remembered the face powder in Julia's hair, the size 8 shoe and shook her head in self-disgust. All along she'd got it wrong. Even with Vivian Orne's car spotted outside the vic's house, she'd still missed it. Right from the first, she'd assumed that they were after a jealous lover, a male, when all along it had been a grieving mother. She'd almost blown it, big time.

'We've got to go and see Innes,' she said, grimly.

chapter fifteen

They were at Gregory Innes's office within five minutes, Tommy wondering nervously if the PI would try to make a break for it, or try any rough stuff, if cornered. He didn't look like the type who'd put up a fight, but he could run like a rabbit, as Hillary already knew. So when they reached the top floor of the converted Victorian house, he went through the door first.

Hillary let him.

Gregory Innes's office was surprisingly light and airy, due to the high ceiling and large windows. He'd kept the walls painted a clean white, had laid down hard-wearing neutral-coloured carpeting, and kept the furniture to a minimum. Grey filing cabinets glowered gloomily against nearly all four walls, and an old-looking computer took up space on what was obviously a desk that had been recovered from a skip. It certainly didn't need 'distressing' at any rate.

'Detective Inspector Greene,' Gregory acknowledged unhappily, his eyes darting from the big constable to the woman he'd hoped never to see again. 'I must say I never expected to see you here.'

'Cut the crap, Innes,' Hillary said, walking straight to his desk and pulling out one of the two facing chairs. 'Tell me about the Ornes.'

Gregory Innes sat back down, hard, and gave a somewhat cheesy grin. 'They were clients of mine. Not that I see what business it is of yours.'

Hillary slowly sat down, keeping her dark eyes fixed on the PI as she opened her briefcase and pulled out the Orne file. Innes paled as she put it on the desk before them. 'And before you ask,' she said softly, 'this was retrieved from the safe deposit box you rented this morning, with a court order, all nice and legal.'

Innes licked his lips and wondered how he'd missed the tail. It couldn't have been that fat slob who'd trailed him the first time. They had to have put a second man – or woman, onto him. Damn. Damn, damn, damn.

He felt the sweat break out under his armpits and told himself not to panic. 'I never thought otherwise, Inspector,' he said with a smile. 'Perish the thought that a copper would ever overstep the line.'

'I told you before,' Hillary Greene said curtly, in no mood for playing games, 'cut the crap. Right now a search warrant is being sought for both this office, your house, your car and your bank records. I'm betting we're going to find that you've been banking substantial sums of money just recently. Unless you've kept it as cash? And I wonder what the corresponding bank records of Mr Orne will show?'

'Now just a minute,' Gregory whined. 'I told you, the Ornes were clients. If they've been paying me money, it's only my fee.'

Hillary smiled. 'Really? So you've no objection if we question the Ornes then? Ask them what you were hired to do?'

The greasy skin on Gregory Innes's nose and upper lip shined obscenely in the afternoon light. He seemed to sense it, for he rubbed his mouth with his hand, trying to think of a way to find out just how much they knew.

'That would be rather cruel. They've recently lost a child,' he mumbled eventually.

'Yes, I know,' Hillary said, tapping the folder. 'A little boy in need of a bone marrow donor. They came to you to track down a rumour that a donor had been found, but was refusing to go through with the surgery required.'

'That's right,' Gregory said. 'When the mother came to me, it broke my heart. I agreed to it right off, even though I knew the chances of success were low. Medical records, donor details, all that sort of stuff, is guarded like gold, you know.'

Tommy Lynch shifted uncomfortably on his chair. During his short time in the police he'd seen many things that had disgusted him, outraged him, or moved him to pity. Pregnant mothers hooked on dope, killing the babies inside them or dooming them to be born with addictions too, whilst peddling their bodies for more money to feed more junk into their veins. Foreign women sold into sexual slavery. Paedophiles. Batterers of eighty and ninety-year-old women. Any manner of grubby, dirty, petty, vengeful episodes that made him wonder if the human race would ever survive. But Gregory Innes was making his flesh crawl in a way that was peculiarly new to him.

'I'm sure you did it all out of the goodness of your heart, Mr Innes,' Hillary said sardonically. 'How much do you charge an hour? Or should I say, how much did you charge the Ornes? Desperate people pay well, I expect?'

Innes flushed an ugly red.

'So, you traced the donor, right. It was Julia Reynolds.'

Innes stuck out his chin. 'Whatever your opinion of me, Greene, I'm a good PI. It wasn't easy, I can tell you. But I did it.'

'Hmm. And reported back to Mr Orne?'

Gregory Innes opened his mouth, then snapped it shut. 'Well, I wasn't going to keep it a secret from my client, was I?'

Hillary nodded, wondering why he had just prevaricated. 'And when you heard that Julia Reynolds had been killed, you were naturally curious? A little worried perhaps? A man with a conscience might feel as if he'd delivered up the woman for slaughter?'

Gregory again wiped his hand across his mouth. Hillary found it almost impossible to guess what he was thinking. She strongly doubted he felt any personal responsibility or remorse for what had happened to Julia Reynolds. But what else was going on behind those self-pitying eyes?

'Naturally, I was anxious to see if the Ornes could have been responsible. That was what I was doing on the farm – trying to establish, one way or the other, any possible involvement by my former client. If I'd found anything, of course, I would have brought it straight to you.'

Hillary laughed. She couldn't help it. Beside her, she saw Tommy look away, and out of the corner of her eye she could see his big fists clenching and unclenching in hidden anger. But she had no real worries that Tommy would lose control.

'So what did you find out, Innes? You being such a hot shot PI and all? Sherlock Holmes having nothing on you, and all that. Were the Ornes involved?'

'No. No trace of them.'

'So when the search warrant arrives, we'll find no records of any telephone calls to their house, say? After all, you finished with their case – what was it – two weeks ago? According to your files, it was all paid for, done and dusted. And if you found nothing to worry about at Three Oaks Farm, you'd have had no reason to call them back. Right?'

Innes felt the sweat begin to trickle down his back. This cow just wasn't going to leave it alone. But Vivian Orne wouldn't talk. She couldn't. They could prove nothing. All he had to do was brazen it out.

'I might have called, just to see how they were doing. Their little boy died, you know.'

'Ah. A condolence call. How nice,' Hillary said. 'Tell me about Dr Crowder. Did you break into his files to find out the name of the donor, or just bribe him?'

Innes shrugged. 'You'd have to ask him that.'

Hillary smiled grimly. 'He wouldn't happen to be someone else you're thinking of blackmailing, would he, Mr Innes?'

Gregory flushed. How did the bloody bitch know? Was she reading his mind? 'I think I've said all I'm prepared to say, Inspector. I'd like you to leave now.'

Hillary smiled. 'I'm sure you would, Mr Innes. Knowing a search team, and a search warrant, are on their way, I'm sure you'd love to have some time to yourself. But I don't think so. DC Lynch, stay here with Mr Innes. If he attempts to leave or use the telephone, you may arrest him on the charge of conspiring to pervert the course of justice.'

She rose, reached for the folder, and put it back in her bag. 'I'm off to visit Mr and Mrs Orne.'

Tommy stood up. 'Guv, you've got no back-up,' he said, a shade desperately. He'd seen Hillary in this mood before. 'Let's wait until the locals get here. Take a couple of bobbies with you, at least.'

Hillary hesitated. 'Tell you what, use the phone, and ask for a patrol car to meet me at their house.'

'Right, guv,' Tommy said, much relieved.

Hillary drove fast and made surprisingly good time to the Ornes' address. She was pretty sure a local patrol car would have got there ahead of her, and hoped they hadn't jumped the gun, but when she pulled up outside the house in the leafy suburb, there was not a sign of a jam sandwich in sight.

She got out of her car and checked her watch. She'd heard on the radio that there'd been a big smash up on the motorway not far from here. Could be her call had been given low priority – baby-sitting coppers from another force was hardly a plum job. Might be that the patrol car had simply got snarled up in traffic. It happened.

She'd just have to wait.

She reached into her bag for her mobile phone and checked back at HQ, where a bemused Janine filled her in on Mr Max Finchley's entrepreneurial spirit.

From what Tommy had told her about Mrs Finchley, Hillary could guess what had driven the construction worker to such extremes. Men married to monied women who never let them forget it, tended to do stupid things. In Max Finchley's case, playing – literally – with dynamite.

She grinned and wondered how many more such bad puns Janine had had to cope with from the others at the station. Word would have got around like wild-fire about her unusual bust.

She gave Janine a quick run-down on the situation and

asked her to pass it on to Mel. Not surprisingly, the pretty blonde sergeant was spitting mad at not being in on it with her, and Hillary wouldn't be surprised to see her turn up some time later that afternoon, depending on how things went.

It was as she was putting away the phone that Hillary spotted Janine's car, and had one of those brief Twilight Zone moments, when she wondered if her junior officer had somehow magicked herself north.

Then she realized that it was Frank who was been using Janine's car today.

Frank!

Shit! What was he doing here? Now she thought about it, he'd been conspicuous by his absence at the bank. But how the hell had he known to come here? He hadn't been able to see the file in the safe deposit box. Or had he?

'You stupid git!' Hillary whistled between her teeth, and quickly sprinted for the gate. If she knew Frank – and unfortunately for her, she did – she wouldn't put it past him to have pulled a fast one. Do a bit of the dirty, trying to get ahead of the investigation and put one over on her. Frank would dearly love to be able to show her up in front of the team – and anyone else who might be watching. Like the new super for instance. But if the Ornes were killers, the stupid clot might just have got himself killed. And think of all the paperwork she'd have to do then!

She ran along the side of the path, instinctively forgoing the front door. She was sure that Frank wouldn't have gone in all guns blazing, and she wasn't about to either. She slowed down as she rounded the back of the house and, her back to the wall, took a quick peak around the garden.

In spite of everything though, she wasn't really expecting trouble. Not real trouble. She expected to see a garden as well kept as the front patch was. A shed, maybe some garden furniture. A cat. A woman pottering about with the autumn pansies. Something of that nature.

She didn't expect to see her sergeant peering in through a window, hands cupped around his face to keep out the light, while someone else sneaked up behind him, eyes fixed on the back of his exposed head with a raised garden shovel in his hands.

'FRANK!' she yelled, launching herself around the corner, and heading straight for the man with a shovel.

In her time, Hillary had come in for her fair share of physical confrontation. By far the worst had been back in the old station house in Headington, when she and two other constables had confronted a man with a six-inch long butcher's knife. He'd sliced one of her fellow constables' forearms right to the bone, and she could still remember his angry cry of pain, and the sickening sight of gushing blood.

But this seemed almost as bad.

In spite of the rush of adrenaline to her head, she could plainly hear the voice of the retired sergeant major who'd been her physical training instructor back in the old days. His method of fighting had been dirty and extremely politically incorrect. And he'd taught her to think just like him. So she was going through her options even as she ran.

She saw Frank jump out of his skin and turn, but his gaze stopped on her as she hurtled towards him. He looked guilty. No doubt he knew he'd been rumbled, and must have always dreaded his boss catching him out in something really bad.

The silly sod! It wasn't her he had to worry about for once.

'Behind you,' she yelled in clarification, still pelting forward full tilt, wondering if she should do a slide and ram her thighs into the back of the perp's knees, up-ending him, or go straight for the raised arm. The shovel was the immediate threat, but her upper arm strength would be no match for a man's. She might not be able to prevent him from delivering a blow.

At least she had one thing going for her. Terry Orne had frozen on the spot. Her yell had had as paralysing an effect on him, as it had on his intended victim.

Now Orne's mouth gaped stupidly as a smartly dressed woman in a dark two-piece suit, with a sleek cut of brown hair and a fiercely angry face, rushed at him like an approaching valkyrie on speed. Terry Orne, like most decent men, wouldn't have dreamed of hitting a woman. So he quite simply had no idea what to do next.

Hillary, however, did.

A man with both arms upraised over his head was just asking for it. Still running, Hillary turned sidewise, jamming her two hands together to form one huge fist and, swinging back, hit Terry Orne with a massive whump in the middle of his belly.

Orne dropped the shovel with a gurgling 'ooofff' and dropped to his knees. And promptly began to lose his meagre breakfast of conflakes and toast.

Frank, now turned all the way around, saw the man drop the shovel and went white. He abruptly sat down on the patio, ignoring the dampness seeping into the seat of his trousers and sucked in a huge breath.

Frank had seen what a shovel on the back of someone's head could do. He had never been that close to death before. A punch up at a football pitch with your colleagues at your back and a hoard of pissed off Millwall supporters in front of you was fun. But unless a bastard pulled a knife, not life-threatening. Handling antsy suspects at the nick could be exhilarating, but you knew you always had back up, if you called for help. Negotiating domestics was a pain, but Frank knew how to handle himself with the worst of boozed up, fist-happy husbands.

But having a shovel walloped down on the back of your head when you weren't looking – now that was staring eternity in the eye.

He swallowed hard, his gag reflex kicking in as he watched the man who would have killed him, being sick all over the lawn. He leaned forward, letting his hands dangle between his knees and hung his head low, taking deep breaths. Little black dots danced on the back of his closed eyelids. He felt definitely iffy. Like he was going to pass out.

'Frank, you all right? You got any pains in the chest?'

He opened his eyes abruptly and lifted his head, only to find Hillary Greene crouched in front of him, one eye on the dropped shovel, one on the suspect, and one (how the hell did she have three eyes?) on him.

'What?' he said hazily.

'Are you having chest pains?'

'No.'

'OK. I'll ring for an ambulance anyway,' she said, and got up, bringing the phone to her ear.

And in that moment, Frank suddenly realized that his misery was only just starting. Because now the fact that he'd only been a second or two away from death was nothing when he compared it to the fact that it had been Hillary Greene who'd saved him.

Hillary Greene.

No, this was just too much. This just wasn't fair. For two pins, Frank could have cried.

The sound of the ambulance arriving within three minutes – Hillary wondered if that was a record – was what finally brought Vivian Orne out of the house.

She'd been on her way to the front window in the lounge to see where the ambulance was going, and which of her neighbours was in trouble, when she'd been side-tracked by the sight of strangers in her back garden.

Now, as she stepped out into the cold autumn air, her gaze went from the fat man sitting comically on her patio, to the poker-faced woman watching her and then, finally, to her husband, who was kneeling on the grass, alternately retching and groaning.

'Terry, love, are you all right?' she heard herself ask stupidly, starting towards him. 'What's going on. Who are you people?' Then, with a sharp edge of fear, 'I'll call the police.'

Hillary reached for her ID and held it up. 'We *are* the police, Mrs Orne. I'm Detective Inspector Hillary Greene, this is Sergeant Frank Ross.'

At this, Terry Orne's head shot up and he regarded Frank with a look of surprise. 'You're not the bastard on the phone?'

'Eh?' Frank said, also lifting his head to look across at the man who'd tried to kill him. The man who *would* have killed him. Curiously, Frank felt no desire to rip the bastard's head off.

He was still trying to come up with ways and means of turning this around. Suppose he told everyone back at the nick that *he'd* laid out Orne? No, it wouldn't wash. Orne himself would probably deny it. Besides, Frank knew, Hillary would have her own version and he had no illusions as to who would be believed.

But there had to be a way to down play it some. After all, there was not a mark on him. He could say Hillary was blowing things up out of all proportion. Yeah, that might work. Play the hysterical-woman card. There'd always be some who'd believe it. Not many, but enough to raise doubts. Right now, that was the only crumb of comfort he had.

The thought of being grateful to Hillary Greene never even crossed his mind. And Hillary, for one, would have been astonished if it had.

Right now, though, she had other things on her mind as she looked at Vivian Orne, a lean, stringy-looking woman with surprisingly wide shoulders and large feet. What had Innes's file said about Vivian Orne's occupation? Aerobics and dance instructor. Which meant muscles. You had to be strong and fit for that. And Julia Reynolds had been drunk and smaller and not at all physically a match for Vivian Orne.

Back at the bank vault, she'd assumed the Ornes were in on it together. Now, she believed it possible that Vivian's husband really had no idea of what she'd done.

'I thought you were the one who'd been bothering my wife,' Terry Orne said, gasping a bit through blue-tinged and vomit-speckled lips. He was still staring at Frank as if it was all *his* fault.

'I never even met your wife, dummy,' Frank snarled. In his ears, he was beginning to hear the jaunts and jibes that would ring around the Big House. Frank Ross, the one who needed to hide behind his boss's skirts. And worse. Much worse.

It was more than he'd be able to bear. Perhaps now was the

time to quit. He'd put in enough time to get his full pension. Maybe eke it out with a part-time job. Night watchman was a doddle, they said. Yeah, maybe now was a good time to quit. He could devote all his time to tracking down Ronnie's loot. Perhaps put a tail on his kid.

'The man you're thinking of is a Mr Gregory Innes,' Hillary said, looking from husband to wife. 'Isn't that so, Mrs Orne?'

Vivian Orne slowly reached her husband, and, ignoring the wet and muddy grass, knelt down beside him. Wordlessly, she put her arms around him. She wasn't sobbing, but Hillary could clearly see huge tears running down her face.

'Who's Gregory Innes?' Terry Orne said.

'Do you want to tell him, or should I, Mrs Orne?' Hillary asked. She knew that now was the optimum time to strike. They were off balance and vulnerable. Briefly, she felt a flash of distaste for what she was doing. Had Tommy Lynch been here, she knew he'd have looked away with a hastily hidden grimace of disgust.

Had Janine been here, she'd be scribbling in her notebook, but even she, Hillary suspected, wouldn't have felt any sense of satisfaction about this situation: the Ornes had been through so much already.

But long ago, a mentor of Hillary's had said something to her that had stuck with her, and remained inviolate, through all the shit life in this job had thrown at her. He'd been an old desk sergeant, retired from the field, but too bored to quit altogether. He'd been like a sage to Hillary back then, she and others of her generation, this man who must have been on the fringes of many a murder case.

Quite simply, the old man had told her, a victim of murder could rely on no one but the investigating officer to fight his or her corner. The family and friends of a murder victim might, for some reason, abandon them. The victim might never even be identified. The case might be open and shut, or never solved. But the dead can't ask questions, or justify themselves, or hunt the guilty, or prosecute, or do any other thing a living person could. The dead needed you.

And, right here and now, Julia Reynolds needed Hillary to do her job. And do it she would.

'Mr Innes is a private investigator, Mr Orne,' Hillary said softly, but quickly closed her mouth when Vivian Orne raised one hand.

She had a long, strong face, that went well with a no-nonsense cut of dark hair and brown eyes. Her arms, hard with muscle, still bore the traces of a late summer tan. But she looked gaunt. She looked like a woman who'd just buried her child.

'I hired him to find a donor, Terry. One of the nurses at the hospital let it slip that one had been found, but wasn't going to go through with the surgery.'

Terry Orne began to wretch again. But his stomach was already empty, and he began to cry instead.

'And he found her,' Vivian carried on, her voice as dead as the look in her eyes. 'It was a girl. A girl out Oxford way. She wouldn't go through with the procedure though. The doctors tried everything to persuade her. But she just wouldn't. She let our Barry die. I couldn't take it. I had to see her, face to face, to let her know what she'd done. To show her our Barry's picture. I wanted to hear what she had to say for herself.'

'What do you mean? Who?' Her husband stared at her with a growing fear in his eyes that made even Frank look away.

'The girl. The one whose bone marrow would have saved Barry,' Vivian said. 'Mr Innes gave me her address. I went to her house, but she was being picked up by this man. She was going to get married. Or at least, that's what I thought. She came out dressed like a bride. Can you believe it, Terry? A bride? Our Barry was dead, would never grow up, would never have a bride of his own. And here she was, this heartless bitch, going to get married.'

Terry Orne looked dazed, as if he was unable to follow what his wife was saying.

'But of course, she wasn't getting married. I mean, it was dark. You don't get married at night, do you? No, she was going to a party. A bloody party!' Vivian's lovely sense of numbness finally went as she wailed the final words with a cry of anguish.

Terry Orne closed his eyes then shook his head. 'Viv,' he said wretchedly, urgently, 'Shut up. Don't say another word.'

But his wife couldn't stop. Not now.

'I followed them to this big farmhouse. I could hear the music inside. I didn't know what to do. I was all fired up, ready to face her. I'd been screwing myself up to do it ever since Mr Innes gave me her name and address. I knew it was too late – Barry was already dead, but I had to go through with it. I just couldn't put it off.'

'Viv, what have you done?' Terry whispered.

'At first, I just wandered around. I found the cowshed, and all those beautiful cows. I walked around a bit, but it was dark, and I kept coming back again and again to the farm-house. Then I realized Mr Innes had given me the phone number of her mobile, as well as her land line. I was sure she'd have it with her, and she did.'

'You rang her?' Hillary asked, surprised. No witnesses had mentioned seeing Julia use her mobile.

Vivian Orne glanced at her blankly. 'Yes. She was in the loo. I heard it flush.'

'But how did you get her to meet you in the cowshed?' Hillary asked. 'Wasn't she afraid of you? Afraid to face you?'

'Viv, for pete's sake, don't tell her. We need a lawyer,' Terry Orne yelped.

But Vivian Orne was still staring at Hillary although, in reality, Hillary rather thought that the other woman was seeing that night instead. That night she'd hung around whilst a party was going on, and a woman inside, who'd let her son die, answered her ringing mobile phone.

'I told her I'd make it worth her while, of course,' Vivian Orne said simply. 'I told her I'd pay her to talk to me. I told her I was the mother of the little boy who'd died. I told her I had over a thousand pounds in cash in my purse. I just wanted to talk to her.'

'And she *agreed*?' Hillary asked, stunned.

'Yes. She was drunk, I think. You know how belligerent drunk people can be? Anyway, I was already halfway up the path, the one that leads to the shed, when she came out of the house. She could see I was a woman alone. I don't suppose she felt particularly afraid of me. Why should she?'

Vivian Orne wiped the tears from her eyes. 'I didn't go there to kill her, you know. It wasn't on my mind.'

Hillary nodded. She hadn't gone armed. No jury would convict her of premeditation, at least. 'So she followed you, and you went into the cowshed?' she prompted. 'What happened then?' She needed to get the whole story out, with Frank as a corroborating witness, before her husband succeeded in getting through to her instincts for self-preservation and shut her up.

'It was beginning to drizzle and she didn't want her dress to get dirty. Besides, the cowshed had lights, and she wanted to count the money, so it wasn't hard to get her inside.' Vivian spoke without any sort of emotion in her voice at all now. Not scorn, not hatred. Not even surprise.

Hillary had come across this phenomenon before. She suspected that Vivian Orne had gone over and over that night for so long and so often, that now every emotion had been wrung out of it. It simply was. Things had just happened as they'd happened.

'Did you have any money?'

'No. She became angry. The girl.'

'Julia Reynolds,' Hillary said. 'Her name was Julia Reynolds.'

Vivian Orne nodded, but said nothing.

'She was drunk, like I said,' she continued listlessly. 'I asked her why she'd refused to save my son. And she said she was scared of needles.'

At that Vivian gave a harsh laugh. 'I told her that they could have arranged to give her gas - like at a dentist. But then she said she had this thing about hospitals. Couldn't stand them, she said. So I asked why she carried a donor card if that was the case, and she said she'd forgotten about it. That she'd forgotten she still had it in her purse.'

Vivian shook her head. 'Can you imagine that? To me, to us,' – she reached across and took her husband's hand – 'that donor card meant everything. We spent months and months, hoping for a call. Hoping someone, somewhere, had registered as a match for our son. Praying for a miracle. Can you imagine?'

Hillary could. That was the problem.

'So, what happened?' she forced herself to ask. 'What made you strangle her?'

'Viv!' Terry Orne said, going white. 'Viv?'

'Shush,' Vivian Orne said, sighing heavily. 'It was when she told me that she didn't want to have a scar,' she said, matter-of-factly, turning once more to look at Hillary. 'She said she was getting married soon, to a rich man's son, and couldn't have an ugly old scar on her back.'

Hillary couldn't meet her eyes any longer and looked away. They collided with Frank Ross, who also looked quickly away.

'I just went for her,' Vivian Orne said. 'She'd turned away from me and was walking away, as if I was nothing. As if I meant nothing. As if *Barry* had meant nothing. His death meant nothing. I just went for her pretty, worthless neck and squeezed and squeezed and, well, that was it. I felt her scratching the backs of my hands, but it didn't seem to hurt. Then she went all limp. I let her fall to the floor, then I went out and got in my car and came home.' Her voice was utterly exhausted.

Hillary nodded. 'I see.'

Vivian Orne looked up from her position beside her husband, who was still staring at her helplessly, as if not sure who she was.

'Are we going now?' Vivian Orne asked quietly.

'Yes. We're going now,' Hillary said, just as quietly.

chapter sixteen

Mike Regis looked along the towpath with interest. He'd been to Thrupp once before, but had only got as far as The Boat, a pub where Hillary had celebrated the closing of a tricky murder case last year.

It was beginning to get dark, and the sky had that pearly luminescence so typical of approaching winter. Trees, beginning to lose their leaves, sighed alongside the canal, and leaves, floating down, littered the khaki-coloured waterway. A pheasant in a neighbouring field was calling noisily, and as he trudged along the muddied towpath, Mike couldn't make up his mind whether or not he liked the place.

People used to bright lights and city streets would call it bleak, but there was something about the gaily coloured moored craft, with their paintings of flowers, castles and water birds, that defied such a word. Smoke, real woodsmoke, belched aromatically from thin chimneys, and mixed with the scent of cooking.

He found the Mollern easily enough. Hillary had explained that Mollern was the old English country word for a heron – as Brock was a badger, and Reynard a fox – and that the boat had been painted in the bird's grey, black, white and old-gold colouring. It was the only barge like it in the line. It looked well-kept and maintained. On the top was a big tub of brightly blooming winter pansies that danced their velvety heads in the breeze. It looked very picturesque, but as he approached it he eyed its narrow confines with something akin to unease. It reminded him of nothing so much as a giant pencil box.

Did people really live their lives in that narrow, tiny space?

He stepped awkwardly onto the small square length of deck and leant forward to tap on the door. It made him feel like some character from a fairy tale tapping on the entrance to a troll's cave.

The door opened, and Hillary looked up at him. He saw a surprised look flash across her face, and instantly noted how tired she looked. Almost depressed, in fact.

'Hey, I heard you broke your case. No party?' he asked, wondering for the first time why she and the team weren't at The Boat.

'No one's in a partying mood,' she said flatly. 'Come in, and I'll tell you about it.'

She poured them both a glass of white wine from an opened bottle in the fridge and filled him in on the sad tale. When she was finished, Mike shook his head. He was sitting, somewhat uncomfortably, on the long narrow couch in the living area that also pulled out into a spare bed. Not that Hillary ever used it. She'd invited nobody onto the boat since she'd moved in.

'And this girl, this Julia, simply let the little boy die? She knew about it, I mean? The doctors kept her informed of how weak he was getting?' Mike asked, disbelief ringing in his voice.

'Yes. Both her own doctor, and of course, poor Barry Orne's doctors did everything they could think of to get her to change her mind. But she wouldn't go through with it. I don't think Julia's parents knew anything about it, though. I'm sure they'd have said right at the beginning of the case if they'd known. I feel sorry for them, Mike. It's bad enough to have their daughter murdered, but to learn this about her now seems somehow unbearably cruel. And then there's the fact that there's going to be no public sympathy for them either, when it all comes out. The trail's going to be a nightmare for them. They're in for a tough time.'

Mike grunted. 'I hadn't thought about that. More innocents

getting hurt. Shit, no wonder you've got a long face. It's a real no-winner, isn't it?'

Hillary sighed and nodded.

'And it was definitely the mother who killed her, not the father?' Mike said.

'Terry Orne didn't even know she'd hired a PI,' Hillary confirmed glumly. 'Though we'll have to charge him for attempted murder on Frank.'

Mike grinned feebly. 'I'll bet Frank just loved the fact that it was you who saved his bacon.'

Hillary nearly choked over her drink, and for a moment, laughed uproariously. So much had happened in the last ten hours that she hadn't even considered that yet. Now that she did, it was enough to chase away the blues. 'You can say that again,' she said, when she'd finished chuckling. 'And I'm never going to let the poisonous little git forget it.'

Regis grinned, but his mind was still on his own daughter, and what he'd have done, had she been seriously ill, and discovered that there was a donor, but the donor was refusing to help.

'I suppose your team are still tying it all up?'

Hillary nodded. After taking a formal statement from Vivian Orne, with a solicitor present this time, she'd let Janine take over, by way of a consolation prize for not being in at the kill. Tommy Lynch was still back at the Big House typing up reports on the Gregory Innes interview.

'I'm determined to nail that private dick,' Hillary muttered with feeling. She knew that Janine and Tommy were also just as keen, and wouldn't be letting the grass grow under their feet. They'd be going up north tomorrow and liaising closely with the locals. For once, her team didn't care if another Force took the credit, so long as they got their man.

'He'll do time, and, better still, have his licence permanently revoked,' Hillary said. 'That'll teach him to play footsies with me and the Intercity Express.'

Regis had heard on the grapevine about Hillary's near miss with the train, and made her go through it once again. She'd already shrugged off her disabling of Terry Orne as nothing, but Regis knew it had taken quick thinking and a cool head and steady nerve to bring it off so neatly, and with such a minimum of fuss or damage.

'They'll be putting you up for a gallantry award if you keep this up,' he said when she'd finished.

Hillary shuddered. 'Don't!' she said. Then, putting her wine glass down firmly, took the bull by the horns. 'You didn't just stop by to massage my ego, though, did you?'

Regis smiled. The man had a nice smile, no two ways about it. In the confined space, she could smell his aftershave, even though his jaw looked like it could do with another introduction to the razor. Her dad had been like that – needed a shave sometimes twice a day. And sitting so close beneath a bright light, she could even make out the golden flecks in his dark green eyes. He was wearing old faded jeans and a bomber jacket – he'd obviously been working the streets, and had come here without changing, and she felt a distinct stirring.

She told her toenails to quit curling, and raised her eyebrows questioningly.

'No, I didn't. Mind you, I have no object to massaging anything that needs it.'

Hillary laughed. She liked a man with a sense of humour. She didn't, for one second, take it as a serious come-on line.

'I come bearing gifts,' he said instead and reaching into his inside jacket pocket, bought out a gold and white envelope, the kind that housed photographs. Intrigued, Hillary reached forward and took them, recognizing one of the subjects at once. 'My, my, Mr Thomas Palmer, local chairman of ESAA, no less. And the scantily clad lady kissing him lovingly goodbye is not Mrs Palmer, I take it?'

'She isn't,' Mike grinned.

'I don't see Mr Palmer backing out of his civil suit due to candid shots of himself or his mistress. And these certainly aren't admissible in court.'

'I wasn't thinking of court,' Mike said with a slow smile. 'I was thinking of sending them to leading lights in ESAA. The lady is the wife of a local fox-hunter.'

Hillary blinked, then began to laugh.

When she'd finished, she put the photos away. She'd have to think about the best way to play it.

'So, what made you decide to play Galahad again?' Hillary asked. 'After the way I put a flea in your ear the other day, I didn't expect to see you for dust.'

Regis shrugged. 'I suppose I wanted to play the big man. You know how we get, sometimes.'

Hillary did. Ronnie had liked to play the big man. The trouble was, he came to believe in his own publicity.

'I don't need another big man in my life, Mike,' Hillary said flatly.

'How about a fairly laid-back, nondescript lover then?' The dark-green eyes held hers steadily. 'We're not from the same nick, so no aggro there. Different specialities – so no competition. We're the same age, we think the same. We're both adults. And I really, honest injun,' – he put a hand to his heart – 'haven't slept with my wife for years. In fact,' – he reached once more into his jacket pocket and produced a letter – 'we filed for divorce yesterday.'

Hillary hesitated, then read the solicitor's confirming letter with an odd feeling of both shame and satisfaction. She was unused to either emotion, and quickly thrust it back. 'You needn't have done that.'

'I didn't do it for you,' Mike said bluntly. And even as he spoke, he wondered. Was that strictly true? 'Things needed to be sorted. And Sylvia is old enough to choose which one of us she wants to live with.'

'You're moving out?'

'Yeah. Well, it's easier for me to move, than for Laura.'

Hillary grimaced. 'Good luck with finding another place to live.'

Mike Regis grunted. 'You don't have to tell me. I was thinking of renting a barge, but having seen this one, I think I'll pass.'

Hillary gave a surprised grunt of laughter. 'Well, thanks a bunch.' She looked around the boat, seeing the mellow wood, the cheerful paintwork, the cosy fittings.

'I didn't mean it was an old tub or anything.' Mike held up his hands in a 'peace' gesture. 'I just suddenly realized it's not for me. I feel like a sardine.'

Hillary nodded. She knew how he felt. When she'd first moved in, she'd hated it. But the place had begun to grow on her. Anyway, if Palmer folded over the ESAA case, she might be getting her house back soon. The thought, for some reason, didn't actually make her feel as happy as she would have imagined.

The Mollern bobbed gently as a passing craft, looking for a last-ditch night-mooring, chugged past.

'So,' Mike said, leaning forward and placing his empty wine glass beside hers, 'about us. I don't want to....'

Whatever it was he didn't want to do remained a mystery, because, like a cliché that didn't know better, her mobile phone suddenly chirruped.

Hillary snatched it up, stuck it to one ear, and snarled, 'Yes?'

'Guv?' Tommy Lynch's startled voice sounded in her ear.

'Tommy. Sorry.' She quickly modified her tone. 'What is it?'

'I think you'd better come back in guv. We've just had word. Roger Greenwood has attacked his Dad. It's bad, I think. He's in the hospital. Theo Greenwood, that is. The JR. We've got Roger Greenwood downstairs. He's in a right state.'

Hillary heaved a sigh. 'OK, I'm coming in.'

Without a word, Regis got up and left her to it.

Theo Greenwood was still in casualty at the JR, and as soon as they walked in, held up a hand to fend them off. He was bleeding profusely from the head, and a nurse and junior doctor were in the process of applying stitches.

'You lot can sod off as well,' Theo Greenwood said, his sickly pallor at odds with the power and anger of his voice. 'I'm not pressing charges against my own son, so you can forget it.'

Hillary nodded. 'Care to tell me what happened?'

'Nothing. Just a family argument. A misunderstanding. Nothing to do with you lot.'

Hillary, knowing a lost cause when she saw it, shrugged, and motioned Tommy to come away.

'Back to the station, guv?' Tommy asked. But Hillary shook her head. They'd already taken Roger Greenwood's statement before coming to the JR. It had been a simple enough story. An anonymous phone call had led him to a meeting with a young woman who claimed to be a girlfriend of someone called Leo Mann. Roger had never heard of him. The girl, Lucy, had laughed, and told him that his girlfriend had been shagging her boyfriend silly, and Roger had almost walked out on her at that point. It had been enough to make Lucy back off, the thought of losing all that money suddenly tempering her indignation.

But what she'd told him had made Roger sick to his stomach. His own father, and Julia. He didn't believe it. It had taken Lucy some time to convince him, and when she had, he'd handed over the money in a daze.

He'd driven back to the Hayrick Inn, torn between the desire to laugh and cry, and alternately not believing it, and then believing it only too well. It explained, if nothing else, the way the old man had been so dead set against them marrying.

By the time he'd confronted his father in his study, he'd been in no mood for a little chat, but had worked up a fine head of steaming rage. At first, Theo Greenwood had tried to deny it, only reluctantly admitting it when it became obvious that his son wouldn't be fobbed off. It had been then that Roger had clobbered him with an angle-poise lamp. Just the once, right on the crown of his head.

'No, no point going back in now,' Hillary said eventually, in answer to Tommy's question. 'If his father isn't going to press charges, I can't see any point wasting more time and manhours on them. Keep the son in overnight, then turn him loose. It'll do him good to sweat for a while.'

Tommy nodded, relieved. He'd felt rather sorry for the young bloke. To find out your own dad had been boffing your fiancée was enough to make anyone see red.

'Can I drop you off, Tommy?' she asked, getting behind the wheel, but the thought of turning up at his mum's house with Hillary in tow, made him blanch.

'No thanks, guv. There'll be a bus along in a minute.'

Hillary frowned. 'OK.' She wondered briefly what was eating him, then shrugged. It was none of her business.

At the roundabout at the bottom of Headington Hill, she waited in a small queue, her mind moving restlessly over the past few days.

Well, they had the killer, the case was done and dusted, and ready to be presented to Jerome Raleigh all wrapped up with a bow. It was good work, neat, tidy, and nothing for the CPS to whine about. As a good way to impress the new boss, Hillary knew she couldn't have done better.

She knew Janine was in a happy mood, and had been hinting about a romantic weekend away. Personally, Hillary wasn't sure just how keen Mel would be to go. Unless she was misreading her old friend, the signs didn't look good on that front.

Frank was in misery, everyone at the station teasing him unmercifully, and that alone made it feel as if all was right with her world.

Then there was Regis.

A potential laid-back, nondescript lover.

She smiled gently and nosed forward as the car in front shot off. She might even have got ESAA off her back. That left only one thing in her life that still needed sorting.

On impulse, she went straight across the roundabout and took the Marston Ferry Road into town. She parked outside her favourite internet café and walked in. She'd long since memorized the numbers underlined in Ronnie's book, and quickly logged on to the bank in the Cayman islands that she thought Ronnie might have used. The White Horse bank went with the Dick Francis novel and the password of Stud. Or maybe Stallion.

Looking around very carefully, sure that the teenagers and serious-looking academics that made up the majority of the café's customers had about as much interest in her as a donkey would have in a motorcycle side car, she logged on.

Holding her breath, she went through the usual rigmarole and the bank's safety measures, and finally found herself staring at a menu of options. So she'd been right: it was this bank.

She used the mouse to log onto the 'Check Status of Account' option and pressed.

The computer asked for numbers. Once more Hillary looked around. Nobody was looking her way. One woman, not a teen, but an attractive thirty-something, looked familiar, but she was typing ferociously and making notes, obviously working hard.

Quickly, before her nerve failed, Hillary typed in the numbers. The screen blinked, then asked for a password.

She typed in Stud and pressed the enter key. Then felt a moment of panic. What if it was the wrong password? What if the computer started blaring like a car alarm, alerted by the interface on the other end that someone was trying to hack into a bank account? But there was no warning screech. And a second later, the screen went blank, then came up with a single line, confirming number, password, and at the end, a row of figures.

For a second, Hillary thought it said one hundred and thirty thousand pounds.

Her brain registered the one, the three, the zeros. And she sucked in her breath. Not a vast fortune by today's standards, but nothing to be sniffed at either.

Then, with one of those little leaps, her brain suddenly jolted, as if receiving a mental kick in the bum.

It was not one hundred and thirty thousand pounds: There were too many zeros.

Too many zeros.

Hillary swallowed hard, and it actually hurt, her mouth had gone so dry. She coughed a little, and that hurt too – her chest felt so tight.

Too many zeros.

She was looking at, had access to, an account in the Cayman Islands that held one million, three hundred thousand pounds Sterling.

Hillary felt a cold frisson run down her back and looked up quickly. And saw Paul Danvers staring at her.

For a second, Hillary was sure that her heart had actually stopped beating. A sound roared in her ears, and a tight sharp pain lanced straight down the middle of her chest.

A heart attack.

Paul Danvers smiled. 'Hey, Hillary. Didn't expect to see you here.'

Hillary scrambled for the mouse and clicked on the exit option, then pressed the key to go back to main menu.

She forced herself to stand on legs that felt like nothing. No bone, no sinew, no cartilage. She felt as if she was floating on cotton wool.

The pain in her chest slowly eased. Her hearing returned to normal. Paul Danvers wasn't here to arrest her – he was just a guy who'd happened to run into someone he knew. And he couldn't possibly know what had been on the screen. It had had its back to him all the time.

She glanced down at the computer, which was now innocently showing the screen saver bearing the café's logo. She glanced quickly left to right. Nobody had seen. Nobody cared.

'You've met Louise right?' Paul said, nodding over to the attractive hardworker, who, hearing her name looked up and smiled vaguely.

Louise?

Right, Hillary suddenly nodded. She'd seen her with Paul at the court. A barrister. The girlfriend.

'Right, yes. Hello.' Her voice sounded scratchy with relief. So that was why he was here. To meet up with the girlfriend!

She cleared her throat. *Get a grip, girl. Get a grip.*

Louise smiled and tapped the face of her watch and held up five fingers to Danvers, who nodded back his understanding.

'She's got a big case on at the moment,' Paul said. 'Patent violation.' His voice was rich with pride.

Hillary nodded. She was going to be sick. If she didn't get out of here right now, she was going to be sick.

'Well, I've got to get back to the station,' she heard herself say, and reached forward to turn off the computer. Even as she did it, she wondered what the hell she was doing. The café owner looked over in surprise. She knew the moment she was out the door that the computer would be turned back on. She should have left it as it was. She knew, in her head, that nobody could trace what she'd been doing. It was only guilt that had made her want to switch it off, forcing a reboot.

'You might have heard, we closed our case,' Hillary said quickly, seeing Paul's eyes go to the computer and a puzzled look draw his brows together in a frown.

As hoped, the news instantly distracted him. There was nothing more interesting to a copper than hearing about a successful solving of a case. With a bit of luck, he'd put her down as one of those dinosaurs who knew as much about computer etiquette as the Queen knew about digging ditches.

'Yeah, I did. Congratulations.'

Hillary pulled on her coat, and grabbed her bag. 'Well, loose ends to tie up, and all that.'

She mentally groaned. Had she really said something so inane? No wonder he was looking at her as if she'd suddenly lost her marbles. Just smile and get the hell out!

She smiled and got the hell out. She walked to her car, fumbled with the key in the lock, then collapsed behind the wheel. She opened the door once more and leaned out, but didn't actually lose her lunch. After a few extra deep breaths of good old Oxford air, she straightened up and sat back in her seat.

She made no attempt to start the engine.

Instead, she stared blankly at the cars parked all around her. A bus went by. The lights were on in all the shops, displaying far-too-early Christmas wares. People came and went. The world was doing its usual thing of carrying on regardless.

Whilst Hillary Greene sat and wondered what the hell she was going to do with a million quid.